RISING

BOOK ONE AFTER THE THAW

TAMAR SLOAN

HEIDI CATHERINE

SEQUEL HOUSE

For Sean and Evan

NOVA

"*D*on't touch me! I want Nova! Where's Nova?"

Nova spins around as the quiet in the infirmary is shattered. Old Sam staggers as he pushes away those who are trying to help him. He crashes into a shelf, scattering bandages and metal instruments.

Rose scuttles to pick them up. They're nothing more than strips of hemp and relics from old first aid kits, but supplies are precious in the infirmary. To be honest, supplies are precious no matter where you are in Askala.

Shiloh reaches out to steady him. "Sam, if you just take a seat—"

"No!" he roars. "I want Nova!"

Shiloh jumps back, her eyes wide with alarm as Rose rushes to her. They both look to Nova, even though she's the youngest in the room. With a small smile, Nova indicates they step back. There's no point them bearing the brunt of Sam's tantrum if they don't need to.

Nova nods to Shiloh who, with a last glance at Sam, rushes out the door. Although she's only slightly older than Nova, the pretty dark-haired girl is still a little intimidated by the

Unbound. Nova places the scalpel she was sterilizing high up on the shelf behind her, doing a quick scan of the infirmary, making sure there's nothing else the old man can hurt himself on.

Grabbing the tray of supplies she had at the ready, she steps around the table, heading to the grizzled old man. "Sam, I think everyone on the Oasis can hear you."

"Ah, there's my angel." Old Sam visibly relaxes, which only has him swaying more. He blinks through the blood congealing on his face.

"Let's get you cleaned up, shall we?" Nova wraps her arms tightly around his waist, noting he's even thinner than last time. "You haven't earned any pteropods these last few weeks, have you?"

Sam grunts. "What the hell for?"

Nova lowers him into a chair, stumbling a little as Sam almost takes her with him. Rose takes a step closer, but Nova shakes her head imperceptibly as she straightens. If they can give Sam what he needs right now, then that's a good thing.

Especially considering the cut on his forehead.

Taking some strips of material, Nova mock frowns at him. "What if I wasn't here? It's not even my day to be in the infirmary."

"I knew you'd be here, love. You're always here when I need you."

Nova shakes her head with a smile, ignoring the tension that comment elicits. She dabs at the cut on his head, trying to get a sense of how deep it is underneath all the blood. "One day I won't be able to patch you up, Sam."

There will come a time when the injury he presents with won't be something Nova has the capacity to fix. He needs to take better care of himself.

Sam grunts again. "I'll deal with that inevitability when it comes."

2

Nova suppresses a frown. Many of the Unbound talk like this—everyone in Askala is aware life is short, but it's like the Unbound don't care.

Seeing the cut is a shallow one, Nova presses down to stem the bleeding. Sam doesn't wince at the pressure, and Nova hopes he hasn't damaged any nerves. Although, judging by the swaying and the smell of his breath, it's probably just the wine the Unbounds manage to brew from the wild berries found in the forest.

She picks up a pair of tweezers, gently probing. "Good thing it won't need stitches," Nova murmurs.

Sam's bleary eyes glare at her from under his bushy brows. "Sure is."

Nova doesn't look away even though she feels her cheeks heat. They both know she couldn't have stitched him up. Sam is Unbound. And not only that, he's an Unbound who doesn't contribute.

Conscious to keep her back to Rose, Nova sends a warning look to Sam, hoping he notices through his drunken haze. What she did last time must stay what it is, a secret.

Sam knows as well as she does—needles and thread are precious. They must be saved for those who'll be part of Askala's future.

"How did this happen, Sam?" Nova asks, although she already suspects the answer.

Sam's gaze slides away. "Lost a game of cards. I'm pretty sure the other guy was cheating."

Nova's lips twitch. "Pretty sure?"

Sam grins, exposing yellowed teeth. "Sure enough to teach him a lesson. Even if he didn't card swap, he won't think of trying it next time."

Nova shakes her head as she smiles. Someone else might be turning up in the infirmary yet. When her mother had gone to see if the weavers could spare any more strips of fabric and left

Nova in charge, she hadn't actually expected there to be any patients coming in.

Deftly and gently, Nova bandages up the cut on Sam's head. She steps back to check her handiwork then nods. It's as good as it's going to get considering how little they have.

Nova's read the books in the Oasis's library. She's spent hours pouring over texts describing marvels like band-aids and dressings and antiseptic.

She rests a hand on Sam's shoulder. "The cut wasn't too deep, I think you'll be fine."

"Of course I will. I've been patched up by an angel."

Nova smiles as she shakes her head. "We'll need the bandages back when you're done with them. And if you notice any soreness or redness, maybe that drink of yours will have enough alcohol in it to disinfect the wound."

"Thanks, love. You're one of the good ones."

Not sure what that means, Nova helps Sam to his feet. Maybe he's talking about the Unbounds. Every Bound knows kindness is central to the colony.

"Oh, and Sam." He turns toward her at the door, swiping his bracelet to open it, then clutching it to steady himself. "They always need help in the gardens. You could earn yourself some pods."

Sam grunts as he turns away. "I thought the plants in those sad squares of soil were as extinct as everything else on this forsaken planet."

Only one crash echoes down the hall as Sam stumbles away. With a sigh, Nova begins to clean up. The cloths will have to be boiled, washed, then hung in the sun. After the soap, its harsh rays are the best sterilization they can get.

Rose rushes over to help. "You're so calm with him." She brushes her brown hair out of her face. "But then again, you're calm with everyone."

4

Nova shrugs. "There's enough sadness and fear in our world. I don't want to be someone who adds to that."

"You're going to make a good Bound, Nova." Rose holds out her hand. "I'll take all that to the laundry."

Nova nods, scanning the table to make sure it's clean. She passes Rose the tweezers. "We'll need to wash these, too."

Nova startles when the tweezers clatter to the ground. She glances at Rose's outstretched hand. The one the tweezers just slipped through.

Her left hand.

The one missing the second last finger.

"Sorry." Nova hates that she blushes. Unbounds having nine fingers isn't a new development in Askala, the ruling has existed her entire life. Maybe it's because she spends all her time outside the infirmary with Bounds. Her mother is Bound. Her friends are Bound.

Soon, she and Kian will be Bound.

She hopes.

Rose waves away the awkward moment. "It's fine. You'd think after almost a year, it would be habit to just use my right hand for stuff like that."

Nova smiles, hating it even more that she looks away. "I'm sure it takes time to get used to."

They busy themselves tidying up, and it doesn't take long before the infirmary is back to pre-Sam order.

Rose stretches her back. "I'd hate to see the guy who thought he'd try and cheat Old Sam."

It would have to have been an Unbound. Not only wasn't it a smart idea, but Bounds know the value of honesty. "Let's hope he or she wasn't too badly hurt."

Because if they were, then the medical attention they can give them is limited.

The door opens and Nova turns with a smile, only to freeze

as she registers the person standing there. Her stomach feels like it just landed between her feet. She knows the cocky tilt of those shoulders. The red hair is unmistakable. A rare feature in Askala.

Dean.

Trying to hide the trembling, Nova tucks her hands into the pockets of her apron. There are few people who can ruffle the calmness Nova has perfected.

The brother of the man responsible for her dad's death is certainly one of them.

Dean grins, just as she expected him to. The man has never acknowledged the damage his brother wrought. He acts as if Ronan never existed. "Seem to have got me a cut on my hand."

He holds up his right palm, where blood oozes from a gash.

Nova nods curtly. "If you'll take a seat, we can have a look at it."

Rose reaches for more bandages. "I can do this one, Nova."

Nova's muscles feel like someone has woven steel through them. Shaking her head is hard, and the motion is stilted, but she can't let Rose do this.

When she's Bound, this will be her duty.

"It's okay, Rose. I've got it."

Dean sits in the same chair Sam vacated not long ago. He stretches his arm out on the adjacent table, facing his palm up. "Seems Old Sam isn't too keen on losing."

"Hmm." Without looking at him, Nova sets to work. Dean's brother was a cheater and a liar, and everyone in Askala knows the importance of genetics.

Focusing on the task at hand, Nova notes this cut is deeper, a jagged gash slicing right across Dean's palm. Quickly and efficiently, she cleans the wound, then places a wad of cloth over it.

Dean leans over to peer at it causing Nova to jerk back. "You don't think it'll need stitches?"

Nova busies herself getting the next bandage. "It'll take some

6

time to heal. You're going to need to rest it or you'll reopen the wound."

"So, it needs stitches."

For the first time since Dean arrived, Nova meets his gaze. Something bubbles in her gut. "We don't have the supplies to provide stitches."

"It's just that I kinda need my right hand, you know?" Dean holds up his left hand, the stump of his ring finger a garish gap between the others. "I help out in the kitchens. It's how I get my pods."

Pteropods. The beautiful, glowing butterflies of the ocean that taste like salty bile and are the main source of nutrition at Askala. Bounds, the ones chosen to breed future generations, are allocated weekly rations.

The Unbound must earn them.

It was Dean's brother who'd lied about being Bound and killed the entire breeding population of pteropods a generation ago. It's because of Ronan that Dean and all the other Unbound are missing a finger. They'd had to ensure an Unbound could never masquerade as a Bound again. The loss of the pteropods was just too devastating.

Nova tries not to frown. Collecting the new pods is what killed her father. She never even got the chance to meet him.

The injustice triggers a familiar spear of heat through her gut. A selfish choice that led to so much loss.

Except Dean is still a fellow human. A breathing, bleeding, feeling soul just like Nova. Some part of her hurts for his loss and all the other Unbounds. She's already decided she'll spend her life taking care of them just as much as the Bound.

The battle within her not resolved, Nova looks away. "Perhaps you'll be able to help in the lab."

From the corner of her eye, Nova sees Dean frown and she tenses. She's not sure how she'll react if he objects. Steeling herself, she wishes she'd let Rose do this.

The door opens again, and relief fills Nova when she sees who's standing there with Shiloh. Her mother's eyes widen a little as she registers who's in the infirmary, but she quickly gains her composure. She walks over and inspects the bandaging. "I see you've taken good care of everything while I was gone."

Nova nods. Making her mother proud is what's driven her since the first time she brought her to the infirmary when she was a child.

"Hey, Thea." Dean turns his hand both ways to show her mother all angles, his gaze steady on Nova. "She said I need to rest it."

The unsaid words hang in the air. *Because you won't stitch it.*

Thea nods, her face serene. "Exactly what I would've recommended. Along with fewer card games."

Dean chuckles, the tension draining out of him. "Well, that ain't gonna happen, now is it?" He stands, cradling his bandaged hand against his chest. "Next time, I'll just need to be quicker."

With his sleight of hand, or getting out of the way when Old Sam takes a swing? Nova frowns at the thought. Her mother would never think such a thing.

"Thank you, ladies," says Dean. "As always, you Bounds take your responsibilities seriously."

Nova's about to call out she's not Bound yet, but with a jaunty wave, Dean's gone.

The moment his distinctive red hair disappears down the hall, Nova sags. Her mother slips an arm around her. "You did good, Nova."

"How can you just smile at him like nothing's wrong?"

Her mother squeezes her shoulder before beginning to clean up. "It was his brother's actions, not his."

"But it doesn't even bother him. He lives his life like none of that matters."

Her mother shrugs. "Maybe it doesn't to him. He's Unbound, that's his right."

Nova clenches her jaw. Everything her mother's saying is true. When Unbounds lose their finger, they also lose the ability to bear children. In return, they gain a life of care and privilege. If Dean wants to spend his life cheating at cards and acting as if his family isn't responsible for a catastrophe that molded the future of Askala, he's entitled to that.

Except Nova has had to live her life without her father.

The tension is back in Nova's muscles, every fiber a battleground of emotions. She tries to ignore it, to be more like her mother, but the feeling doesn't go away. Frustrated, Nova concentrates on tidying up the next pile of bloody rags.

Her mother reaches out to pat her shoulder, smiling at her. "You go. There's little to do here."

Nova looks up, reading the meaning behind her mother's words. Like magic, the tension dissolves. Her mom knows there's one person who can help her feel better. All he has to do is look at her, his soulful dark eyes full of promise and laughter, and everything's right in Nova's world.

"Are you sure?" Excitement tingles across Nova's skin.

"You're not even supposed to be here today, remember?"

Shiloh steps forward, her pretty, tanned face smiling. "We've got this, Nova."

With a quick kiss on her mother's cheek and a smile for Shiloh, Nova heads to the door, swiping her bracelet over the scanner. "Thanks, you two. Let me know if there's anything you need, though."

Nova can already feel her heart rate pick up in anticipation.

The way to the upper deck is so familiar Nova could navigate it blindfolded. She's done this walk every day of her life, all because the infirmary is at one end of the beached cruise ship the colony calls home, while Kian spends his time at the other.

Although it's overcast, the promise of a storm carried on the

9

wind, Nova lifts her hemp scarf around her head and tucks her blonde hair in as she leaves the bowels of the Oasis. It's always been an annoyance to be so fair-skinned. Not only does she stand out amongst the hues of caramel and copper that color most people of Askala, it also makes her more vulnerable to the sun.

She remembers the first and only time she thought she could be like the others. She and Kian were seven or eight, and their parents, probably tired of their noise bouncing around the narrow corridors of the Oasis, had sent them to the gardens behind the wall. They'd played tag and tried to catch the rabbits that managed to sneak in, but the animals were so small they'd escaped from their traps. Nova had got tired of her scarf catching on branches or slipping over her face, so she'd thrown it aside.

That day was the first time Nova was in the infirmary as a patient, rather than her mother's helper. Kian had helped cool her with damp cloths as it felt like her skin was being cooked from within. The blisters were unavoidable, but she was lucky they didn't become infected.

Nova sighs, pausing to gaze out over Askala. The forest reaches for the horizon one way, the ocean the other. Both are so beautiful it has Nova catching her breath. Both are so dangerous, it sends a shiver down her spine.

Those childhood memories feel so long ago.

That's because they were before.

Before they'd realized the Proving was a very real part of their future, rather than just a hushed discussion beneath the bows of a mangrove pine.

Before their friendship had taken its inevitable trans-formation.

The one they can't act on, no matter how strong the pull.

Not until they're both Bound

If they're both Bound...

Shaking her head, Nova heads for the pteropod pool.

"Of course we'll both be Bound," she mutters aloud. Their parents are Bound, their grandparents were Bound. They both want nothing more than to serve Askala.

The image of Dean and his injured hand rises uninvited. She didn't treat him with the same warmth she showed Old Sam. A part of her wanted to shout at him that his brother took her father. That her mother was forced to raise her alone. That he can act like it doesn't matter, when it really does.

Nova wipes her hand down her face, wishing she could somehow brush these thoughts away.

Bounds don't feel like this. Bounds are kind and loving and intelligent. There's no room for anger or bitterness in their hearts and minds.

She doesn't enjoy feeling like this.

She doesn't want to feel like this.

But she does.

Which worries Nova. How much of the calmness that Rose commented on is the real Nova, and how much is an act?

What if she fails the Proving?

The Proving that begins in a few days.

Nova reaches the pteropod pool and a quick scan tells her there's no one there. To think the large square cavity was once used for something as frivolous as swimming and nothing else. It was the actions of those short-sighted ancestors that resulted in the pool now being used for something far more practical. And essential.

The blue water glistens under the sun, islands of green phytoplankton calmly bobbing on the surface. Below, masses of small, glowing bodies glide through the water on opaque wings. This place is the lifeblood of Askala.

Kian's mother oversees it, having taken over from her mother just after the pteropods were wiped out. She's done an incredible job of reestablishing a healthy population.

Pulling in a calming breath just like her mother taught her when faced with something especially confronting in the infirmary, Nova reminds herself Kian won't be far away. He tried to convince her not to leave and help out in the infirmary in the first place. She could sense his impatience for her to return from the moment she left.

Heading to the nearby stairs, Nova figures he must be in the water testing room, probably preparing for the incoming storm. Weather changes in Askala are not only fast, they're unpredictable and extreme. What looks like a light shower can turn into a violent storm, while masses of black clouds can do nothing but shade the world for three days.

Taking off her scarf, Nova ties it around her shoulders even though it's far from cold. Maybe she should take the back corridor just in case Kian is coming from the library, where she left him.

For now, it's best to assume this one is going to bring everything those black clouds promise. Angry winds and rain full of wrath. She can't contain the shiver.

The last one brought changes to the landscape no one could predict.

Why does it feel like it's a harbinger of what's to come?

KIAN

"*The* pH is good?" Kian's mother pauses in tapping away at the tablet to tuck a strand of dark hair behind her ear. She doesn't look up, nor does her frown ease, as she waits for an answer.

Kian swirls the vial as he stares at the contents. He doesn't need to hold it up against the colored slips of paper to get his answer. He's done these enough times to know the light green liquid is just where it should be—acidic. "Yep. pH is good."

"Temp?"

Kian checks the dial, then checks again. "Not too hot, not too cold."

His mother lets out a breath. "Good. They should be all set, then."

Kian brushes her arm. "They'll be fine. This is nothing we haven't seen before."

His mother relaxes enough to smile at her son. "I know, I know. It's just that they're kind of important."

Kian grins. "Good thing the pteropods have us looking after them then, isn't it?"

She smiles as she rolls her eyes. "Yes, it is."

Kian heads to the back of the room to grab the net rolled up in the corner. "Shall we?"

"I was just waiting for your fath—"

The door swings open with a bang, propelled by the wind outside, and Kian's father fills the doorway. "Sorry, Amity, there was a disagreement among the Unbounds."

Kian watches as his mother noticeably relaxes. "It's okay, Magnus. We only just finished."

His father enters the small room, and as always, it feels like it shrinks. He's always been tall, but the years of leading Askala have meant he's developed a presence. When Magnus enters a room, no matter how big or small, everyone has a new focal point.

His father walks straight to his mother, his hand lifting to touch her face. "You're worried."

She leans into the hand cupping her cheek. "I always worry with the storms, you know that."

Kian watches his parents look at each other like they have all the time in the world. He knows some unspoken communication is passing between them. He's never seen two people so closely connected.

Apart from himself and Nova.

His father nods as if he just answered a question. "We won't lose them again, Amity. We've made sure of that."

Kian's mother presses her lips to her beloved's palm. "I think the pteropods would be too scared to die on your watch."

There are few people who can make Kian's father smile. He gives the responsibility of Askala's future the weight it deserves. Some days it seems to permanently pull down his brows.

But his mother is one of them. His father's lips tip up. "They wouldn't dare."

Kian holds up the net. "Ah, in case no one's noticed, there's a storm coming."

His parents turn to him, both smiling now, and Kian grins

14

back. It's always been nice knowing he's another one of the few who can bring a smile to his father's lips.

His father walks over to him, slapping a hand on his shoulder. "We'd best get going then."

Kian leads the way out, the sound of the wind already a muted roar outside. Above deck, the black clouds are hanging low over the ocean. Periodically, a fork of lightning streaks down, flashing through the rolling gray.

His mother touches his father's arm. "I'll just do a last check."

She's gone before either of them answer, and they both know she needs to do this, even though there's nothing left to check. The routine last lap around the pool that holds the pteropods is probably more about burning off nervous energy than checking the pods. Kian stands beside his father as they watch Mother Nature vent her fury over the sea.

Kian tingles with excitement. The storms are such an impressive display of Earth's might. "It's going to be quite the show."

His father angles his chin up, letting the wind push his black hair out of his face. "Why do these happen, son?"

Kian's cousin, Dex, has started to surreptitiously roll his eyes at these constant questions. Kian can't blame him, his father can be pretty intense about them.

But Kian gets why his father does this, which is why he answers it like it's the first time he's been asked. "Humans released five thousand gigatons of carbon dioxide into our atmosphere. The carbon trapped heat in ways never seen before. Oceans warmed. Sea levels rose." Kian pulls in a breath as he watches the manifestation of human short-sightedness. "Weather events became more extreme."

Flooding, drought, cyclones, wildfires. No one was safe.

No one could escape the legacy that humanity had created.

"Exactly. We can never forget, Kian. It's why we do what we do."

Kian's response is always the same. In the beginning, it's what he knew he was supposed to say. But he was still young when it became a promise. No, a pledge. "We'll make sure this never happens again, Dad."

His father relaxes as he always does at hearing those words. "I know you will."

Kian's mother returns and they get to work. Quickly and efficiently, they unroll the net, then take a corner each. The gusts of wind tug at it as they spread out, stretching the net the length and width of the pool.

The fine mesh will keep the islands of phytoplankton, the food that keeps the pteropods thriving, from being ripped away in the storm. It also means that if there's a deluge of water and the pool floods, precious pods won't be washed away by the overflowing water.

If they can get the net attached.

The wind multiplies, catching the free corner and flapping it about like a flag. It splashes the surface of the pool, scattering a clump of phytoplankton. Kian can almost feel his mother's anxiousness. If they can't feed the pteropods, they can't feed the colony.

"I'll grab it as soon as I tie down my corner!" Kian calls out over the roar.

Working as quickly as he can, Kian wraps the rope around the hook installed along the edge of the pool just for this purpose. His parents are doing the same at each of their corners.

He's finished and is just about to run to the remaining corner when he pauses. Squinting against the wind, he instinctively straightens.

Nova.

He could almost sense she was returning. Not because of any psychic ability, but there seems to be a time limit on how long they can be apart. After that, their souls seek the other out.

For precious seconds they stare at each other across the distance. Reconnecting. Reaffirming.

Rejoicing.

Then they're both running toward the wildly flapping corner. The moment they're there, they both realize there's no way they can reach the writhing net a few feet away. It flicks the water, hitting the surface over and over again.

Nova looks to Kian. "You got me?"

Kian grins. "Always."

He grips her hand, reveling in the way they fit together so perfectly. Nova places one foot as close to the edge of the pool as possible then leans out. Kian angles back in counterpoint, planting his feet into the ground.

Slowly, but with a surety that comes with trust, Nova leans further and further out, stretching her arm toward the net. Kian locks his muscles, becoming her foundation.

The net flicks past Nova's straining fingers and she makes a grab for it but misses.

"Almost, Nova!" Kian shouts.

Nova leans out a little further, gaining another inch over the pool. Kian's heart swells, loving the way she never doubts that he's got her. A gust of wind buffets him, tugging at his loose clothing and he grits his teeth. She's right. Letting Nova go is something he'll never do.

The next flick of the net and Nova snatches it. Kian whoops with victory as he reels her back in. Within moments, they've secured it.

They step back, taking in the mesh that's now stretched over the pool. They've done everything they can to protect the pteropods against the approaching deluge.

His mother is waving at them. "Let's get inside, you two."

Taking each other's hands, they race after Kian's parents. Below deck, Kian shuts the door behind them, instantly cutting off the thundering wind.

He stands beside Nova, his parents in front of him, chest heaving a little. "Well that's an interesting way to get a new hairstyle!" Kian pushes his fingers through his shoulder-length hair. He inherited his mother's Inuit genes, meaning the black strands have probably meshed together to make a raven's nest on his head.

Nova reaches up, brushing the wayward strands back after they promptly flop over his forehead. "Crazy hair suits you."

Kian turns to her, and as always, his breath hitches.

Nova is the sort of beautiful that everyone notices, and not just because she's one of the few fair-skinned people left. Even if everyone in Askala were the same, Nova would stand out.

Despite being windswept and flushed, with strands of blonde hair yanked from her braid and framing her face, she's exquisite. Her sky-blue eyes sparkle as she smiles, a smile Kian wishes he could capture and carry with him always.

His father clears his throat. "Good job, you two. You look like you've done that before."

Kian grins down at Nova. They spent many an afternoon practicing that same move over the edge of the lake, always pushing how far they could reach.

It was after the first time Nova fell in that he noticed her newly developed curves...

Nova giggles, her hand tightening around his. "Good to know it came in handy for something."

Kian's mother smiles at them. "Sometimes the pair of you function like two parts of a whole." She turns to his father. "We should probably check on the gardens before the storm sets in."

His father nods. "Yes, we'll need to make sure the fences are secure." He glances at Kian and Nova. "You stay here. You'll need to check the net every now and again to make sure it stays fastened."

"We've got it, Dad."

Kian says the words, knowing he won't let his father down. His heart is promised to two things. Nova. And Askala.

His dad pats his shoulder as they leave, his mind already at the gardens situated at the edge of the forest. "Thanks, son."

With his parents gone, Kian turns to Nova, wriggling his dark brows at her. "We make a good team."

Nova rolls her eyes. "You said that when we were twelve and we thought mangrove pine soup would be edible."

Kian chuckles as he remembers how bad it smelled, let alone tasted. "And when we were fourteen and we tried to get a raven's egg."

Nova grins. "That one was your idea, and you wouldn't listen when I told you a broken leg isn't as treatable as it used to be."

"We almost got it, though." Kian takes a step closer. "And we'll make an even better team at sixteen."

"We are sixteen, Kian."

Kian shifts in closer, his voice dropping. "I meant Bound sixteen."

Nova's tongue flicks out across her bottom lip. "Oh."

Kian's gut clenches as his gaze is drawn there. He's spent so long wondering what Nova's lips feel like. What they taste like.

Their gazes lock and the air heats. It's like the small room just became pressurized. Kian's hands twitch by his sides, desperate to hold her in a way he's never held her before. Their bodies angle closer, their heads naturally coming together.

Except they're not Bound.

Yet.

Simultaneously, they step back. Nova pulls in a steadying breath, mock glaring at Kian. "You've got to stop doing that."

Kian grins. "It's like trying to fight gravity."

Nova shakes her head and creates more space between them. "I'll head back to the infirmary. Last time we had a storm that

19

looked like that, one of the Bounds slipped over and cut their knee trying to check on the lab."

Kian pouts. "You could stay and help me here."

Nova's eyes twinkle as she shakes her head. "You know time alone isn't a good idea."

He jams his fingers through his hair, smiling ruefully. "As always, you're the voice of reason."

Nova steps toward the door, her hand brushing his as she passes. Even that simple contact flares the awareness that never seems to dial down. "I'll see you in the hall at dinner."

Kian watches her leave, realizing it's getting harder and harder to stop. Thank Terra the Proving is only a few days away.

After that, there'll be nothing that will keep Kian and Nova apart.

DEX

*D*ex stands at the closed door of the lab, deciding he's never been more bored or lonely. He should be used to it by now. Not so much the boredom, but the loneliness. It seems like *everyone* has a *someone*.

Except him.

He'd hoped to hang out with Kian in the days before their Proving, but his cousin hasn't had as much time for him since his responsibilities with the pods increased. And since Nova became... well, the more curvaceous version of the Nova they used to play tag with as kids. And who could blame him? That girl redefines the word beautiful. Both inside and out.

But Dex is relieved that in this case history won't be repeating. His feelings for Nova are firmly in the friend zone. Sadly, for his father life wasn't that simple when he was young. Rumor has it he'd been madly in love with Kian's mother, but had lost out to his younger brother in the race for her affections. Just as Dex knows he would if his feelings were different and he tried to compete for Nova's heart.

His aunt Amity and uncle Magnus are each other's someone. Just like Kian and Nova.

Dex is more like his own father. Destined to be alone.

Knowing he's not allowed to enter the lab until his Proving, he decides to head to the beach. A storm is coming and there's no better place to watch it roll in than standing on the edge of the water. His father would forbid this, of course. He's supposed to take cover in the safety of the Oasis. But there's no way his father will ever know, given he's locked himself in the lab.

As Dex takes the well-worn path to the beach, thoughts of his mother race through his mind, just like the black clouds filling the sky. She'd been his someone. His father might spend every spare moment at the lab, but his mother had doted on him. He can no longer remember her face, but the memory of her love lingers.

If only he could remember the night she was taken from him. If only he could've stopped it.

He'd been very young, but the Bounds in the next cabin said they'd woken to hear his mother begging for Dex's life. They'd rushed to her aid but had been knocked over by an Unbound who was escaping down the corridor with a hood pulled over his head and a knife in his hand. They'd picked themselves up and gone into the cabin to find that although Dex had been spared, tragically his mother had not.

Ironically, her name had been Mercy.

She'd died protecting him, which meant that she was no longer his someone, leaving him to be nobody's anything.

As the dirt beneath his bare feet turns to sand, a gust of wind draws his attention to the sky and he's pleased to see the storm is gathering strength. It feels right that the sky's angry. It helps to make up for the lack of anger his father seems to feel about the injustice that was dished up to them that night. His father chooses instead to spend endless hours in the lab designing the Provings that Askala's sixteen-year-olds must face each year. Perhaps if he hadn't been working the night their world imploded, things would have turned out differently.

Soon though, his father will need to leave the safety of the lab. Because this year's Proving will be a special one, requiring all the High Bounds to stand down from their prestigious roles and make way for the next generation. Dex knows his father hopes he'll be included in that group, but Dex refuses to talk about it. He doesn't even know if he's Bound yet.

First, he must face his own Proving. He's tried to find out what the tests will be, but as a High Bound who takes his role seriously, his father refuses to give him any clues, confident he can pass it by himself.

Dex isn't so sure.

Because unlike the eight other teens being tested his year, not one of them is like him. Nobody has the same disadvantage. Disability is probably a better word for it, but he's never liked to apply that word to himself. He's determined not to let what happened to him the night his mom died, hold him back.

Blinking back tears, he breaks through the trees and walks out to the narrow beach. As he stares at the swirling rust-colored ocean, he tries to accept that pain is as much a part of the landscape as the decaying hulk of the Oasis. One day, when the rot in the ship reaches critical mass, they'll have to build a new home. Not an easy prospect with resources so scarce. At least if he's Unbound, this won't be a problem he'll need to solve.

The storm picks up a new energy and Dex throws back his head and drinks in the feeling of being alive. He'd much rather be out here than breathing the stale air of the Oasis. Perhaps another tornado will pick up the giant ship and throw it back into the sea. Except this time, instead of being filled with wealthy passengers, it will be eaten by the acidic ocean and wipe out Askala once and for all. What a tragedy that would be after all the hard work that's been done to build the world he's lucky enough to live in today.

He's about to sit down on the sand when he spots something in the distance. Squinting, he looks harder. Is that…? It can't be.

He looks again. It is! It's a hand, waving frantically above the rise and fall of the angry sea. Scanning the water from left to right, he sees more shapes bobbing on the surface. People. Lots of people. No, not people, he reminds himself.

Remnants.

It's been so long since anyone from the Outlands has tried to make their way to Askala that they'd started to wonder if any of these leftover people remained.

But there's proof in front of him right now that there are still survivors.

Dex runs to the post on the shore that marks the spot where a bridge once connected Askala to the Outlands. Before Magnus had it burned down as his first act of power when he became their leader.

Picking up the ancient horn that hangs from the post, he presses it to his lips and blows deeply.

The sound surprises him. He's never heard this horn, let alone made the sound himself. It's high-pitched and echoes over the sand, being swept up by the wind before it has a chance to reach the Oasis.

If the Bound can't hear his call, nobody will come to help. And then what will he do? If any Remnant touches the shore, they're entitled to stay. That was why Magnus burned the bridge after the pteropod population was wiped out. They didn't have enough resources to sustain themselves, let alone an outsider.

But, do they now?

He blows the horn again, this time using every last bit of breath he has to push the sound through it. If they didn't hear that, he has no hope. Should he run back and raise the alarm? Or would it be foolish if the one set of eyes they have on the Remnants turns away?

Letting the horn fall back against the post, he gets as close to the churning water as he dares. It won't harm him if he touches it briefly, but extended contact is highly dangerous. The acid would burn him, trying to dissolve the skin from his bones. Then it would start work on the bones themselves.

How are those Remnants surviving out there? They must be in agony.

He sees what remains of the raft they must have traveled on. The timber planks are steadily tearing apart.

The people are getting more frantic now. Heads are bobbing up and down, as they come in and out of sight. Even from here, he can see their skin turning a lighter shade of the angry red ocean. For one foolish moment, Dex considers swimming out to haul them to shore, but then he remembers the story his father told him about the time his aunt Amity tried to do that and not only failed, but she'd almost lost her own life. It's been drummed into him since he was young. Never enter the water.

Never.

But standing here just seems so cruel.

Returning to the horn, he tries again. The wind is stronger now and swallows the sound like a hungry leatherskin.

The thought of these thick-skinned sharks has Dex racing back to the shoreline as he scans for the ominous gray fins. It's not often the leatherskins are offered a feed like this and he's certain they won't miss their chance. Not many aquatic animals survived global warming. What wasn't wiped out by the destruction of humans did a good job of wiping each other out. Only the toughest creatures survived.

The rain starts and Dex winces at its sharpness. If the Bounds hadn't heard the sound of the horn before, then there's no point trying again now. He's well aware of how loud the sound of rain is as it pelts the old cruise ship. His only hope is that someone was in the gardens and was able to raise the alarm for him.

A flash of lightning has Dex jumping and he wraps an arm around himself, determined not to leave his post as he waits for the boom of thunder to follow.

His wait is short, evidence of how close the storm is.

A Remnant's cry skims across the water and reaches his ears. Holding up his right hand to shelter his eyes, he looks out and sees a girl. Or a woman, perhaps. Her long dark hair is wrapping itself around her face and she's trying to claw it away as she kicks against the water, somehow keeping herself above the surface. She's much closer than any of the others, although still far enough away that it will take a miracle for her to make it ashore. Each time she gains a bit of distance, a current sweeps her back.

Her skin isn't pink like the others. It has a dark, glossy appearance. It's impossible to tell from this distance but it almost seems like she's coated herself with something. There's a silver disc strapped to her throat and it catches the light, glinting like she's some kind of beacon. A raven flies above her, attracted by the reflection, but afraid to get too close. The ocean would love the chance to drag its feathery form into its depths.

The other Remnants are slowly disappearing under the water. Each time Dex scans for them, there's one less to find. A dozen become ten, then five, and now he can only see three others besides the girl.

In all the times he'd imagined what a Remnant attack might look like, he'd never thought it would be like this. He'd been told the Remnants were vicious and selfish and would stop at nothing to take what they'd all worked so hard for in Askala. But these helpless Remnants bobbing in the water don't look like that. They look like... people. Desperate people without a hope.

He jumps as he feels a thump on his back, and his hand falls to his side. It's Kian.

"I've been looking for you," Kian shouts over the noise of the storm. "You must be mad to be out here!"

Dex nods, pleased his cousin noticed his absence. Then blinking raindrops from his lashes, he points. "Remnants."

"Sweet Terra!" says Kian. "We need to call an alert."

Dex rolls his eyes, although his cousin can't see it, mainly because his gaze is glued to the ocean. "Tried that already. Twice."

There are only two Remnants above water now. Plus, the girl, who seems to have made it a little closer.

Kian grips his arm, almost as if he senses Dex's urge to run into the water and drag her ashore.

"Is she going to make it?" Dex asks, not really expecting Kian to have any better idea then he does. They're both equally inexperienced when it comes to Remnants.

Kian shakes his head. "Not a chance. Look!"

Dex follows the direction Kian's pointing and sees two gray fins slicing through the water. The waves aren't a problem for these beasts. If anything, they give them an advantage.

The girl has seen them, too. Whatever she's put on her skin may be protecting her from the acid of the water, but it's going to do little against the rows of sharp teeth that line the enormous jaws of a leatherskin.

"We've got to help her!" cries Dex, wresting himself away from Kian.

"We can't," his cousin says. "We might not be made Bound if we help a Remnant ashore."

"This isn't the Proving." Dex wades out into the water. He has so much less to lose than Kian. If Kian fails his Proving, he'll miss his chance to be with Nova, who's certain to be made Bound. But what does it matter to Dex? He's not sure he wants to be Bound if it means watching a girl drown.

His ankles tingle as they submerge in the warm salty water, but he pushes himself outward.

"Dex!" Kian shouts. "Get back here."

Then he hears the sound of the horn. Kian is trying to help him in the only way he can. He tried to tell him the horn was useless.

"I'm sorry!" he shouts back to his cousin, hoping he hasn't gotten them both in trouble.

There's a scream and Dex looks up just in time to see a leatherskin toss a Remnant in the air like he's some kind of puppet instead of a fully-grown man.

Dex runs further out into the water, watching as the shark catches the man in its open jaws. Red liquid gushes over the triumphant mouth of the leatherskin before it dives under the water, taking what's left of the man with it.

Dex tears away his eyes and drags in a deep breath, willing his heart rate to slow. That poor man! Remnant, he corrects himself. That poor Remnant had been a fool to try to come here. He must've known the dangers. But had he deserved to die like that?

The girl looks more panicked now. She sees Dex in the water and holds both her hands in the air, waving at him for help.

He holds up his right hand, wishing he could return her gesture properly. Holding this one pathetic hand in the air feels like a symbol of his loneliness. Because in this world where everyone has a someone, even his hand is missing a partner.

Lifting what remains of his other arm, he stops in the water and stares at the space where his left hand should be. What makes him think he's going to be able to save anyone? When that girl called to him for help, she didn't realize who she was calling. A half-man, forever maimed by the Unbound who took his mother away.

Unlovable. Pathetic. Hopeless. A freak. It's no wonder he feels so alone.

Because not only did that Unbound take his someone away.

He took away his chance for him to ever find someone else. Who would ever love someone with a stump for a hand no matter how kind their heart is?

He hadn't been able to save his mother. He hadn't even been able to save himself. But maybe, just maybe, he might be able to save this girl.

WREN

*W*ren takes in a large gulp of water and winces as the acid burns her throat. She'd planned to keep her mouth firmly closed if she ended up in the ocean. And her eyes, as much as possible. But here she is with both her eyes and mouth wide open, clawing at the relentless cruelty of the waves as they beat at her, determined to drag her to their toxic depths.

But she's not going to give up. If she dies out here, she'll die trying until the very last moment when her body no longer has anything left to give.

She mustn't panic like she did earlier when she'd seen the leatherskins circling. That had cost her dearly when the undertow had taken advantage of her distraction and pulled her out. Further from land. Closer to the sharks. Miles away from hope.

But then she'd noticed someone wade out into the water and she'd become certain she still had a chance. Clinging to this feeling, she seals her eyes and mouth as another wave sends her tumbling. She keeps calm as she waits for the ocean to relinquish its grip and allow her back up to the surface. This isn't anything like swimming in the inland lake where she'd trained.

Thank goodness she's fitter than she's ever been. She had plenty to eat as she'd layered her small body with muscle, preparing for exactly this moment. She'd lifted heavy logs, climbed trees, and run for miles. But nothing in the world could have prepared her for this. The ocean's an even tougher trainer than Cy.

More demanding. Less forgiving.

The wave spits her out, only for another one to grab hold and drag her down again. She has just a moment in between to draw in another breath, grateful now for the way Cy had held her head underwater to strengthen her lungs. She'd kicked and struggled against his hand, but right now, she holds still. Eventually the water will allow her back up.

Feeling the hold loosen, she propels herself upward, her lungs screaming for air.

"Assholes!" she cries when she breaks through the surface. It feels good to curse without Cy here to reprimand her. Let him climb aboard a raft and watch it break apart and see what kind of language he uses.

She was sure the raft would make it further than it had. It was made from mangrove pine, for goodness sake! That stuff lasts for years in the water. But they didn't think hard enough about the twine they'd used to hold the planks together. It seems dipping it in sap wasn't good enough.

At least the sap is working better on her skin. She doesn't feel like she's being affected at all. Apart from her throat. And her eyes. Oh, for the love of god, her eyes hurt! It's like someone's lit a fire in her pupils.

The rain is pelting down now and she lifts her face to the sky and tries to catch some drops of fresh water. But it's no use. There's only one way she's ever going to feel better again and that's if she gets herself the hell out of here. If she doesn't survive, then that whole trip will have been for nothing. The rest of her companions are already as good as dead.

She's sad about that reality, but nowhere near surprised.

She'd known they weren't going to make it the moment she'd laid eyes on them. Not one of them had trained for the journey in the same way she had. They had no idea what dangers they were likely to face. It's hard enough for her and she was ready for it. Well, she thought she was.

Dragging herself through the water, she tries to swim on an angle to get out of the rip that seems to be taking so much pleasure in dragging her further out to sea.

Something bumps her roughly on her side and she spins around to see a leatherskin whip past her. Cursing once more, she draws in a deep breath and prepares to fight. Known for their enjoyment of playing with their food, the leatherskins are brutal. But she can be brutal, too. She's had to be. It's called survival and it's a game she knows how to play well.

Treading water, she waits for the leatherskin to come at her again, as she knows it will. It's expecting her to be scared, which of course she is, but it's not expecting her to put up a fight. Although, surprise feels like the only thing she has on her side here. She just has to hope it's enough.

A huge gray fin emerges from the water beside her and she acts quickly, knowing she has one chance at this. She lunges for the fin and grips it hard, swinging her body up and over until she's straddling the giant beast. The shark struggles and squirms, trying to flip her from its back as it snaps its hungry jaws in the air.

Damn this sap on her skin! It might be protecting her from the acid, but it's making holding on impossible. The powerful muscles of the beast are thrashing beneath her and her hands slide up the fin. If she lets go, she's as good as dead, but she's been taught to never give up. Never. Even when death seems certain, sometimes it's not.

In one quick movement, she reaches down and pulls out a small but sharp knife she has in a holster around her waist. Holding onto the fin with one hand, she slams the knife into the leatherskin's side, only for the blade to bounce back at her. There's a reason these sharks have survived in water so acidic. Nothing can penetrate those thick hides. She'd been foolish to even try.

The shark dives down and as Wren is pulled underwater, she's left with a choice. Hold on and be dragged to the ocean's depths, or let go and put herself in the path of that snapping jaw once more.

The decision is made for her as her hands slip from the fin and she shoots back up to the surface finding herself alone. Vulnerable. But with some fight still left.

It takes her only seconds to realize the shark has moved her out of the rip. She's further from shore now, but it should be an easier swim. If she lives long enough to make it.

She puts the blade of the knife between her teeth and takes a few strokes toward land, praying for a miracle. Please, let the leatherskin have become distracted. She's sure she can make it, if only it leaves her alone.

A giant mass slams into her middle, flipping her high into the air and flinging the knife from her teeth.

This is it. It's all over.

The pain of her defeat grips her bruised core, crushing what's left of her hope. But as gravity makes its claim on her and the giant jaws open up beneath her, she decides that this isn't how it ends for her.

Reaching out and grabbing the knife as it flies past her, she lands on the rows of sharp teeth, screaming in agony as she drives the knife into the roof of the leatherskin's mouth. Please, let the blade be long enough to reach this evil creature's tiny brain.

The leatherskin's jaws go instantly slack and knowing she reached her target, she rolls herself out of its mouth and back into the water, a pool of blood bubbling around her.

She did it! Her heart might be beating out of her aching

chest and the smell of fear might be clinging to her skin under-neath the diminishing layer of sap, but somehow she took on a leatherskin and won.

Not knowing if the blood belongs to her or the shark, she tucks the knife back in the holster and kicks toward land once more. She has to make it before the other leatherskin sees her. There's no way she has the strength to do that again. Or the luck.

Her strokes are strong and determined but quickly weaken as the adrenaline wears off.

Hearing Cy's voice in her ear, urging her on, she swings an arm high above her head and drives it down, cupping her palm as she pulls herself through the water. If she just keeps going, she can make it. Each stroke is bringing her closer to her goal. A goal that people had told her was impossible. But impossible doesn't mean the same thing to Wren as everyone else.

Impossible just means she has to fight harder.

A flash of lightning strikes and she instinctively grabs hold of the pendant around her neck. A crazy thing to be wearing in the water during a storm, but she couldn't risk losing it. This is her link to home. To Cy. But more importantly, to Phoenix.

Her pupils aren't just on fire now, her entire eyeballs feel like they've burst into flames. She pauses her swimming to rub at them, unable to tell how much further she has to go. She can do this. She has to do this.

Squeezing her eyes closed, she pushes on, startled when something grabs the back of her shirt. Her heart thumps hard in her chest as she tries to work out if it's a person or a shark.

"I've got you," says a deep voice.

She feels every one of her muscles go weak all at once. Like they'd lasted as long as they had to and are now refusing to go on.

She looks up and through her blurred vision, she sees a guy. Perhaps the same age as herself. He's tall, but scrawny with mousy brown hair that's hanging limply over his protruding ears. He only has one hand, something that would make her curious in any other circumstance.

"Stand up," he says, shouting over the wind. "It's shallow here. You're losing a lot of blood. We have to get you to shore."

She can't quite believe he's saving her. She'd been told the people here would do anything to prevent her making it to land alive. They hated outsiders, going so far as to call them Remnants. A disgusting name. How can any innocent person be considered a leftover?

Deciding she's dreaming, she allows her eyes to close. Perhaps she's no longer alive and this is some kind of death angel dragging her to the pits of hell.

"Stand up," the guy insists. "I can't get you to shore alone."

She sighs and summons the energy to open her eyes and scramble to her feet. Of all the people to save her, trust it to end up being a boy with one hand.

"Climb on my back," he says, bending over. But he's so much taller than her and it feels like climbing a mountain.

"I can't," she says, using the words she hates the most. But for the first time in her life, they feel true. She's completely depleted.

He crouches in the water and winces as it laps at his waist. "Hurry!"

She does as she's told and climbs onto his back, holding on as he stands and stumbles toward the shore. It's just like keeping hold of the shark. Because she trusts this guy about as much as she trusted that leatherskin.

But at least he's not trying to kill her. Which means she'll also let him live.

For now.

He reaches the shore and falls to his knees. She slides off him and lies on her back on the sand, panting for breath as the rain tickles her face. Her eyes are stinging, but now that she's out of the water, there's a small amount of relief.

Blood is pooling around her, but there's not as much of it as she'd feared. Most of what she'd seen in the water must've come from the shark. With any luck she'll get out of this with a series of superficial cuts and bruises. She draws in a deep breath and winces. And perhaps a broken rib or two.

Her vision clears just enough for her to see there's another guy standing over her. This one has dark hair. And two hands. He's one of those handsome sorts she doesn't trust. Come to think of it, she really doesn't trust anybody.

"I'm going to get help," he says, running away from them.

She turns her head to see her savior is also lying on his back, rubbing at his eyes with his one hand.

"Thanks," she says, feeling like some kind of acknowledgement is required. Her throat is on fire and it's hard to get even that simple word out. Or perhaps she's just not used to thanking people.

The guy's hand falls to his side and he blinks at her. "My pleasure."

This makes her smile, and she wonders if he meant to be funny.

"I've never seen anything like what you did out there." His red eyes are wide, his voice full of awe.

She clears her throat so she can respond. "That's because you've never met me."

NOVA

*N*ova is folding bandages beside her mother, wishing she was somewhere watching the storm with Kian as they like to do, when the door to the infirmary flies open.

Shiloh darts in, her dark hair plastered to her face. "Thea! One of the Unbound just knocked themselves unconscious trying to climb the lookout."

Nova shakes her head. The lookout is nothing more than a ladder that spears up into the sky, now used to monitor the empty horizons. According to the stories, it used to lead to a slide, although it was long ago destroyed by an angry storm. Those were the days humans seemed to think frivolity was a right.

Nova's mother straightens. "That's not unusual. They've probably been enjoying their berry wine and thought the storm would add an extra challenge."

Nova goes back to her bandage folding, telling herself she's glad she's never tried the stuff. The Unbound seem to like risk-taking. It's like they don't care whether they live or die.

Shiloh's gaze flickers to Nova before returning to her mother. "Well, it's…ah…Dean."

Nova shoots up. "He's probably reopened his wound."

Her mother's hand falls lightly on Nova's shoulder. "I'll go."

Nova hesitates. She should go—she was the one who treated his cut in the first place. And it's more important that her mother, the more experienced healer, stay back.

But it's Dean...the one person who makes her feel far from a future Bound.

Before Nova can respond, her mother is heading to the door. "Shiloh, you come with me. Nova, you stay here, in case someone comes in." With a soft smile over her shoulder, she's gone.

Nova flops back into her chair. She should've gone.

A Bound would've gone. They wouldn't have thought twice. Shiloh certainly didn't. Dean's relationship to the one person who almost destroyed Askala wouldn't have mattered.

But it was her father who lost his life trying to repair that damage, leaving her mother unable to bear partnering again after the loss of her beloved Tareq. Would even a Bound forgive that?

Kian's face, with his earth-colored eyes so full of love and faith, floats through her mind. His handsome features are never far from her consciousness. There's no doubt in his mind that they'll pass. That she'll pass. He's told her over and over she only worries because this is so important to her. To both of them.

Nova sighs, picking up the next threadbare slice of cloth. All she can do is have faith he's right.

This time when the door flies open, Nova makes a decision as she leaps to her feet. It must be Shiloh. Her mother needs help, and this time she won't hesitate.

She'll help whoever it is, no matter who they are.

Except it's not Shiloh. In fact, it's someone she's never seen before.

The bloodied girl who stumbles through the door is short

enough that initially Nova thinks she's a child, but then she registers the muscled body and realizes she must be older.

Nova jumps forward to help her, already assessing her injuries, but Dex is just behind, grasping the girl's shoulder.

She shakes him off with a sharp movement. "I'm perfectly capable of walking." The girl glowers at him. "I have two legs, you know."

As the girl realizes what she said, she tenses her jaw, but she doesn't drop her gaze.

Kian is right behind Dex, a frown darkening his features. "He was just trying to help."

The girl juts her chin, dark hair sticking up in wet spikes. "It's not help if I don't want it."

Nova pauses at the steel laced through the girl's words. There's something different about her. Although she's small, her bare arms are corded with muscle. And her clothes, they're not the flowing, neutral colored hemp they all wear. Nova peers a little closer. They seem to be made of scraps of thin material... and leather. But it's not just the clothes or layers of muscle that make this girl stand out. She's a little...obnoxious.

Nova's hand flies to her chest. Sweet Terra, she's a Remnant!

The girl spins around, suddenly on high alert. The assessment she gives Nova with red-rimmed eyes that almost look too large for her small face is quick. She relaxes a moment later. "What? Never seen a bit of blood before?"

In fact, the cuts were the first thing Nova saw. Streaked across the girl's midriff, they've shredded the leather vest she's wearing. Beneath, gashes and grazes peek as if they're behind curtains. Everywhere, there's blood. A dark, pithy blood, darker than Nova's ever seen before.

She resists frowning as she wonders what that means. "I've seen blood before."

The girl shrugs. "Not that it matters. I don't need hel—"

She sways, one hand flying to her head while the other

reaches out blindly, only to find nothing to steady herself. Nova is by her side in an instant. She feels the girl tense, probably getting ready to push Nova off in the same way she did Dex, but her legs give out.

Nova grabs her around the waist, her fingers slipping through the blood, and leads the girl to the nearest cot. The girl lets her, but the moment Kian and Dex step in to help she growls.

Nova looks at her in surprise. She doesn't think she's ever heard a person growl. She doesn't think Kian and Dex have either, because they both stop, eyebrows high in their hairline.

The girl relaxes back into the cot. "At least you guys are smart enough to know when to back off."

Kian frowns, just as Nova thought he would. This Remnant obviously doesn't realize that the people of Askala don't talk to each other like that.

Nova feels some of her tension soften. This poor girl. Who knows what she's seen and gone through in the Outlands. How she got here is going to be an interesting story, but she's here.

Which now entitles her to stay.

The girl's sharp gaze is flitting around the room with the speed of a hawk. She sees Nova looking at her, and she stares back, her jaw at the same tilt since she came in. Everything about her is strength and determination.

But as Nova keeps looking, she notices what others wouldn't. The lines of tension fanning around the girl's eyes. The lips that are a little too pale. The slightest tremble as the girl drapes an arm across her waist.

She's in pain, and she doesn't want to show it.

Helping her isn't a choice. Nova stands and turns to Kian, but before she can say a word, he shakes his head. "I'm not leaving."

Of course, he knew what she was going to say. And of course, he's not going to agree. Protectiveness is synonymous with love for Kian, and they've all heard what Remnants are capable of.

But the infirmary is Nova's territory, and this girl needs medical attention. She points to the door. "Then you'll have to step outside. I need to tend to her wounds."

Kian starts to shake his head, but Nova raises a brow. The girl's clothes are barely hanging on, and Nova is going to have to remove what's left to dress the cuts. Kian and Dex can't be in the room for that.

Kian opens his mouth to object, but Nova plants a hand on her hip. "She has a right to privacy."

"If she was here to hurt anyone, she would've done it by now," Dex offers. "Let Nova treat her, we won't be far away."

Nova throws a grateful glance to her friend. Dex has always had a special place in his heart for the injured birds of this world.

"The door stays cracked, and I'm going to be right on the other side of it," Kian huffs.

Nova rolls her eyes. "That's fine."

Kian's earthy gaze twinkles. "In that case, I'd be happy to."

Nova shakes her head. It's so easy for Kian to slip back to his default—an easy confidence that everything will turn out okay. Faith and optimism are part of his DNA.

Kian glares a warning at the girl, who does little more than roll her eyes, before leaving the room. Dex follows him out, glancing over his shoulder at the last minute. Nova goes to offer him a smile, hoping to reassure him, too, but Dex doesn't look at her. His focus is on the girl lying on the cot, who's staring at them like she's willing them to leave. With a frown of his own, he tucks his handless arm into his chest and leaves, stopping the door from sliding completely shut.

Slipping into the role she knows and loves, Nova heads to the shelves to get some supplies. The cuts will need to be cleaned and bandaged, and the girl will need some fresh clothes.

Her hand pauses as she reaches for a small basin. What if she needs stitches?

Hoping her mother isn't far away, Nova decides she'll treat this girl as if she were anyone who would come to the infirmary before their Proving—as a potential Bound.

Remnant or not.

Nova returns, not surprised to find the girl still watching her with her sharp gaze. Remnants probably don't trust easily.

Nova smiles. "My name's Nova. Welcome to Askala."

"I know where I am. I'm the one who swam through an acid ocean to get here, remember?"

Nova's smile widens. It's like talking to Old Sam. "And you are?"

"Wren." She starts to cross her arms only to wince. The tightening of her face is only slight, and quickly suppressed, but Nova doesn't miss it.

Taking the seat beside the cot, she places the tray of bandages beside her. "I'd like to take a look at your wounds. Is that okay, Wren?"

Every muscle in Wren's small, athletic body tenses. "Do I get a choice?"

Nova's brows shoot up. "Of course you get a choice. I won't touch you without your permission."

"Good. Because I'm pretty sure I'm fine."

Yep. Very much like Old Sam. Nova leans back, giving Wren some space. "Tell me, how did you get here?"

Wren has done what no Remnant has achieved since the bridge was burned—made it to Askala alive.

Wren's glance slides away. "There were several of us. We built a raft, but the blasted thing fell apart quite a distance from shore."

Nova nods. Others have tried to reach Askala using anything that floats, but every Remnant has fallen victim to the acidic ocean...and the leatherskins. "So you swam?"

"Didn't really have a choice, did I?"

Nova looks at Wren again, surprised at the sense of respect she's feeling. This girl is strong in a way no one in Askala is, probably because she's been chiseled by the fight for survival. But Nova can sense that her strength is deeper than the power-house of muscles that make up her small frame.

"That's very impressive, Wren."

It's Wren's turn to be surprised, but she quickly masks it behind a frown. "Well, it almost wasn't thanks to the leatherskin."

Leatherskin? The word has Nova focusing on the ribbons of cuts along Wren's midriff. She'd assumed they'd happened on the rocks that aren't far off the beach. Askala isn't surrounded by stretches of sand and gently rolling waves. Not when the island they live on was created by a rising ocean. Instead, the land drops off sharply into the sea. Below, is rocky soil and a continental shelf bordered by what used to be hills and valleys.

And Wren survived not only an ocean the color of watery blood that corrodes skin and bone, but also a deadly shark that would've been over twenty feet long!

Nova leans forward again. "I'd really like to take a look at your cuts. I wouldn't want them to become infected." She smiles gently. "Leatherskins aren't very good at brushing their teeth on a daily basis."

Wren nibbles on her lower lip, the first sign of vulnerability Nova's seen since she half-barged, half-stumbled through the door. "Fine, then. But I keep telling you, they're not that bad."

Nova doesn't answer. If Wren had to fight off a leatherskin, then there's no way these cuts are only superficial.

Nova quickly wets a rag before Wren can change her mind. Carefully, she peels back a shred of leather. The first thing she notes is that Wren isn't as dark-skinned as she initially thought. Instead, she's coated with some sort of sticky substance, like the honey she's read about. Then she sees the cuts. Angry welts slice up her side, one of them streaking from her hip to her ribs. Nova frowns. There's dried blood smeared across her gummy skin, but the cuts themselves aren't terribly deep. Most have stopped bleeding and have already started the healing process.

"Are you sure it was a leatherskin? I would've expected the cuts to be deeper."

Wren narrows her eyes at Nova. "I jammed my favorite knife into its brain, I'm pretty sure I'm sure."

"Oh." Nova focuses back on the cuts to hide her surprise. Wren fought off a leatherskin? And won? "Well, you've been very lucky then. These cuts should heal well."

"Told you."

Nova ignores the smugness in Wren's voice, maintaining her focus. As always, she keeps her touch gentle and even, but Wren never flinches. Nova suspects she could apply quite a bit of pressure before any sign of pain were to flicker across this determined girl's features.

As she cleans the wounds, the sticky coating dissolves away, exposing smooth, caramel skin. Just as she suspected, the cuts aren't deep, which is probably a good thing. She doubts Wren would've accepted an offer to have them bandaged.

As she works, something strikes Nova. Wren certainly isn't the child she thought she was when she first entered. "How old are you, Wren?"

"Sixteen."

Nova straightens as she realizes what this means. "You're very lucky, then. You're just in time for this year's Proving."

Wren's lips tense. "So I can prove what?"

Nova pauses, suddenly wondering how this all sounds to an outsider. She suspects the Remnants know as much about Askala as they do about them—fragments of information tied together with guesses and assumptions.

"It's a series of four tests over seven days."

Nova's about to say more when Wren pushes up, stifling another wince as she sits on the cot. "What sort of tests?"

"Tests of intelligence and empathy. It's how we pick our leaders."

"You value smarts over strength? That explains why you're all so weedy and weak."

Nova stands up and takes the tray to the bench. "Of course we do. The future of Earth depends on kindness and sacrifice, not those who hunger for power. That's what created the world we're barely surviving in."

Wren arches a brow. "And if you fail?"

Nova was hoping Wren wouldn't ask that question, but it seems Remnants are smarter than she's been led to believe. "You're unable to lead." Nova straightens as she turns to face Wren. "And unable to breed."

"You what?" Wren leaps to her feet. "You sterilize them? That's awful! And you call taking part in the Proving lucky?"

Despite her size, Wren's dismay and disgust hit Nova like a tidal wave. Feeling like she needs to drop an anchor, Nova pulls in a steadying breath. "It's not as simple as that. Bound and Unbound are both fortunate in their own way. The Bound must take on great responsibility along with their ability to pass down the genes that will ensure Earth's survival. They must also care for the Unbound so they can live a life of ease. They're not shunned or looked down upon."

Wren snorts. "And this comes from the people who call us Remnants."

Knowing it's going to take time for Wren to see the good that Askala is founded on, Nova decides against arguing. Wren has gone to great lengths to make it here, so she must want to be here. She'll soon learn that she is, indeed, lucky.

Glad that her sense of calm is returning, Nova sorts through their spare clothing. Wren might be the same age as her, but she'd be closer to a child-sized outfit. "The room next door is a washroom. There'll be a basin of water for you to finish cleaning up." She extends her arms. "Here's some clothes. And make sure you put the bracelet on. It's how we open doors around here. Just press it to the sensor. I'll put some food out for when you return."

Wren takes a step back. "What's the catch?"

"The catch?" Nova asks in surprise. "There are no catches. They're really just robes made of hemp." She holds out the clothes further. "Maybe a few buttons, but that's it."

Wren relaxes, like she just figured it out. "You want me to owe you."

Now Nova is genuinely confused. She glances down at the bundle she's holding. "Owe me what?"

Wren's eyes, the ones that are rounded and soft, yet always so sharp and alert, look from Nova to the stack of clothes in her hands. "You're just giving me clothes and food?" she asks incredulously.

"You need them, and we have enough to spare. Why would I not?"

For the first time since she arrived, Wren is speechless. Frowning, she glances down at her ripped clothing. Torn pants hug her legs, while the remaining shreds of cloth and leather barely cover her torso.

Nova takes a small step forward. "Your clothes will take too long to dry, and these will protect your skin from the sun."

With a frown that seems too big for a girl named after such a dainty bird, Wren strides forwards and takes the clothes. "Fine. But there'd better not be a skirt in there."

Nova shakes her head with a smile. "Pants, like the ones I'm wearing."

Wren grunts and heads to the door, stopping as it slides open. Nova isn't surprised. Kian would've plastered himself to the other side, listening in like a hawk.

Wren curls her lip at him. "Wanting a peep show, were you?"

46

Kian scowls, but it doesn't hide the deep flush that creeps up his cheeks. "We look out for our own." He moves closer to Nova. "I'm not surprised a Remnant didn't realize what that looked like."

Instead of looking affronted, Wren grins. "A Remnant that will be at this year's Proving, from the looks of things."

Kian stiffens like he's been slapped, which has Wren turning back to the exit, her grin tipping up in victory.

Nova blinks, not sure how to take this girl. She's everything a Bound isn't—suspicious, defensive, even rude. But there's a gutsiness about her that she can't help but respect. No wonder she managed to make it to Askala when no one else has.

Dex appears in the doorway, his face a little flushed. "I'll keep an eye on her. You two decide who's going to let the others know."

The High Bound. What will they do when they discover a Remnant has made it to Askala? That a Remnant will be taking part in this year's Proving?

Wren gazes at Kian coolly. "Yeah. You'll need to tell your breeders—I'm mean leaders—that burning the bridge hasn't stopped us."

Nova sucks in a breath. *Us.* She'd been so focused on trying to help Wren that she hadn't considered the consequences of her arrival.

If Wren has made it to Askala, could other Remnants?

Kian comes to stand beside Nova. "Any Remnants who come in peace have always been welcome."

Nova instantly relaxes as his shoulder brushes hers. Although Kian's words were meant as a warning, he's also showing Wren they're a people of love and peace. Wren may be strong, the other Remnants may be, too.

But Askala is stronger.

Nova manages a smile. Kian has always had enough faith for the both of them.

Wren is about to leave when she pauses at the door. Dex steps back so she can pass, but instead of walking through, she turns back to Nova. "How old are you, Nova?"

Nova's heart lurches. "Sixteen."

"So, you'll be part of the Proving, too?"

Nova nods, her throat feeling tight. "Yes, I will be."

She stops herself from glancing at Kian and Dex. We all will be.

"So you're lucky too, huh?" Wren's eyes have taken that assessing slant again, for some reason putting Nova on edge. "You think you'll pass?"

Nova straightens her shoulders. "My mother is Bound." High Bound, no less. "And I've worked hard to embody everything Askala stands for."

And the one who holds my heart, the one who's watching me right now, will almost certainly be Bound.

Wren turns toward the door, shaking her head. "So, what you're saying is, you don't know."

KIAN

*T*he Remnant disappears into the room adjacent to the infirmary, the door sliding shut behind her.

Kian stares at it for a few seconds, his gut hot and hard, before turning to Nova. "Ignore her. Don't forget the Remnants think there's nothing more important than their own survival."

Nova looks up at Kian with her sweet, blue eyes and he feels his heart thud a little harder. "She's right. None of us know if we'll pass."

Kian strokes his fingers down her soft cheek. "I know, okay?" He spreads his fingers, his other hand rising to cup her cheeks. "Askala was built on love, remember?"

He savors the rush that always comes when Nova smiles. Kian's reminding her of the words he said when they were fifteen, standing beneath the boughs of a mangrove pine.

Askala was built on love.

We were forged from love.

Our future will be filled with love.

"I remember," Nova whispers.

The glance at her lips is reflexive. Yearning pulses through his veins. What would it be like to show Nova how he feels rather than just tell her? Her blue eyes darken, telling him these emotions are swallowing her just as completely.

Dex clears his throat. "You'd better go tell your dad, Kian."

They both step back, guilty even though this is nothing Dex hasn't seen before. They're not meant to let these feelings get so strong before the Proving. It's only after the tests that the youth who are the future of Askala can even consider what had been filling Kian's mind.

Kian grins. After that, it's encouraged. He turns to Dex. "I'll wait here a bit longer."

Dex is already shaking his head, probably expecting Kian to say that. "This is important, Kian."

Kian is about to suggest Dex should go, but he quickly changes his mind. Dex was the one who helped the Remnant out of the water. Without him, there's a high possibility she wouldn't have made it. As much as he's not sure how he feels about that, Kian doesn't want quiet, awkward Dex to have to explain his actions to the leader of the High Bound, Kian's own father, Magnus.

Or Dex's own father, another of the High Bound.

Except that means leaving Nova with the girl. Although she's been nothing but rude and obnoxious, she's still a Remnant, and who knows what she's capable of.

Or what she wants with Askala.

Dex steps forward, gripping Kian's arm. "Wren's injured. She's not a threat."

Nova nods. "There's a bed in that room. I wouldn't be surprised if exhaustion catches up with her the moment she sits down."

Dex squeezes his arm. "Plus, Nova will look after me if anything happens."

Kian grins as his muscles unwind. Dex has mastered the art of subtlety and humor, and he loves that about his cousin and childhood best friend. He's telling Kian that Nova is perfectly capable of looking after herself, quietly pointing out that he's getting overprotective.

Dex arches a brow. "I mean, you could always ask Nova to come with you."

Kian bursts into laughter. They both know that would be a waste of breath. There's no way she'd leave the infirmary unattended. Nova has always loved with a passion, and that includes her drive to heal others in this little room.

Nova flushes a delightful shade of red. "Someone has to be the responsible one around here."

It's then that they hear the voices down the hall, and Kian realizes the decision has been made for him. Thea and Shiloh are on their way back, which means he can go.

"I'll see you two at the dining hall for dinner?"

Nova smiles the smile that only seems for him. "It's a date."

Kian takes her hand and squeezes it making a promise to himself. Soon, after the Proving, it will always be a kiss good-bye, rather than a touch.

Dex rolls his eyes. "I like you two and everything, but I can only hold one hand at a time, so it won't be a triple date."

Kian chuckles, for the umpteenth time, wondering if Dex is really as casual about his missing hand as he makes out. Their entire life, he's joked about it. At the same time, Dex has rarely talked about how he lost it.

Or his mother.

Shaking the thought away, he heads in the opposite direction to the voices. Right now, they have a Remnant to deal with, which means he has to find his father.

A quick check of the pod pool tells him he isn't there, and that the storm has almost blown over. His mother isn't there either, which means they're probably both in the boardroom. That's where his father goes when he's not busy doing something else. The people of Askala know this, meaning they can usually find him if they need to.

Kian realizes it's a good idea. Right now he needs to talk to him.

He navigates the maze of corridors and flights of stairs that make up the Oasis, letting his fingers brush over the walls with their cracked paint as he goes. The smell of mildew gets stronger the further in he heads, but he still thinks of it as an old friend. This decaying skeleton has been their protection since Askala was born.

He's almost at the boardroom when the sound of children squealing and laughing has Kian simultaneously smiling and wincing. He's pretty sure the paint wasn't peeling throughout the cruise ship until his younger siblings were born.

He rounds the corner to where the room opens out to find them running around on the frayed carpet, arms outstretched and interlinked like three crazy cogs.

Kian makes a point of pretending to sneak past. He really doesn't have time for this, but there's also no way he'll get past them without the usual treatment.

Holly sees him first, her six-year-old scream feeling like it just punctured his ear drums. "Kian's here!"

Willow joins her sister, quickly gaining on her seeing as she's two years older. "Come on, Jasper, before he gets to the door!"

Kian stops, his eyes wide with horror. "Not the Triple Treatment! Anything but the Triple Treatment!"

A trio of giggles precede the three bodies coming at him, Jasper doing a pretty good job of keeping up despite being the youngest. They crash into him one after the other, and Kian scoops them up. "Ha! Now I've got you!"

He spins them around as they wriggle like puppies in his arms.

The squeals do the impossible and rise in pitch. "Put us down!" Willow shouts.

"Yeah! Or we'll tell Nova that you kissed a cockroach!" Holly bellows in his face.

Laughing, Kian stops and lowers them back to the floor. "You guys are gross." And they obviously know his Achilles heel.

A door opens to his left and his mother comes out. "You three, I told you to keep it down." She sees Kian and stops, shaking her head. "Well, there was the problem."

Kian throws his hands up in surrender. "Hey, I was just walking through."

His mother rolls her eyes. "You taught them everything they know." Her smile fades as she registers it's unusual for him to be here. "Why aren't you with Nova?"

Which is a fair question. If he's not helping his mother with the pods, everyone knows where to find Kian. Beside Nova.

He sobers. Today is different. "I need to talk to Dad."

A stillness envelops his mother. She's spent her whole life being in tune to others' feelings, and as Kian is her firstborn child, the connection is even stronger. He doesn't need to say anything else to let her know something significant has happened.

She sucks in a breath. "Is it the pods?"

Kian shakes his head, wishing he could explain, but he needs to tell his father, their leader, first. "They're fine. I just came from there."

His mother relaxes. "He's alone, so this is good timing."

Jasper tugs on Kian's pants. "Wanna play blocks, Kian?" Kian smiles down at his little brother, loving how he stretches out the 'e' in his name—Keee-an.

His mother swoops in before he can respond. "Come on, you three. Kian needs to talk to Dad."

She ushers them back to the middle of the carpet, where a collection of wooden toys sits. She runs her fingers through Jasper's hair, a fond smile lighting up her face.

His mother had two miscarriages after he was born thanks to malnutrition. Without the pods, many women didn't have the strength to see their pregnancies to term. His mother is natu-

53

rally a loving woman, but Kian suspects those losses made his three younger siblings all the more special.

No wonder her first fear was the loss of the pods.

His stomach tight, Kian knocks on the door, then enters. His father is in his usual seat at the head of the large oval table that dominates the room, focused on the ledgers before him. Those columns hold the lists of all those in Askala. Bound and Unbound.

And now there will be a third. For Remnants.

His father looks up and a smile breaks across his face. "Kian." He looks behind him. "Is Nova with you?"

Kian almost rolls his eyes, but a part of him likes that everyone realizes he and Nova are two halves of a whole. It's like knowing that dawn and dusk are inseparable, or love and happiness. He indicates with his thumb over his shoulder. "No. She's back at the infirmary."

Kian enters and closes the door behind him. Pulling in a breath, he decides to get straight to the point. "A meeting needs to be called."

His father shoots to his feet, but Kian raises his hand. "It's not the pods. They're fine."

His father had to endure the loss of two children just as his mother did. As the leader of the High Bound and Askala, he would've felt another layer of responsibility for their deaths along with the many others.

He sits back down slowly, as if he's being careful not to disturb the fine balance their survival depends on. "Something else has happened."

Kian frowns, thinking of the girl and her thinly veiled antagonism. "Yes. During the storm, a Remnant made it to Askala."

His father's eyes widen before his eyebrows slam down. "A Remnant? How?"

Kian takes the seat beside him, as if his legs are about to give out under the weight of this. "There was a raft with several of them, but only one, a girl, made it. She's strong."

And surly. And ungrateful.

His dad jams his fingers through his dark hair. "So, only one was successful." He glances at Kian sharply. "Is she...well?"

"Injured, but no signs of disease."

The Outlands were once defined by malaria, typhoid, and dysentery. A global greenhouse had been a breeding ground for many diseases.

"And she's definitely the sole survivor?"

"She barely made it herself."

His father rubs his chin. "Did anybody help her ashore?"

Kian pauses, weighing up what he should say, but confident his cousin didn't do the wrong thing.

"Dex helped her right at the end. She was practically on land by then, anyway."

His father's eyebrows shoot up but he doesn't say anything. It's possible other Bounds would've done the same. Watching suffering is something most struggle to do.

With a sigh, his father leans back. "Then there are unlikely to be others."

Kian nods, wishing that was all there was. "She's sixteen, Dad." Their gazes connect. "She's entitled to take part in the Proving."

Looking back to the ledgers, his father strokes his chin, and Kian waits. Magnus is known for his steady mind and ability to make necessary decisions. He'll realize this girl is a threat.

Pushing himself up, his father begins to pace. "Callix will need to be notified. The tests begin the day after tomorrow." He stops and turns, looking like he's talking to himself more than Kian. "We'll need to ensure she has adequate food. Who knows when her last meal was."

Kian doesn't say anything as he thinks of the muscles layered on the girl. She didn't look like she was starving.

"I'll talk to Amity. She should probably be given a couple of pods."

Pods? He's going to give her pods?

"And she'll need a room. We'll see if there's anything on our floor."

Kian has to contain the gasp. That's with the Bound! "Dad." His father continues to pace, so Kian repeats himself. "Dad. How can you be so…accepting?"

Doesn't he realize that this girl will be there with them, taking the tests of the Proving?

His father stops, his gaze steady. "She set foot on Askala, Kian. She's entitled to our hospitality."

"But—"

He strides to the door. "I'm going to talk to her. And Dex."

To tell him he did the wrong thing? Or congratulate him? Kian blinks. "But—"

This girl is an outsider. She doesn't understand the choices they must make. She'll think of no one but herself.

"There's nothing to worry about, Kian. We'll welcome this girl, and she'll take the tests." His father pauses at the door, his dark gaze steady. "Before the bridge was burned, not one Remnant ever passed the Proving."

The door closes with a *click* and he's gone. It takes a couple of seconds for the ramifications of what his father said to hit him.

Kian straightens, his hands gripping the table. His father is right. There's nothing to worry about.

A Remnant doesn't have what it takes to pass the tests of the Proving.

By the end of the seven days, that Remnant will become Unbound, like every other Remnant has. She'll go to live out her years on the upper decks of Askala.

Standing up, relieved to feel a smile spreading across his face, Kian pushes back his chair.

By the end of the seven days, he and Nova will be free to be together. They'll be planning a future filled with love and children.

Deciding he has time to play blocks with Jasper before heading to the dining hall, Kian lets the smile dial up to a grin.

By the end of the seven days, most likely, he'll never see that Remnant again.

DEX

*D*ex takes his seat at the table and draws in a deep breath. The moment he's waited for his whole life is here. He's about to begin the first of the four tests that will determine his future.

It's time for his Proving.

There are eight others at this chipped, round table. He knows all of them, of course. Askala isn't so huge that anybody gets to be a stranger. But some he knows better than others.

There's Kian, the one he knows best. And with two High Bound parents, he's the one most certain to succeed. Dex is happy for his cousin. He'll make a wonderful Bound.

There's Nova, too. Seated next to Kian, like she can't breathe without him by her side. She'll succeed, too. Everyone knows her mother is the kindest soul in Askala. And although her father hadn't been a High Bound, he'd been smart. And brave. Surely those genetics were passed down, even if her father hadn't been there to watch Nova grow.

Then there's the Remnant he'd helped pull from the water. Wren.

A girl so unlike anybody he's ever met. Feisty. Brave. Strong.

And altogether fascinating.

Kian doesn't share Dex's opinion of her, though. He looks across at his cousin and has to suppress a smile at the way he's glaring at their newest arrival. He'll get used to her in time. If he even has to. Wren is the least likely out of all of them to pass these tests.

The other five participants have been sneaking glances at Wren, their eyes filled with a mixture of curiosity and fear. That's exactly how they should be feeling. They'd be fools to turn their backs on her.

But Wren isn't bothered by any of them. She's sitting with her arms crossed and her eyes glazed over as she stares at the floor, a clear message that she doesn't want to be here. She's the only one of the nine of them who has zero interest in passing this test. She's made it known she'd prefer to be Unbound. There's no way she wants to work toward preserving Askala. Dex wonders if she realizes exactly what Askala is. It's not just a place. It's a fight for a better world. For Earth. If Wren had her way, they'd rebuild the bridge and let every last Remnant across.

She's wearing the same hemp clothes as the rest of them, her shiny pendant peeking out from the neckline of her shirt. Her injuries have healed surprisingly quickly. There's barely a scratch on her now, which seems odd. Although, there's something about the way she's sitting that tells him she's still fighting some pain. Not that she's the sort to admit it. He'd love to find out what she's been through to have hardened her heart to the world like this. Not to mention who taught her to fight a shark armed with nothing but a small knife.

He tucks his stump under his good arm, resisting the urge to drum his fingers on the table. This test is taking forever to get started. How long does his father intend to keep them waiting?

A guy called Jay is sitting across from him. Tall and thin, he's in danger of hyperventilating if things don't get moving soon. He's always been a nervous sort, but Dex has never seen him like this. Shiloh, the pretty one who works with Nova in the infirmary, is beside him and she puts her hand on his arm and gives him a warm smile.

"It's going to be okay," she says. "Whatever the result, we're going to be alright. There's no pass or fail in the Proving."

Jay nods, although it's obvious he's unconvinced. They all are.

Especially Wren, who snorts and shakes her head. "If there's no pass or fail, why are they bothering to put us through this?"

Dex opens his mouth to answer, but Kian beats him to it, pushing back his chair and standing with wide eyes. "You don't understand anything. These tests are necessary for the fu—."

The door slides open, silencing Kian, who sits back down and folds his hands in his lap.

Smart.

He knows he needs to keep his emotions in check. As difficult as this is under the circumstances. Dex has never heard so much shuffling and sighing and tapping of feet. If nerves were tangible, there'd be no room left to sit at this table. The air is heavy with it. Their futures are all dangling on the frayed threads.

Dex's father walks in carrying a large box. He sets it down on the center of the table with a thud that makes Shiloh jump. Now it's Jay's turn to return the favor and he puts a steadying hand on her back.

It's strange for Dex to see his father here. In his element. He lives for these tests. Dex is almost sad for him that this is his last one before he has to step down and let the next generation take over. But he's not sad for himself. He might actually get to spend some time with his father now.

Unless...

He shudders, fully aware his father would like Dex to take over from him and run the future Provings. It's strange to think that in only twelve months, it could be him putting down a box on the table and making a group of potential Bounds jump in their seats.

But first he has to get through this first test. Then the next three. The thought punches dread deep into his gut.

His father has Lana with him, one of the other High Bounds who helps with the Provings. She has dark eyes that smile out from her friendly face. This is no doubt one of the reasons she was chosen for this job. Not many people have the sort of face that can soothe your fears with one heartfelt glance. And looking around the table, they could all do with a little soothing.

Jay has removed his hand from Shiloh's back and is rocking his reedy body in his chair, muttering something. If he doesn't get his act together, he's got no hope of surviving this week.

"Welcome to the first test of your Proving," says Dex's father, stepping away from the table to stand beside Lana. "This box contains a set of square blocks. Your task is to see who can build the tallest tower. No working as a team. Everyone must build alone. As you're aware, we'll be observing you."

"May the Proving serve you well." Lana beams at them. "Please wait for the buzzer to sound before you begin."

A few of the participants smile back at Lana, including Nova. Wren hasn't lifted her eyes from the floor. Kian is staring at the box, no doubt wondering how he's going to build the tallest tower, while ensuring Nova gets to do the same. That rule banning teamwork isn't going to be easy for them to abide by.

For once, Dex is glad to be alone in this world. The Proving is going to be hard enough to get through as an individual. It's strange to think that both his parents have faced this test and passed. His father has never talked about his Proving, and his mother never got the chance to tell him about hers. But surely, he has a chance? Even with one hand. Especially if the tests are all like this.

His father catches his gaze and nods at him before he disappears out the door. This leaves Dex wondering if he's set up all the tests to take his missing hand into account? He's not sure why, but this thought grabs hold of the dread in his gut and twists it into angry knots.

Jay reaches for the box and drags it toward him.

"The buzzer, Jay!" says Nova. "We have to wait."

"I forgot." Jay pushes the box back as if it's on fire and Dex is certain he catches a smirk on Wren's face.

"This is taking forever," says Felicia, an impressive set of curls bobbing from the top of her head. Has she pinned them like that just for the Proving? Dex doubts his father is going to give her extra points for grooming. "How long do we have to wait?" She directs her question at Dex, crossing her arms and pouting.

Dex shrugs, annoyed she's singled him out. "How would I know?"

"Because Callix is your dad." She rolls her eyes.

"Of course. Having friends in high places is very *handy*." He waves his stump at her. "My dad's told me all about the tests. I'm just here for my good looks."

"Dex!" Kian shoots him a warning look. "Don't joke like that. She might believe you."

"Sure, it's a joke," says Felicia, touching her hair gently to make sure it's staying in place.

"My uncle would never tell Dex the answers!" Kian's face has turned pink and Dex pauses to admire his cousin's fierce loyalty. "It's forbidden for Callix to even talk about the tests. Dex knows as much as we do about what's happening this week. Nothing!"

"Okay, okay!" Felicia holds up her hands. "I was just joking, too."

There's a tutting noise from the other side of the table and Dex sees that Wren has finally lifted her head. "You idiots do realize that this is part of the test, don't you?"

"What do you mean?" asks Felicia.

"This!" Wren waves her hands about. "The test started the moment you walked inside this lab. They'll be watching you to see how you interact at all times, not just after the buzzer rings."

Felicia falls quiet and sits back in her chair.

"They're watching you, too, Wren," says Shiloh, straightening her back. "Not just us."

"They can watch me all they like." Wren stands up and pokes her tongue out at one of the cameras, before turning around and wiggling her behind.

Dex imagines his father's face right now and suppresses a laugh. Wren really isn't taking his precious tests very seriously.

But Nova is less amused. "Wren! Stop th—"

A loud buzzer swallows up the rest of Nova's words. Wren takes her seat and resumes her crossed-arm position like she never moved.

Kian reaches for the box this time and takes off the lid. "We need to count how many we have."

"We have a genius in the room," says Felicia.

Dex groans. This girl is going to drive him crazy over the next seven days. Surely, she can't possibly become Bound with an attitude like that?

Kian takes the blocks out of the box, one by one, counting them as he goes. Large and square, they look like they're made from the wood of the varnish tree—a species so invasive, it's widely used in Askala. Pale and smooth, the blocks look easy enough to build with.

"Is there anything inside them?" asks Jay, looking at the blocks like they might be filled with cockroaches.

Kian shakes one near his ear and sets it back on the table. "Pretty sure they're empty."

Dex sits quietly and waits, turning over potential strategies in his mind. The task seems simple enough, but clearly, it's not. There's no way these blocks will divide evenly by nine. And even if they do, there's still no winner. This task is about

63

building the tallest tower. Making them all the same achieves nothing.

"Fifty-six blocks," Kian announces.

"That doesn't divide by nine," says Thom, who's been quiet until now. He lifts his shaking hands and counts again, using his stocky fingers as counters. Dex can't help but hope Thom doesn't rely on them for counting too much if he becomes Unbound.

"It divides by eight, though," mutters Kian, shooting Wren a glare.

Dex tries once again not to laugh at his cousin's clear distrust of their newest arrival. Surely, he realizes that if she hadn't arrived, there'd be a different number of blocks in that box? They were never going to divide evenly between the participants.

"Apologies for breathing," says Wren, the only one who hasn't yet grabbed a block. "Just pretend I'm not here and take seven each."

Dex's eyebrows shoot up, surprised at her ability to calculate numbers in her head. So much for Remnants being stupid.

Small towers are being built, slowly and cautiously, with apologetic looks being cast around the table each time a hand darts out to grab another block. Except Felicia, who already has a tower of eight blocks. She doesn't seem to have thought much of Wren's suggestion.

There's a crash and Dex looks up to see Jay has knocked over his tower while reaching for another block. Dex would've thought with arms as long as his, this wouldn't have been a problem. But Jay's shaking is clearly his downfall here.

"Just take your time," says Nova helping him pick up the blocks he dropped. "We all need to try to stay calm."

"She's right," says Shiloh. "Let's just think this through. There's a lot riding on this test."

Dex nods in agreement. The only problem is that nobody is

really sure what the test actually is. Or how much time they have.

Drawing in another deep breath, Dex tries not to buy into Jay's nerves. Nova's right. They have to keep calm if they have any chance of outsmarting this test.

His tower is four blocks tall and he looks at the diminishing pool of free blocks before reaching for his fifth.

"Too slow!" Felicia swoops the block out from under his open hand and adds it to her tower.

At first, he's annoyed, but then he thinks again. This task is supposed to measure intelligence and empathy. Building the tallest tower might prove someone is smart enough to succeed, but does it prove that they're kind? The way Felicia is behaving makes the answer obvious.

He looks around the table. Most participants have five blocks towering in front of them and are debating amongst themselves what they should do next.

Except for Wren, who's still sitting with her arms crossed and hasn't reached for a single block. And Nova, who has a tower in front of her made up only of two blocks.

"You take this one," Nova says to Kian, pointing to a block that's easily in her reach.

"No working in teams!" Felicia points at them, then looks at the camera. "Did you see that? They're working as a team!"

"We're not!" Nova's mouth falls open. "I just…"

"She's trying to show that she's kind," says Thom. "Not a bad strategy, actually."

Dex suppresses a sigh. "Nova isn't trying to show she's kind. She *is* kind."

But Thom isn't listening. A new frenzy has started around the table and now everyone is trying to offload their blocks to each other, determined to show how selfless they are. Not wanting to be seen as the only selfish one, Dex pushes his blocks forward.

Soon, all the towers have been broken down and the blocks are back in the center of the table. It's like they really do contain cockroaches now. Nobody wants to touch them.

Wren is openly laughing, seeming to be enjoying herself at their expense. Her dark hair has been washed and combed since Dex saw her in the infirmary. It still looks unruly but frames her face in a flattering way. She certainly looks a lot better than Felicia with her strange set of curls. Not that he expects Wren would like anyone to tell her that. She'd probably chop off her hair with her knife at the first hint of a compliment.

"You guys are hilarious!" Wren says.

"Why don't you build a tower?" Dex asks her, genuinely curious about her take on this impossible test. "If you don't care, then show them how selfish you are. Take all the blocks."

"I'm not playing your stupid games." She shakes her head. "Where I come from, we spend our time working for our survival. We kill bears, we build shelters, we fight our enemies. We don't sit around tables building towers out of blocks. Do you know how pathetic you all look?"

Dex winces at the sharpness of her words, wondering if she has a point.

"The future of Askala depends on these Provings," says Kian. "A future that's far more important than anything you Remnants have to do."

"Do *not* call us that," spits Wren, her face dancing with anger. "Or I'll think of a few choice words to call you."

"I don't doubt that," says Nova, placing a hand on Kian's chest to keep him in his seat. "But he didn't mean it as an insult. It's just the name our ancestors gave you."

"Then it's time to think of a new name," says Wren. "A *kind* one, since you all seem so desperate to think of yourselves that way."

"Come on," says Dex. "We're getting distracted here. If Wren doesn't want to join in, why don't we take her suggestion to all build a tower of seven blocks?"

Maybe that really is the best solution here. For them not to have one winner, but for there to be many winners. A demonstration of having behaved in the interests of the greater good. Dex swallows, hoping it's the right answer.

There are a few nods around the table and they start counting out blocks, taking seven each. Except for Nova, once again, who's pushing her allocation of blocks toward Kian, desperate to see him win this task.

Kian is shaking his head at her, urging her to build her own tower, neither of them wanting to speak out loud, no doubt fearing another attack from Felicia.

As Dex re-builds his tower he sees Nova offer Shiloh a block. But just like Kian, Shiloh shakes her head.

"Nova, it's better for everyone if you hold onto your own blocks," says Dex, worried about what Thom said earlier. What if it looks like Nova is trying too hard to appear kind? Not everyone knows how pure her heart is.

Nova's eyes sheen over and she nods at Dex, stacking her blocks into a tower, seeming just as uncertain as he is that this is the right answer.

A loudspeaker crackles to life and Lana's cheery voice beams across the room. "You have thirty seconds to complete your task and build the tallest tower. Good luck!"

Dex looks at his tower and sits back in his chair to wait. Everyone is finished, even Felicia who seems to have accepted that there's more to this game than she first assumed. They all have towers made from seven blocks in front of them.

Everyone, except Wren.

"Please, Kian," Nova whispers just loud enough for Dex to hear. "You can win this. They said *tallest* tower. Take one of my blocks."

Lana's voice fills the room again. "Ten seconds to go!"

There's a flurry of movement and Dex sees Kian make a grab for Nova's blocks and add them to the top of his tower.

There's another movement to the left of him and Dex looks down to see his entire tower is now perched on top of Felicia's.

The buzzer sounds and they all jolt as if it delivered an electric shock.

"Time's up," says Lana. "Please place your hands in your lap and wait for us to return."

Dex looks around the table. Fourteen blocks each for Kian and Felicia. Zero for Nova, Wren and himself. And seven for everyone else.

How on earth is his father going to interpret these results?

WREN

*W*ren sits in the dining hall of the Proving, still unable to believe that food is being put in front of her with no expectation of her doing anything in return. Although, it isn't quite what she's used to. More vegetables, less … bears, but when she hasn't had to work for it, she's not complaining.

At least she gets to take a break from playing stupid games. That test with the blocks was ridiculous. Well, ridiculously clever, really. Something that had seemed so simple had turned out to be so telling when it came to peeling back layers and revealing true personalities. It had been fascinating to observe.

Nova and Kian had looked out for each other the entire time, until Kian made a mysterious run for first place at the end. Not surprising, really. She'd already figured out that Nova's far kinder than this guy who seems to have laid claim to her heart.

As for Felicia… well, she's a lost cause, as are most of the others, whose names she can't remember.

Except Dex.

She looks at him across the table now. He's eating a raw carrot. Skin on, of course. There's no way they're peeling or cooking any of the goodness out of what they've grown. It's amazing they've succeeded at growing anything, really. He washes the carrot down with a drink she's noticed they all take once a day. Apparently, it halts their fertility until after the Proving. They don't seem to be insisting that Wren drinks it. She's not sure if this is a compliment or an insult.

Dex sees her looking at him and shoots her a quick smile.

She glares at him. Just because he saved her life doesn't mean she has to be nice to him. Although, she has to admit she does like him a little bit. He's kind of funny. Nobody back home has time for a sense of humor. They're too busy trying to stay alive.

Dex is smarter than he thinks. That was obvious in the test. He thought before he acted, weighing up the possibilities before he made a move. It's just a shame Felicia stole his blocks right at the end. Served him right in a way, though. That's the first lesson in basic survival. Never lose your focus. Not even for a second. Sleep with one eye open. Treat everyone with suspicion. Otherwise...a pain in the ass can sneak up and steal your blocks when you least expect it.

"How do you think we did?" asks one of the female participants whose name Wren can't remember. Flower? Moss? Petal? It has something to do with nature.

"Well, Kian and Felicia had the tallest towers," says the tall lanky guy sitting next to her. "Looks like they would've scored the highest."

Felicia beams at this news and Wren stuffs something green in her mouth and winces at the taste. What is this crap? Chewing it anyway, she swallows it down, takes a sip of her water, and shoves in another piece.

"Kian would've scored higher than Felicia," says Dex, eating the same green substance, only seeming to be enjoying it.

"Why do you say that?" snaps Felicia. "We both ended up with fourteen blocks."

Dex shrugs. "Because you had different reasons for taking

the extra seven. You took my blocks because you wanted to win. Kian took Nova's because he knew it would make her look generous. Am I right?"

All eyes shift to Kian, who shuffles in his seat.

"Kian! You didn't," says Nova. "I thought you did it because I convinced you to try to win."

"It's complicated," says Kian, avoiding Dex's eye.

Wren continues to eat, enjoying this conversation. She's certain the cameras that are still pointing at them are continuing to whirr. Not that these fools would realize their test is continuing. Do they really think this week is about four simple tests? She's certain it's far more complicated than that. Why else aren't they allowed to leave this sterile lab until the week is over?

"I should've known." Nova hangs her head. "I should've taken your blocks."

"No," soothes Kian, wrapping an arm around her. "You did the right thing."

"You're a genius, Kian!" Dex bursts out laughing. "Here we all thought you were being selfish and the whole time you were trying to make Nova look good. And in doing so, you've made yourself look like the most selfless creature to walk the earth. Brilliant!"

Dex's words do little to cheer either Nova or Kian. But they do amuse Wren.

Felicia has gone quiet, poking her food around her plate with her finger. "So, you don't think I got a good score then?"

"Who knows," says Dex after a pause, despite every one of them at the table all being very aware that she'd likely scored the worst out of all of them.

"What about her?" Felicia points at Wren, her bottom lip quivering. "I must've done better than she did."

"Leave me out of this." Wren holds up a hand and shakes her head. "You all know I want nothing to do with these tests."

"Well, that's sort of bad luck," says Kian. "Because you're stuck with the tests. Just like for the next seven days, we're stuck with you. So, you may as well make the most of it."

"That doesn't answer my question." Felicia is looking at Kian now. "How do you think she did?"

But it's Dex who answers. "I think Wren's another one who accidentally scored well."

"What?" Wren pushes back her chair and leans across the table to get in Dex's face. "And how did you arrive at that conclusion?"

Dex also leans forward, not seeming intimidated by her in the least, until their faces are only inches apart.

"Because you didn't touch a single block," he says. "You left them all for us, so we could win."

"That's not why I left them!" She pulls back and slams herself into her chair, trying not to wince as a sharp pain bolts through her ribs. Her skin may have healed over, but bones are far harder to repair.

"It might not be why you left them," says Dex. "But that's how it could look. What an empathetic soul, leaving them all for us."

Wren glares at Dex, hoping he'll choke on the next piece of that green stuff he eats. "It's *not* why I did it."

"Well, that's just great," says Felicia, drawing the attention back to herself. "So, she and Kian get the top scores and one of them had fourteen blocks and the other had none. How are we supposed to know what to do in the next test? This is impossible! Beaten by a Remnant!"

Wren is out of her chair once more, fury pumping through her veins. She strides to Felicia and grabs her by the throat, lifting her until she's standing in front of her, choking for air, her ridiculous curls bouncing on top of her stupid face.

"What did you call me?" asks Wren, trying to shake an answer from her purple face.

Two strong hands grab Wren's arms from behind and she lets go of Felicia, spinning around to find it's Kian holding her.

"Let go of me!" She spits, watching her saliva land in the middle of his forehead and slide down his nose.

He does as she asks and shoves her aside.

Damn it! Her ribs!

She catches her balance and pulls back her shoulders, putting her hands on her hips in an attempt to look larger than she is.

"*Do not* put your hands on any of us." Kian wipes the spit from his face and glares at her.

"Then, *do not* call me that word." Wren holds out her index finger, pointing at everyone around the table, one by one. "Do you all understand me? We are real people on the other side of that ocean, not some kind of leftovers. Got it?"

"You're not behaving like a real person." Felicia clutches at her neck, which has some impressive purple streaks down it. "You're behaving like an animal."

"Oh, shut up, Felicia," says Wren.

Felicia's eyes widen, not used to being insulted in this boring world she lives in.

"Trust me," says Wren. "I only said what everyone else has been thinking all day."

With that, Wren leaves the dining hall and heads to the bunkroom, needing some space from this group of idiots.

She can't win. Or rather, she can't lose. If Dex is right, all her efforts today have had the opposite effect. Not participating has made her look kind. Possibly clever, too. Hopefully, her actions just now with Felicia have proven otherwise. Because she might be clever, but she's definitely not kind. Nobody's ever taught her how to be.

She climbs onto a bottom bunk, wondering how anyone can sleep on something so soft. Hauling herself back out again, she grabs the blanket and crawls underneath, stretching out on the hard floor.

Better. Much better. Closing her eyes, she imagines she's sleeping on the dirt with Phoenix beside her. She'd love to know what he's doing now. Is he missing her?

Her hand flutters to the pendant she wears around her neck and she knows she's got no chance of finding out news on anyone she loves. Not stuck inside this lab.

"Wren?"

She stills her breathing, not wanting to be found. Even if that voice does sound like it belongs to Dex.

There's the shuffling of feet and she turns to see Dex lying on the floor next to her. From this angle he looks fully formed, his missing hand on the other side.

"What happened to your hand?" she asks, not expecting an answer, but unable to help herself from asking.

"Felicia ate it," he says, keeping his face serious. "You really should watch out for her."

Wren smiles before she can catch it, so she turns her face away instead.

"Don't let them get to you," he says. "Not Felicia, not anyone."

"I really don't like that name you people call us." She turns back to face him.

"I hadn't noticed." He blinks at her, holding back a grin. "Maybe you should let everyone know."

This time she catches her smile before it gets away from her.

"Is Callix really your dad?" she asks, surprised she has so many questions for him. It's not like she actually cares about the answers.

"Yep, that's my dad, all right." He grins at her. "Even though we look nothing alike."

"So, is Lana your mom?" She tries to remember Lana's darker features, to see if they fit more closely with Dex's face.

"Nope."

"Where's your mom, then?"

"Dead." He says this word like it means nothing, although she notices the way his gaze flicks away.

"Mine's dead, too." She bites down on her tongue, regretting her words. She wasn't going to tell anyone anything about herself when she came here. She must be more careful.

They lie there in silence for a moment. A silence that should be uncomfortable, but strangely, isn't. Is that what happens when somebody helps save your life?

"Why don't you try in the next test?" he eventually asks, not blinking as he waits for her response. "See what happens. Maybe if you try, you'll do worse than if you don't."

"Is that another joke?" she asks.

"Not this time." He lets out a loud yawn. It's late and sleep is starting to beckon.

"I'll think about it," she says.

"Great. Because I don't know about you, but this floor is hard. I'm going to take one of the bunks." He scrambles to his feet and she's left staring at two ankles.

"Hey, Dex."

"What?" He bends over and now she's seeing a mop of brown hair as his upside-down face hovers under the bunk.

"Can you take the bunk above me?"

His head flips up before she gets a chance to see his reaction. But the squeaking of the springs in the mattress above her, tells her that he heard her just fine.

She doesn't trust Dex. Not even a little bit. But if she has to have anyone sleeping above her head, then it may as well be him.

"Goodnight, Wren." The croak in his voice reminds her of Phoenix.

"Night."

She lifts her hand to her cheek, surprised to find it's wet.

Maybe what she needs to do is channel her inner Felicia for the next test. Try to be that person they all expect her to be.

A selfish Remnant. The leftover scum of the world.

Although, that might all depend on what the next test is. Surely each one is going to be more difficult than the one before?

What on earth could Dex's dad have thought up for them to do next? And does Dex have a point? Should she try? It seems it can't do her more harm than not trying did today.

"Hey, Dex," she calls up to him.

"Uh-ha," comes his sleepy reply.

"You'd better get some good sleep up there. Because tomorrow I'm coming for you. You won't know what hit you in the second test."

"Good for you, Wren."

She can hear the smile in his voice. But that's just because he hasn't figured out yet how much of a threat she really is.

Askala better watch out. Because when Wren decides to do something, nothing and nobody are going to stand in her way.

NOVA

$\mathcal{N}$ova flicks her hands, trying to work off some of the energy that's zinging through her body. Despite its simplicity, she's not sure she passed the last test. When there didn't seem to be an obvious answer, giving her blocks to Kian had been a no-brainer. If no one could win, then he should.

But then he'd taken the blocks and built one of the tallest towers. And he'd done it for her, and for everyone else.

It's exactly what a Bound would do.

Which means when the door before them opens, she needs to make sure she gets this test right.

No one had been expecting the announcement over the loudspeakers this morning, meaning they'd all jumped as they sat in the dining hall, eating breakfast. With seven days for four tests, they would have to be close together. But everyone assumed there would be a day in between each one.

Maybe part of the Proving is to test their resilience. Maybe the tests are all over in four days, leaving them three days to wonder whether they've passed…

Now, they're crowded in a corridor of the lab, a closed door before them. Callix's voice had been calm and pleasant as he'd told them to report here. Felicia had led them, striding away with her shoulders back and her curls pinned carefully into place. Nova had held back, finding Wren beside her. She'd wondered how she was feeling, but Wren's face had given nothing away. Before Nova had a chance to ask, Kian had ushered her away.

She'd rolled her eyes. Kian really doesn't like that girl.

At the rear of the group of nine teens, Nova looks around. Jay is swallowing reflexively, Felicia's shoulders are still back in their power pose. Nova fiddles with the edge of her collar. This feels like the first time her mother asked her to help with treating a bleeding Unbound. There'd been excitement at the chance to prove herself, to get it right. At the same time, she'd been so scared she'd get it wrong.

Kian's hand slips around hers. "You've got this."

Nova's about to deny she's feeling nervous, but she's never lied to Kian. Plus, he'd see right through her. She grips his hand tightly. "What makes you so sure?"

He grins, his dark eyes glinting. "Because you've got me."

Nova shakes her head as she smiles, impressed that Kian can not only be feeling calm enough to crack a joke, but that he got her smiling, too.

Dex leans in. "More importantly, you've got me."

This time, Nova almost giggles. How did she get so lucky to be surrounded by such supportive friends? By so much love? "Looks like I've got it in the bag, then."

Kian nods. "That's my girl."

Shiloh takes a step back to join them. "They're right, Nova. You have nothing to worry about."

Her pale blue eyes with their dark lashes flicker to Kian, and Nova has to stop herself from stiffening. Did Shiloh say that for Nova's benefit, or for Kian's? Trying to push away the unkind thought doesn't work. Shiloh's become less and less subtle with her feelings toward Kian the closer they've gotten to the Proving.

Kian doesn't seem to notice, because he leans down toward Nova. "See? It's practically unanimous."

Shiloh smiles, and Nova's struck by how pretty she is. With the dark hair and caramel skin of most people in Askala, she's a classic beauty. What's more, she's kind. And smart. She probably did say that for Nova's benefit, wanting to help out another participant, just like she's volunteered to help in the infirmary.

Nova sobers. These tests aren't about who your friends are, or how much you're in love with one of them. They're whether you're smart and kind enough to lead Askala.

Whether you're like Kian and Shiloh.

Before Nova can think any further, the door opens and Callix steps out. "Welcome." He greets them warmly as if they've just arrived at the dining hall. "Inside is the second test of the Proving. Please come in."

Felicia strides through and the others follow. Nova watches as they each file in, frowning when they seem to pause. What in sweet Terra is in there?

Kian releases her hand, and she instantly feels its absence. He disappears through the door, Dex throwing her a wink as he follows. Nova holds back, watching to make sure everyone's okay, conscious this isn't just stressful and scary for her.

Wren is the last to go and Nova indicates for her to go past, but Wren just arches a brow. "Are you always like this?"

"Like what?"

"So...generous?"

Nova flushes, wondering if Wren meant to give her the compliment. "I try."

Wren strides past, glaring over her shoulder. "Because if you keep going, the world is going to walk all over you."

Nova's jaw slackens but she catches herself. Wren doesn't

realize what she's talking about. Generosity and kindness aren't weaknesses. They're what humanity needs more of.

Nova has just stepped through when the door closes behind her. Stifling a startle, she looks around the room and her eyes widen.

This time when her jaw slackens, she doesn't stop it. Several others have done the same. There's no way she could be this lucky.

What used to be a small room in the lab has been outfitted to replicate the infirmary. Shelves line the side walls, the hemp shreds they call bandages stacked on them. Just like the space she spends so much time in, cots line the left, a handful of chairs dispersed throughout, a table in the center.

Except there's one glaring difference. A curtain hides the back wall, directly behind the table. Dual holes have been cut through it, and two arms jut through and rest on the table, more cloth covering them from the forearms down. Whoever is behind is completely hidden.

Nova's gut clenches, dreading what might be under there. People only come to the infirmary when something is wrong.

Callix walks over to the table. "Two members of Askala have been injured." Callix points to the first arm. "One is Unbound."

Everyone would've realized that pretty quick—the missing ring finger would be undeniable.

He indicates the second one. "The other is Bound. Your task is to treat them as best you can."

Callix heads for the door, smiling at several of them as he passes. "May the Proving serve you well."

He's gone before anyone can respond. It's possible a few people haven't blinked. The click as the door is locked pierces the silence.

Nova glances around, waiting for someone to take the lead. They need to find out what's under that cloth. It's not likely to be significant, but time isn't a luxury one has when it comes to injuries. Nova tenses. Surely they're not bleeding under there…

There are a few shuffles, but no one moves. Kian is frowning, while Dex is looking a little pale. Wren is assessing everyone with her eagle gaze. Jay actually takes a step back.

It's Shiloh who makes the first move, moving toward the table, which is all it takes to spur Nova into action. Although Shiloh has helped out, the infirmary is Nova's domain. This is her opportunity to show she has what it takes to be Bound.

She strides through the people in front of her, stopping at the table. With a confidence she isn't feeling, she pulls back the cloth. Nova stifles the gasp as she registers what's underneath it, but several others are unable, the sound of their shock firing behind her.

Each of the arms has been cut, a large diagonal gash slicing through the skin. Blood oozes onto the metal beneath them.

Nova doesn't think. She dashes to the shelves and grabs a wad of cloth. Within seconds she's clamped the hemp around each arm. "We need to stop the bleeding."

Kian is by her side in a blink. "What can I do to help?"

Nova angles her chin at the arm on her right. "You take that one. We need to keep up the pressure."

Kian nods, and without flinching, wraps his hand around the cloth that already has blood seeping through. Nova frowns. The cuts must be deep.

"What are the rest of us supposed to do?"

Nova doesn't need to look up to know it was Felicia who spoke. The whine in her voice is unmistakable. She grits her teeth, not sure how to respond to that. There are only two arms to treat.

Dex shifts closer to Felicia. "Maybe this test is about recognizing who's the best person for the job. Not about each one of us trying to prove ourselves."

Felicia opens her mouth only to shut it on a frown. It's obvious that doesn't sit well with her.

Wren shrugs. "For what it's worth, I think he's right. And that Nova is the best person for the job."

Nova turns away before her flush shows. She hates that she's conscious that Callix would've heard that.

Focusing on the task at hand, she carefully peels back the bloody wad of bandages so she can inspect the wound. The bleeding has eased, showing her a deep gash through the flesh. Her shoulders drop.

They're going to need stitches.

And the arm she's looking at belongs to an Unbound.

Shiloh steps up. "Can I help?"

Nova nods. "You take over here. I need to inspect the other wound."

On the Bound.

She steps in close to Kian and does the same, discovering it's as she suspected. The cut is the same length...and the same depth. Nova turns to the others. "They both need stitches."

Looking around, she watches their faces turn pale. They all know Unbound don't receive the same level of medical care. What little resources they have must be saved for those who will breed.

Jay swallows. "So the cuts are pretty deep?"

Nova nods again. "Yes. And long."

Jay's face goes from gray to white. He swallows, his Adam's apple bobbing in his long neck. "Oh."

"I know this is tough, but we need to decide what to do. They've lost enough blood as it is."

Nova's eyes widen as she watches Jay begin to sway. Dex must see it too, because he rushes toward him, catching Jay as his body crumbles. He flops onto Dex like a jellyfish, making him stumble. Wren darts over, and together, they navigate unconscious Jay to the nearest cot. He flops down, lanky legs and skinny arms tumbling over the edges.

Wren steps back. "He fainted just talking about blood?" she asks incredulously.

No one answers, wondering what this means for Jay. Nova looks away. "Place him in a comfortable position on his side. The cuts take priority."

Dex nods quickly and does as she asked, navigating the use of his stump in a way only someone who's lived with it most their life could.

Seeing Fern at a loss in the corner of the room, Nova indicates with her chin. "Fern, can you keep an eye on him?"

Nova glances at Wren, hoping this infirmary is as exact in its replication as it seems. "There should be a metal tray on the third shelf behind you. It contains the supplies we'll need for the stitches."

Nova notes that Wren doesn't hesitate, and despite the ticking clock hanging over their head, it almost makes her smile. Wren knows this is important and she's not letting her hostility for Askala get in the way.

Except Felicia beats Wren to the shelves. Stepping in front of Wren, she grabs the tray.

Wren jerks back, holding her hands up. "It's all yours, Ms. Pushy."

Felicia pauses as she realizes what she just did in her haste to be helpful. She looks down at the tray, obviously wondering if she should hand it to Wren.

"Felicia." Nova can't help the sharpness in her tone. These two men need medical attention. "Bring it here."

With a start, Felicia rushes over and passes Nova the tray. Nova sits it on the table and looks down. Despite the urgency, she pauses.

"What's wrong?" asks Kian, as always so in tune with the slightest changes in her.

Nova looks up, dread a black blossom in her belly. "There are only enough supplies to treat one person."

Someone in the group inhales sharply, and Nova turns to scan them. Everyone is wide-eyed as they realize this is the decision they must make. Do they really have to choose to sew the Bound and leave the Unbound?

"Ah, Nova?"

It's Shiloh, her gentle voice sounding strained. Nova turns to find her staring at the arm she's still holding pressure on.

The hand has gone slack. Whomever is on the other side of the curtain has fainted. Nova waits for the arm to retreat, but it stays where it is. Someone must be propping them up.

Bile rushes up her throat as she registers a partially healed cut across the palm that now lies exposed. Sweet Terra, she knows that hand!

This isn't a faceless Unbound. A person who didn't pass their Proving and is now sterile. This arm belongs to Old Sam. Gruff, tough, soft-hearted Old Sam.

Suddenly, Nova's head swims. Did Sam do this for a pod? Because she suggested he try to work for them?

Dex clears his throat. "What does it mean for the person we don't sew up?"

Nova tries to push Sam's face from her mind, but it's undeniable it's him Dex is asking about. "We'll bandage their wound." She hesitates, hating the words that will come next. "But they run the risk of opening again and there is a higher chance of infection. There will be more scarring."

Dex glances at Kian, who's still holding the arm of the Bound. "Well, this sucks," he says weakly.

"You've got to be kidding me!" Wren shoves her way to the front of the group. "You're going to choose one over the other?"

She spits the words out in disgust as she glances around. No one makes eye contact.

Dex shakes his head. "It's not that simple, Wren. One is Unbound."

"Maybe we need to trade places, because it's pretty simple from where I'm standing. They're both human beings."

Shiloh's face is soft with understanding as she looks to Wren. "Don't you see, Wren? The Bound would've done this by choice. They're willing to sacrifice for Askala. The Unbound would only have done this for payment. They're not the same."

Felicia straightens her shoulders, a mannerism Nova is starting to find annoying. "Maybe we're not meant to treat either. Maybe it's kinder not to make a choice."

Kian shakes his head. "I don't think we're meant to do nothing."

Felicia huffs. "Then we treat the Unbound? He looks in worse shape. Maybe they want to see whether we care for the Unbound as we're supposed to?"

Dex's shoulders sag. "I don't think this is some trick question like the last one, Felicia."

Kian looks to Nova. "Plus Unbound don't usually get stitches, do they?"

"Not usually." The words sting Nova's throat. Several months ago she broke the rules for Sam. She couldn't bear to see him suffer more than he needed to.

Kian's eyes darken with inevitability. "I think we treat the Bound."

Dex shifts closer to his cousin. "Kian's right. The Bound is the future of Askala."

Felicia crosses her arms. "I was just going to suggest that."

Every cell in Nova's body rebels. There has to be another answer. She knows the good of the many comes before the need of one, but how is this kindness? How can she leave Sam like this when she was possibly the one who suggested he do this? The Unbound depend on the Bound to care for them.

An idea strikes Nova like lightning and she spins around.

"We'll treat both! I'll just space the stitches out to every second one. There will be enough thread to close both their wounds!"

"But will that be enough?" It's Thom at the back of the room, his voice full of doubt, his arms crossed over his barrel-like chest

Nova waves the concern away. "The wounds will be able to tear open more easily, but they'll just have to be careful."

Kian is watching Nova steadily. "And the chance of infection?"

Nova hesitates. "Will be reduced for both."

Dex shakes his head. "Yet still higher for both."

Wren shoves her way through, looking at the faces around her. "You guys are unbelievable, you know that?"

Kian's frown only deepens. "Please step back, Remn—." He catches himself as Wren's eyes flare. "We have work to do."

She leans forward, knocking the tray in the process. "You seriously think you have the right to treat them as if they're different? Look at that blood! Imagine their pain! They. Are. The. Same." She bites the last words off through gritted teeth.

Nova steps forward, her heart aching. She needs to understand this isn't an easy decision for any of them. "Wren—"

But Wren steps back. "Don't touch me. I thought at least maybe you were different, Nova."

Her face twisted with disgust, Wren spins around. Nova tells herself Wren's opinion doesn't matter. That those words don't sting.

Wren shoves her way through the participants, and Nova watches in shock as she heads for the door. Nova's about to remind her it's locked, but with three swift kicks to the sensor, Wren leaves it shattered on the floor.

Shoving the sliding door open, she storms out.

Everyone stands in stunned silence. It was an unspoken rule that no one leaves the room. The door probably didn't even need to be locked. It's obvious Wren doesn't want to pass—she's literally smashing the rules.

Rubbing her brow, Nova turns back to the table. There's no more time. These wounds need to be treated.

Nova looks to the tray to get the scissors she'll need to cut the thread. She'll have to be careful if she's going to make it last for two wounds, even if she does only every second stitch.

Except the scissors are gone.

Looking around frantically, Nova makes sure they haven't fallen onto the table or even the floor. Surely Wren hasn't taken them.

Surely she doesn't hate them all so much that she'd stop either of these people from being treated.

But it's undeniable. They're nowhere to be found.

Nova looks up to Kian, wishing his frown was unfounded. "Wren's taken the scissors."

KIAN

*K*ian's never experienced the need to punch something, but he finds his hands clenching into fists. This is exactly what a Remnant would do.

Look out for no one but themselves.

He glances around the room. He doesn't have time for such a wasteful emotion. "Are there any other supplies?"

Everyone leaps into action, scanning the shelves, even rifling through the blankets on the cot.

Dex holds one up. "Could we use the threads from these?"

Nova shakes her head. "Not strong enough and not sterile."

He drops it back on to the bed. "It was pretty genius if you ask me."

One by one, the others turn toward those at the table. Several hold up their palms to show they're empty handed.

Damn Remnant.

Kian glances up at the camera pointing down from a corner of the room. Surely the test is over. These two people need treatment.

Except no voice comes through the loudspeakers, giving

them a reprieve. They're waiting to see what the participants are going to do.

Nova flutters gentle hands over his, then over Shiloh's. "Keep the pressure steady. It's what will keep the bleeding under control until we have a solution."

Respect for Nova has Kian straightening. She hasn't lost sight of what they need to do—find a way to help these people.

Jay groans and Fern rushes to help him as he sits up, holding his head. "Is it over?"

Felicia huffs. "Not yet. We just lost the only way to close up these cuts."

Jay blanches. "Sweet Terra, I can smell it."

Kian realizes he's right. The sickly, coppery scent of blood has permeated the air.

Felicia jams her hands on her hips, sending her curls wobbling. "If we don't figure something out, you're going to smell a whole lot more as that poor Bound keeps losing blood."

Jay's eyes roll to the back of his head as he flops back onto the cot. Kian turns away, knowing he'll be looked after by Fern, wincing a little inside. Who knows what this is going to mean for Jay's scores on this test.

Nova flutters her hands over his again, checking that he's maintaining pressure. She looks pained, which makes Kian's heart ache. This would be such a difficult test for her.

What's always been so straightforward for him has always been grayer for her. In his mind, Bound have these rights because they're the people who will heal the hurt inflicted over hundreds of years. It's Bounds who have to shoulder the responsibility and sacrifice.

But Nova has always seen the person beneath the label. The Remnant's words would've struck a chord with her. Unbounds bleed. They feel pain.

Kian hopes Callix notices the way she took charge when

they first entered. Healing others is Nova's calling. Her heart is an endless well of giving.

Another reason he's determined for this test to end well.

Dex is glancing around the room, looking like an idea just hit him. "Is there another way to cut the thread? Like a knife or something?"

Kian wishes he could slap him on the back. "You're a genius, Dex."

Nova's face brightens. "Maybe a scalpel?"

Everyone snaps into action a second time, once again looking for something to get these wounds stitched up.

Kian watches as the others search, feeling the warm arm of the Bound beneath his hand. The person hasn't moved since this all began, the embodiment of patience and faith. His gut clenches at the thought of what he's going to have to do if they find something.

He'll have to tell Nova he thinks she's wrong. They're meant to treat the Bound.

Thom jumps up, holding a utility knife in triumph. "Will this do?"

Nova pulls in a breath. "I think it will have to."

Kian is just about to speak, knowing how much hearing this is going to hurt the girl he loves, when the door slides open.

Everyone spins around to find the Remnant standing there.

The anger flares hot and fast. The nerve of this girl! Chafing against having to stay and hold a wound, Kian wishes he could stop her from entering. He's had enough of her prejudice.

She doesn't get to judge what she doesn't understand.

The Remnant barely looks at him as she strides past, clutching something to her chest. "Here." She passes whatever it is to Nova. "Put this on the wounds."

"Like hell she will."

Nova's gaze flies to Kian in surprise. He doubts he's ever

used language like that, but he's never felt this sort of anger. The Remnant is probably trying to poison the Bound.

She sneers at Kian. "It will heal them."

Kian looks down to see one of the wooden cups they use for drinking, a thick, brown substance in the bottom. "I doubt that very much."

"Of course you do, you narrow-minded idiot." The Remnant turns back to Nova, her voice softening. "It's the sap of the mangrove pine. It's what healed my own wounds so quickly."

Nova's eyes widen. "The stuff you were coated with when you arrived?"

The Remnant nods, then grins. "Remember how surprised you were to hear it was a leatherskin I had a run-in with?"

Nova glances down at the two wounds being covered by Shiloh and Kian. "I thought you must've exaggerated."

The Remnant pushes the cup further toward Nova. "The sap heals wounds. You won't have to choose."

Nova stills, her breath evaporating.

Kian wishes he could move to her side, but he's stuck keeping the pressure on the Bound's wound. "She could be lying, Nova. It's not worth the risk."

Although the Remnant's shoulders stiffen, she ignores him. She places the cup on the table. "All you need to do is spread it on then bandage them up."

Kian can see the hope in Nova's eyes. He shakes his head. Surely it can't be that simple.

Kian can feel the intensity of the stares of the others. Everyone is trying to decide what the right thing to do is.

"I think Dex was right," Nova says. "This test is about realizing who the best person for the job is. And I believe that's Wren."

Nova takes the cup of sap and walks to the Unbound. Kian opens his mouth to say something, but Nova holds up his hand. "He's already lost consciousness, he needs it more."

Carefully, she peels back the bloodied hemp as Shiloh looks away with a grimace. Nova drizzles a line of sap down the wound. She looks around, only to find Dex by her side.

"Need more of these?" he asks with a smile, holding up some clean bandages.

"Thanks, Dex. You're always one step ahead." Nova glances at one of the cameras from the corner of her eye, and Kian realizes she said it for the benefit of those watching.

Probably Dex's father.

Deftly, she wraps up the Unbound's arm. Once she's finished, she doesn't stop to admire her handiwork, instead moving straight onto the Bound. Nova steps in close to Kian and he breathes in her scent. Any anger or frustration dissolves as his lungs fill with the essence that is Nova—crisp pine and sweet soap.

All she wants to do is help others. It's a quality he's always admired.

Gently, she repeats the process. As she lifts the bandages soaked in blood, Kian steps back, giving her some room. He watches as she works quickly and efficiently, her mind totally focused on the task before her.

Within minutes, she's drizzled the sap and wrapped up the Bound's arm.

The Remnant peers over her shoulder. "It'll give them almost instant relief from the pain. There's something in it that numbs the skin."

As if on cue, the arm of the Bound relaxes, the palm opening up like a flower. Kian's eyes widen. The Bound had held their hand in a fist during the entire test, probably bracing themselves against the pain. It seems the Remnant is telling the truth!

Nova steps back, letting out a breath. "All done."

A collective sigh seems to exhale throughout the room. Shiloh is the first to smile. "Well done, Nova."

Nova shakes her head. "It's Wren you should be thanking."

Shiloh blinks as she turns to the small girl, the only one who has yet to relax. "Ah—"

The Remnant puts up her hand. "If any of you had bothered to consider that these two people were equals, that neither was more deserving than the other, then we wouldn't have been in this situation in the first place."

Shiloh snaps her mouth shut. Kian finds his frown returning. Why does this girl have to be so obnoxious about everything?

The door opens and everyone spins around to find Callix standing there. "Well done, everyone. You've completed the second test of the Proving. You may now return to your bunkroom."

Callix smiles as if nothing out of the norm has happened and is gone. Kian blinks, but then realizes Callix probably left before any questions could be asked. If they've run this test before, it never would've finished the way it has.

That's because a Remnant has never taken part in the tests.

There's a shuffling behind him and Kian turns to find the arms drawing back through the holes. He suspects they're marveling at their pain-free wound.

Felicia heads for the door, scowling. "Well, that was fun."

She doesn't wait for an answer before leaving the room. The others follow, Jay holding his head as Fern watches him closely, all trickling out with bowed shoulders. Shiloh offers him an apologetic smile as she passes him.

Kian draws up one of his own, hoping to give her some reassurance. She probably feels as shell-shocked as he does. "You did well, Shiloh."

To Kian's surprise, her smile dials up. "You did too, Kian." With a last glance over her shoulder, she slips through the door.

He turns back, not surprised to find Dex standing beside Nova. She has her arms crossed as she rubs herself as if she's cold. Kian envelops her and she sinks into him. "That was tough."

Dex lets out such a big sigh, it feels like he must've been holding it the entire time the test was going. "That was harder than when Nova got hold of a deck of cards, convinced I could play snap with her."

Kian folds around Nova, enjoying the sensation of their bodies fitting together. When this is all over, they can begin the life he's looked forward to for so long. He and Nova. Dex and whichever Bound he falls for. Friends and lovers and family. All Bound. All happy.

"It wasn't as hard as it should've been."

Kian stiffens at the sound of the Remnant's voice. Why did she have to hang back, too?

Nova turns in Kian's arms. "Thank you, Wren. You saved that Unbound."

The Remnant's arms explode outward. "Do you know that if it wasn't for your awful finger chopping, I would've had no idea which one was which? And that it didn't actually matter?"

Kian's arms tighten around Nova. "Of course you wouldn't know the difference. You don't understand Askala."

"You're right, I don't. I don't understand how you can call yourself kind, and then consider treating one person at the expense of the other. In my world, we treat everyone the same."

"As a threat," Kian grinds out. The same way she's treated everyone at Askala.

Nova rests her hand on Kian's chest. "You'll come to understand why we're doing this, Wren. Until then, I'd love to learn more about this sap."

The girl's animosity doesn't abate. "It's amazing what you can learn when you don't close yourself off from the world."

Kian snaps his mouth shut. Does she know it was his father who made that decision?

Nova slips out of Kian's arms. "Will you show me?"

The Remnant crosses her arms. "Sure. I wouldn't want to seem ungrateful." She glares at Kian.

Dex chuckles and Kian considers scowling at him. Now isn't the time to have a sense of humor.

But he stops himself.

This Remnant did what none of them thought was possible. It seems she healed both the wounds, sparing a choice none of them would've liked to make.

A choice that would've stayed with Nova for a long time.

A choice that may have seen Nova fail this test.

Kian feels like a rod has been rammed down his spine. "Thank you...Wren."

Wren goes from a tightly drawn bow ready to attack, to frozen shock. Recovering, she narrows her eyes at him. "I bet that hurt."

Sensing Nova relax, Kian steps up to her. Wren helped the girl he intends on spending the rest of his life with, and for that he is grateful. "It really did, to be honest."

Something strikes him as he starts to comprehend exactly what Wren has done. A small jolt of joy bursts through him as he rests an arm around Nova's shoulders. "You do realize that you just topped the second test, don't you, Wren?"

Wren reels back like he just slapped her. She opens her mouth, probably about to fire another of her snarky retorts, but then slams it shut. Kian almost chuckles at finally seeing her speechless. Wren's glare is pure fury as she spins on her heel and stalks from the room.

But Wren leaving seems to suck any feeling of smugness straight out of him. Kian's arm tightens around Nova's shoulders reflexively as the next realization hits him.

Wren just topped the second test.

Which means they didn't.

DEX

*D*ex wakes early. Or at least he thinks it's early. It's hard to tell in a bunkroom with no windows. There's a soft glow filtering across the room from the emergency exit light above the door. Just enough that he can see his hand if he holds it up in front of his face.

His right hand.

He'd asked his father several times over the years what would happen to him if he fails his Proving. How can they cut the finger from a hand that no longer exists? Will they take a finger from his right hand instead?

His father has always been adamant that they won't touch his hand. It'd be cruel to take a finger from someone who only has five left. He'll be allowed to wear his Bound ring—if he gets one—on his right hand and that will set him apart enough. He hopes his father is right. If anyone should know, it's him.

Tucking his hand back under his blanket, Dex lies still and listens to the breathing of the eight other participants, hoping the tornado-proofing of the lab is enough to withstand Jay's snoring. How does his family put up with that in their tiny cabin on the Oasis? At least after this Proving, Jay will be given a cabin of his own. Either near his family or with the Unbound on the upper decks. Dex hates that he already suspects that's where Jay's heading. Hopefully he's good with heights.

Kian is making noises, too. Not snoring, but a kind of mumbling. Dex smiles to realize he's saying Nova's name. That guy has it so bad. It would be sickening if it weren't so ridiculously cute. He's even trying to protect her while he's asleep.

Another noise grabs Dex's attention. Well, not so much a noise, but a lack of noise. There's total silence coming from the space on the floor underneath his bottom bunk. Is Wren even breathing?

Leaning over the edge of his bunk, Dex swings down his head to check on her, but the shadows are too dense and all he can see is her blanket. Reaching out he swipes his hand across it trying to get Wren's attention, only to discover the blanket is lying flat on the cold floor.

He stretches out a little more to get to the back corner under the bunk, but without another hand to hold onto the bed, he loses his balance and topples out. Lying on the floor, he winces as he rubs at his forehead, which took the brunt of the fall. It's sore but he's okay. The next test might be a physical one. He can't afford to have any injuries.

Thankfully, he doesn't seem to have woken anyone over the noise of Jay snoring and Kian trying to rescue Nova from a fire-breathing dragon, or whatever it is he's dreaming about. He shuffles over, getting himself closer to Wren's sleeping space and checks for any sign of her. Has she decided to give a bunk a go instead of this hard floor?

He quickly checks the other bunks, only to find she's not in any of them.

Heading for the door, he scans his bracelet and it slides open.

"What are you doing?" Kian sits up, his dark hair a messy halo around his tired face.

"Go back to sleep," Dex whispers. "I'm just going to the bathroom."

Kian lies down and mumbles something unintelligible as Dex slips from the room.

A quick check of the bathroom tells him Wren isn't there. She's not in the dining hall, either. Then he feels a warm rush of air near the main exit. Someone's opened that door very recently and let some of the warmth of the night into this air-conditioned lab.

Which means someone's used this exit recently.

Dex puts his hand to his chest, aware how hard his heart just started hammering. It's one thing for Wren to sneak out of bed at night, but another all together for her to leave the lab. That's strictly forbidden during a Proving. Nobody is allowed to leave, not even his father.

Shaking his head, Dex realizes this is why she's done it. Kian had pointed out to her that she did well in their last test. And that was right on the back of her being aware she also likely scored well in the first test. Instead of sitting the third test, she must've decided to leave. It's a bit hard to pass a test when you're not present.

Does she really not want to be Bound that much? Most people want nothing more than this. Despite the Unbound living a life of being cared for, nobody ever really aspires to be one of them. But, then again, he's never met anyone like Wren, either.

But he'll be damned if he pulled her from the ocean only to have her throw away her life like this without even trying! She could be banished if she refuses to finish her Proving. And *that* is not acceptable. She fought so hard to get here. The least she can do is make the most of it.

Without giving it too much more thought, Dex slams his bracelet to the sensor and strides through the exit into the darkness. If his dad notices he left the lab and asks him about it, he'll just tell him that he thought Wren's disappearance was the third test.

The thought has him walking faster. Maybe Wren's disappearance *is* the third test? Could it be? Surely not.

Now to decide where a Remn—someone from the Outlands might go. Definitely not the Oasis. And not the garden, given the way Wren had screwed up her face at dinner as she'd eaten her broccoli. Which leaves either the forest or the beach.

The beach.

It has to be. It feels right that she'd return to the place where she arrived.

Dex jogs down toward the water, enjoying the burst of fresh air, even if it's so humid it feels like his lungs are filling with water. His nose twitches as he tries to expel the sterile environment of the lab. If all goes well, he'll be back in there shortly. Best to make the most of being outside while he can.

It's a full moon and as he emerges from the trees at the narrow beach, he has to blink as he takes in the spectacular sight of the moon reflecting off the water. The ocean is churning, as always, and the movement of the waves sends beams of moonlight dancing in the midnight air. There really is no sight more beautiful.

Then he sees her. Wren is sitting on the sand with her knees pulled up to her chest, not making any effort to hide herself. She looks like a lost child. The urge to find out why she came here burns at him, but he's aware he has to tread slowly. The startled look on her face when she'd told him her mother was dead had been enough to let him know she hadn't planned to share details of her life.

He sits down beside her and pulls up his own knees. Drawing in a deep breath, he tries to slow the rate of his heart.

"What are you doing here?" she asks, without turning her head. "Don't you know it's against the rules to leave the lab during the Proving?"

"It is." He nods, even though she's not watching him. "Which is why I need you to come back with me."

"There's a whole other world out there, Dex." She points out to the water. "People. Families. Friends. Lovers. All fighting to stay alive. While you—"

"While we what?" He snaps his head toward her, his heart pounding with anger now instead of concern. "While we dedicate our lives to saving the planet that humans destroyed with their greed? If Askala didn't exist, there'd be no hope. At least this way humans have a chance of a future."

"Some humans," she corrects. "Some humans have a chance. The ones you deem worthy with your stupid tests."

"And what's your answer to all of this?" Dex picks up a handful of damp sand and throws it at the water, watching it separate and sink into the acidic depths. "What's your plan to save Earth?"

Wren shrugs, turning to look at him for the first time. "I don't have one. The only plan we have over there is to survive. Survival is everything."

"And you treat everyone the same over there, do you?" He shakes his head, knowing this can't possibly be true. "When you're sitting there eating your bears, or whatever it is you eat, and someone walks up, you just hand over what you have?"

"Of course not." Her voice has dropped to a whisper. This is the most unsure he's ever seen her. "We look after our family first. Always."

"Can't you see it's not so different here? The Bound are a family. So are the Unbound. And together, we're one larger family. You treat people differently over there, depending on who they are to you, and so do we. We just determine this with the Provings instead of by blood. We have to secure our future. For everyone's sake."

"Not for the sake of that Unbound in the test," she says.

"Were you really going to let him bleed out and die, just to save the stitches for someone deemed more worthy?"

"It's not about worth." He shakes his head, trying to find the right words. "It's about survival. You said it yourself... survival is everything."

She huffs, not liking to hear her words twisted. "The survival I was talking about is a little more short-term."

"And can't you see that's what the problem is? We need a vision for the future. A new way of doing things." Finally, she's listening to him!

"You really believe your own bullshit, don't you?" she says, crushing his excitement and sending his shoulders sagging.

"Why did you come here if it's so awful?" He stands, keen to put a little space between them. To think he risked his own Proving for this Remnant. He should have listened to Kian. They're all the same. Selfish and obnoxious.

He'd really thought Wren was different.

"I didn't know what it was like here." She stays in the same position he found her in. Knees hugged to her chest, dark hair flying in the breeze. He hates that he's aware she looks beautiful. "If I knew, I would never have come."

"Could you get any more ungrateful?" Dex combs his fingers through his hair, trying to keep it from falling into his eyes. "We pulled you from the ocean, we fed you, we clothed you, and this is the thanks we get."

"Nova said there was no expectation of anything in return for any of that." Anger flashes in Wren's dark eyes as she looks up at him. "You calling her a liar?"

Dex sighs. "No, Wren, I'm not calling her a liar. It would never occur to someone as sweet as Nova to think she'd have to ask you to be grateful."

"So, that's what you want." Wren scrambles to her knees and holds her hands together in front of her. "Thank you, Dex. Oh, thank you for rescuing me. My savior!"

"Stop that." He turns away, glad she can't see the flush that's burning across his cheeks. He'd asked for gratitude, not humiliation. "All we're asking of you is to live by our rules. And that includes finishing the Proving."

"There's no point." She sits back on the sand and resumes her former position, hugging her knees to her chest. "I don't want to pass."

"Well, for someone who doesn't want to pass, you're doing a pretty good job of it. The first test you came across like some kind of empathetic saint, and the second you made us all look like bumbling fools."

"When are you going to get it?" she asks. "I wasn't trying to make you look like anything. Nothing I do has anything to do with any of you."

"It has *everything* to do with us." Dex paces down the beach, then abruptly returns. "You totally changed the outcome of both those tests. None of us had a hope coming up against you."

"Then maybe you shouldn't have helped me out of the water."

She stares at him, daring him to agree. It's a dare he's willing to take.

"Yeah, maybe I shouldn't have."

She turns her face away from him, but not before he catches the hurt he just inflicted. If he didn't know better, he'd almost think she cared.

Unable to take any more of this, he stalks away from her, heading back to the lab. But the minute he hits the trees, he changes his mind and returns to her at twice the pace he left. He's not finished with her yet.

"You don't get to do this, Wren." He stabs his index finger in the air, wishing all the frustration he's feeling would go rushing out of it. "You don't get to ruin my Proving. If they find out I left the lab, I'll fail. You need to come back with me so you can explain if we get caught. It's the least you can do."

He pauses as she seems to consider this for a moment.

"And you never know," he says. "Maybe you'll actually get your wish and stuff up the next test."

"And if I don't?"

"Is being Bound so bad?" He crosses his arms. The stance he's perfected to make himself look fully formed. "It's gotta be better than being banished."

Wren's spine straightens at this word. "You banish people?"

"Not for a long time, but yes. If you don't follow the rules and finish your Proving, then I guess we'll find out if it still happens."

"I can't end up back out there." Wren shakes her head, fear filling her eyes. "I can't."

"Then don't." He shrugs and turns away from her. "I'm going back. Are you coming or not?"

She's by his side in a heartbeat. Or maybe three given the pounding in Dex's chest. Together, they march from the beach and take the path back toward the lab.

"They're not really going to banish me, are they?" she asks in that strange voice again. The one steeped in fear.

"Not now that you're coming back." He hears his tone soften, wondering why it's so difficult to remain upset with this infuriating girl. "You're doing the right thing."

"You're so serious tonight," she says quietly. "I thought you were supposed to be the funny guy."

"And I thought you were supposed to be the tough girl."

"I am." She takes a step closer to him and nudges him off the path with her shoulder.

"Wren!"

She's laughing now and despite how unsure he still feels, he can't help but shoot her a smile.

At least he's managed to get her to come back with him. Finally, he's done something right. Because there's no denying that part of the anxiety he's feeling is down to the fact that this Proving isn't even close to going the way he'd hoped.

He'd been very unexceptional in the first test, and barely non-existent in the second. Which means the pressure is on now more than ever.

He has two more tests left in which to prove himself.

Two more chances to do his mother proud.

WREN

*W*ren shuffles her feet, waiting for Dex's father to appear and give them their next test.

Lana and her irritating smile had come to collect them this time and lead them out to a walled yard beside the lab to await further instructions. Wren had thought when she'd stepped back into the lab with Dex in the early hours of the morning that she'd have to wait days to breathe clean air again.

There's a large object in the middle of the yard. It's covered in a sheet and they've been told not to touch it. Which means everyone's circling it like a herd of leatherskins, speculating about what's underneath.

Wren can't be bothered making a guess. She already knows what's under there. And it's an object that has her pacing. This isn't something she wanted to encounter again so soon.

"Maybe it's a hoe," says Felicia. "You know, those big mechanical ones that dig up the vegetables."

Wren doesn't even bother to disguise her eye roll. Dex shoots her a quick smile.

Dex.

Her best friend in here. Except he's also her mortal enemy.

Their relationship redefines the word complicated. He's the reason she's alive. He's also the reason she's back in the lab, participating in a test she has no interest in passing.

She hadn't been able to say no to him when he'd begged her to return. Well, it was that and the threat of banishment. She's heard that word before and it punches as much fear into her as the thought of death.

"Maybe it's a new kind of stretcher?" says Nova, her face lighting with a smile. "For the infirmary."

"Pretty big stretcher." Felicia holds her stomach and lets out a laugh, glancing at the cameras as she does so, making sure there's no chance of Callix missing what was just said.

The smile falls from Nova's face. "I just thought it was a possibility."

"And I thought I told Felicia to shut up," says Wren.

Felicia pokes out her tongue and crosses her arms. But thankfully, she also falls silent.

"What is it then?" asks Thom, scratching at his square chin like it's going to give him the answer.

"It's a lifeboat," says Kian, his face turning gray with the gravity of what that might mean.

"Well done." Wren claps her hands, loudly and slowly, wishing it hadn't been Kian to point out something so obvious. "Full points to the boy genius."

Before Kian has a chance to reply, Callix steps through the door that connects the lab to the yard. Lana is close behind him.

"Good morning," he says, a smile reaching his mouth but absent from his eyes. "Welcome to the third test of your Proving. It's great to see you all here."

Wren can't be sure, but she thinks he glances at her. Does he know what happened last night?

Callix nods at Lana and they walk to the covered object and take one end of the sheet each, flipping it away dramatically to reveal... a boat.

Wren sighs. Such a surprise!

"You were right, Kian." Nova smiles up at the guy she loves.

"This is one of the original lifeboats that arrived here on the Oasis." Callix runs his hand over the edge of it as he speaks. Faded orange in color, it looks like it would hold about a dozen people if it weren't for the equipment it's filled with. "It's one of the last boats we have, so you're very fortunate to be given the opportunity to work with it during this test."

Fortunate? Is he delusional? There's no way that boat will withstand the ocean. If it were that easy, Askala would be filled with people like Wren.

"Anybody who goes out in that will be dead in a matter of hours," she says, shaking her head.

"That's right," says Callix. "*Hours*. And it takes less than that to do what this test requires."

"But—"

"Wren, please, let me finish." Callix holds up his hand and scowls.

"Okay," says Wren, taking a step back, hoping she just lost a point for her rudeness. "But I'm not going out in that thing."

Callix draws in a deep breath before he starts again. "You'll need to equip this lifeboat with everything required to perform a successful pteropod harvest."

"But the pteropods are being bred successfully on the Oasis," says Jay, getting that nervous look about him again. "We don't need more."

"Increasing their diversity will increase their strength," says Kian. "We can always use more."

Wren vaguely remembers someone saying Kian's mom is responsible for breeding those squishy little creatures. How strange to think that they contain so much goodness. They tried to give her some to eat when she arrived here, but she'd refused. The idea of biting down on one of them is gross.

Callix holds up his hand again, clearly having more to say.

"In two days, you'll send out a team of three people to harvest a tank full of pods. This is the maximum number of people the lifeboat can safely carry, given the weight of the equipment. Use your time wisely to decide who you'll send to complete the test."

"May the Proving serve you well," says Lana, beaming at them like a death sentence hasn't just been handed out to three of them.

Felicia's hands fly to her hips. "But how does—"

"You have all the information you require for this stage of the test." Callix turns to head back to the lab, Lana following closely behind him.

The door closes behind them and the nine—soon to be six—participants are alone once more.

"Great test," says Wren, directing her words at Dex.

"Leave him alone." Kian steps toward her. "Callix is his father. That's all. This has nothing to do with Dex. Are you responsible for everything your father does?"

"It's okay." Dex puts a hand on Kian's arm. "Leave her. We have other things to discuss."

Kian returns to Nova's side, shaking his head at Wren, as if he still can't believe she's breathing the same air as him. To be fair, Wren's not too pleased about breathing his air, either.

"We need to make a plan," says the mousy girl with the flower name. She's clearly decided she has to step up her game.

"What are you thinking, Fern?" asks Dex.

Fern! That's it. Not a flower name. But close enough.

Fern visibly swallows. "I'm not sure."

"She's right," says Thom. "We have to make a plan. Should we draw names at random?"

"That's a great idea." Shiloh steps forward, as supportive as ever.

Wren takes a step back, deciding to let them finish their niceness contest.

"It's a terrible idea," says, Felicia, putting an end to the contest in four sharp words.

For once, Wren agrees with her. Choosing names at random would make this a fool's mission.

"We need to send our strongest," says Dex.

All eyes turn to Kian. With those muscles bulging out from underneath the long sleeves of his shirt, he's clearly got the most physical strength of anyone on this team.

"She's strong, too."

Wren looks up to see Nova pointing at her. Eight sets of eyes follow Nova's gaze.

"I'm not going. No way!" Wren crosses her arms and takes another step back. "If you guys want to kill yourself passing this test, then knock yourselves out. Going out in that thing is suicide."

"Does anyone know how to swim?" It's Fern speaking again, keen to make up for her fumbled attempt to take charge of this discussion.

"I do," says Kian. "I had to learn so I could help Mom fix the pteropod tank."

"I think it's a given that you're going," says Dex. "Nobody knows more about the pods than you."

Nova gasps. "Dex! Don't! Let's talk this through. Sometimes the obvious decision isn't always the best one. We learned that in our first two tests, didn't we?"

"It's okay." Kian wraps an arm around Nova. "Dex is right. I should go."

"What's your problem, Nova?" asks Felicia. "Worried about lover boy?"

"Of course, I'm worried." Nova raises her voice in a way Wren hasn't heard before. It's good to see her with a little backbone at last. "My father died collecting pods in one of those things. I never even got to meet him."

"Oh." Felicia is struggling for words for once.

Wren winces. Poor Nova. Losing a parent is tough. Having to relive the way they died would be even tougher.

"Sorry." Felicia has found her voice again. "But I still think Kian has to go."

Wren takes a few more steps away from the group and sits down on the patchy grass, wincing as her bruised ribs adjust to the change in position. They feel a little better today, leaving her thinking that maybe they're not broken.

She turns her back to the others. Let them fight it out. This has nothing to do with her. For all she cares, the eight of them can cram themselves onto the boat and go down together.

"I'll go with him." Dex's voice is loud and clear. He sounds certain about this. Suddenly the idea of them all sinking into the toxic ocean doesn't sound quite so appealing.

Wren shifts so that she can see Dex out of the corner of her eye and waits to see what happens next.

"Not him," says Jay. "Sorry, Dex, but we agreed to send our strongest and you…. Well, you're…"

"Missing a hand?" says Dex. "In case you hadn't noticed, it hasn't stopped me doing anything before. I'm just as capable as you are. If not, more."

So, that's why he's so certain. Desperate to prove that a guy with one hand is worthy of becoming Bound.

Dex waves his stump at Jay like he's going to whack him in the face and Wren's heart breaks just a little bit. She's noticed how he crosses his arms to hide his missing hand, clearly self-conscious about it. He might joke about it, but that doesn't mean he doesn't care. She knows all about how it feels to put on an act.

The conversation takes off in circles as each person puts forward their thoughts on who they think should go. Callix must be wetting his pants with excitement with the amount of information he's gathering on them all. Perhaps he's not even intending to send any of them out. This test may be about who they choose, rather than the actual mission itself. Surely Callix wouldn't risk three young lives?

But then again, the lives of those two people bleeding out in the second test had been risked, so perhaps this is more than just talk.

Hauling herself to her feet, she walks to the wall, enjoying the way this strange new clothing she's been given breathes in this relentless humidity. She's never felt more comfortable, even if she does feel a bit foolish. Phoenix would die laughing if he could see her dressed like this. But she could hardly have continued to wear her regular clothes. The leatherskin had made sure of that.

She kicks at a knot of timber in the wall, watching as it splinters away. The shadow of a bird circling overhead catches her eye. Stepping out from the shade of the overhanging tree, she squints into the sun, seeing it's a raven.

Well, that's bloody great! She's been looking for a raven all week and now that one's finally here, she's surrounded by a bunch of Askala-loving diehards.

Tucking her pendant into her shirt, she sighs, desperately hoping she'll be able to sneak out here later when she's alone to catch the bird's attention. Maybe then she can get Cy the message she's been carrying around all week.

If the raven's still here. And if it's one of Cy's.

The morning wears on and by the time the sun reaches its highest point in the sky, they're no closer to selecting a team. Names are being put forward and pulled back and put forward again. The only name that remains constant is Kian's.

With the way he's treated Wren since her arrival, she can't say she's too sad about this. Although, it's a shame for Nova. Her heart will never recover if she loses him.

Looking around the group, Wren is struck with the thought that no matter who goes, there will be hearts that will never recover. Everybody has somebody who loves them. Even Felicia, as hard as that is to believe.

This test is cruel. How could Callix design such a thing, knowing Dex was going to participate? Was he confident his maimed son was safe from selection? But surely, he must have known his nephew would be chosen. None of this makes sense. This test has to be a trick. Nobody will be sent out for real. Callix is just trying to see how the three are chosen.

Not being able to stand listening to these fools for a moment longer, Wren hauls herself to her feet, supporting her ribs with her hand.

"I think we should all go," she says, determined to bring this never-ending argument to a close.

All faces turn to stare at her.

"The boat only takes three," says Felicia.

"Then we'll make a raft." Wren shrugs as she walks toward them. It's about time these fools stepped outside their comfort zone and learned to look at things from a different perspective. "I didn't arrive in one of those things. We can make it from mangrove pine."

"Not the mangrove pine again." Felicia rolls her eyes.

"Let her finish," says Nova. "If we hadn't listened to her yesterday, none of us would have passed that test."

"Maybe none of us did pass," says Jay, tugging at his hair. "Except her."

"Her raft broke up in the water." Kian narrows his gaze on Wren. "I was there. I saw it. This is sabotage."

"We soaked our twine in mangrove sap." Wren moves closer to Dex, then realizing what she's doing, steps back. "It wasn't enough."

"Then what is enough?" Dex scratches his head, biting down on his lower lip.

Wren lets out a slow breath, part of her wishing she'd stayed with her back turned on the grass. But she knows she couldn't have done that. This is her opportunity to show them there's a way to reach the Outlands. With or without the bridge. Askala may have cut themselves off from the rest of the world, but there's no reason for them to remain isolated.

"If we tie the planks together using the smaller, flexible branches of the pine, it should hold," she says, keeping her gaze fixed on Dex.

"Should." Kian shakes his head. "Who here's prepared to risk their life on a *should*?"

Dex takes a step closer to Wren. "I will."

Wren's mouth falls open, although she really shouldn't be surprised. If anyone was going to back her up, it would be Dex.

"You're crazy, Dex," says Kian. "Please, don't do this. This wasn't what your father had in mind when he set this test."

"Exactly." Dex is undeterred. If anything, Kian's argument only seemed to make him more determined.

"You'd listen to her before me?" Kian pulls back his shoulders, steam practically rising from his ears.

"When are you going to work out that Wren's the smartest out of the lot of us?" Dex shakes his head and Wren fights the rush of heat that's made its way to her cheeks. "I'm doing it. You're not leaving me and my one hand behind."

"I'll do it, too." Fern steps forward to stand on Wren's other side. There's no mistaking the fear in this girl's eyes.

"Me, too," says Thom. "I'm in. I think..."

Whoa! Wren shakes her head. It was enough of a shock for Dex to agree to travel on a raft, but Fern and Thom? These people are even more desperate than she'd realized. It's almost like they'd rather die than become Unbound.

"Pick your teams." Fern projects her voice, trying so hard to prove herself that it gives Wren a small pain in her chest. "If you want to go with Kian, stand beside him now. If you want to go on a raft, come and join us here. If you'd prefer to stay behind, stay exactly where you are. The choice is yours."

Wren holds steady, not saying a word as she watches the shuffling of people choosing teams. She looks up at the camera, grinning as she imagines Callix's frustration at his test falling apart.

Nova stands firmly by Kian's side as Wren suspected she would.

Jay starts walking toward them, then changes his mind at the last moment and heads over to Kian. Felicia darts in front of him, trying to get there first.

The two of them cross their arms and stare at each other, weighing up their options. One of them will need to step away.

This leaves only Shiloh left to make her choice. Trust Wren and join her team or stay behind and be almost certain to fail the test. The way her eyes are darting toward Kian, it's fairly obvious what choice she'd like to make, but knows she's missed her chance. Reluctantly, she joins Wren.

"I'm not making you come with me," says Wren, not wanting the weight of responsibility for a reluctant passenger on her shoulders.

"I want to go out." Shiloh speaks clearly, despite the wobble in her voice.

Thom is shuffling his feet now, his indecisiveness almost as annoying as Felicia's rudeness. Perhaps it's better if he does change his mind. It would have to be a strong raft to hold his robust frame.

Then his eyes light up as he sees his way out of this situation. "Maybe the way to pass is to prove how clever you are by staying behind."

"How is that clever?" Felicia rolls her eyes.

"Actually, that's the smartest thing anybody's said all day," says Wren, enjoying watching them all squirm. They're behaving as if they're actually going on this mission. More than ever, she's convinced it has to be a trick. And if it's not, then at least she gets to teach them an important lesson. "Going out there is the most dangerous thing you'll ever do. The only way to guarantee you're not going to die is to stay behind. Callix would never want you all to risk yourselves. I'd call that clever."

Thom puffs out his square chest and nods at Felicia, who seems to be weighing up her options yet again.

"Besides," adds Wren, deciding to tip her over the edge. "Callix was pretty clear about the fact that only three of us should go. Staying behind is a way of showing him you're following the rules."

She hides a smile as Felicia physically retreats like she's been pushed in the chest.

"Yeah," says Thom, glancing at the camera. "Told you it was smart. Staying behind is just as honorable a choice as going. We can't risk everyone and Bounds need to follow rules."

Without a word, Felicia leaves the lifeboat to stand beside Thom, glancing around to see if anybody else is going to follow.

Jay lets out a sigh, relieved at not having to fight for his place on the boat.

"Come on! Join us! You heard what she said." There's a desperation in Felicia's voice that Wren recognizes. There's safety in numbers. Felicia would clearly feel more comfortable if some of the others decided to stay behind, too.

But nobody else moves.

"I'm all good, thanks," says Wren, trying not to smirk.

"I thought you said it was smart!" Felicia puts her hands on her hips and pouts.

"Yeah, but I'm just a dumb Remnant, aren't I?" Wren grins at her, enjoying the discomfort her words bring. "I want to fail, remember?"

"You made the right choice." Thom puts a hand on Felicia's back. "We'll be fine. We're just following the instructions. It's foolish to send us all out."

"So, that's Kian, Nova, and Jay on the boat," says Fern. "Thom and Felicia staying behind. And Wren, Dex, Shiloh, and me on the raft. Last chance to change your mind."

They stand in silence, each reflecting on whether or not they're standing where they want to be.

They've all made their own choice.

They've all sealed their own fate.

Now please, let this be as far as this test goes.

NOVA

$\mathcal{A}$ raft and a lifeboat sit at the edge of the water, and Nova isn't sure which of them looks the sturdiest…or safest. The lifeboat is one of the last remaining vessels from the Oasis. A tired, faded orange, it was built before humans realized the ocean could become a monster with the ability to slowly devour it.

It's been their only way to go out and get pteropods, though. Kian's mom explained to her how each year they need to harvest more to ensure the population in the tank doesn't become inbred and weak.

Those lifeboats are all they've had…until now.

Nova stares at the raft beside it. It took two days of grueling work for the nine of them to chop down two mangrove pines, split them, then lash the half-trunks together, using some of the smaller, more flexible branches. Now, they rest on the sand, the exposed cuts face up, the sap still bleeding from the roughhewn surface.

Wren had pointed out early on that Callix would probably wait until they'd finished this back-breaking work before telling them they didn't actually have to go out.

Nova smiles as she shakes her head. Wren hasn't grasped how far Bounds will go to ensure Askala not only survives, but thrives.

She twists the bracelet around her wrist, wondering how she feels about the crude raft. Felicia keeps sneering at it. Dex is fascinated by it. Kian, despite his reservations, worked hard to help build it. In fact, he was the first to chop down a mangrove pine. But he'd frowned the whole time.

Nova had brushed his arm whenever she'd passed him, feeling the muscles bunch at the touch. She knows he's angry and torn.

No one is sure whether this raft is a good idea or not. It could mean the largest harvest of pods Askala has ever seen... but it will definitely mean putting far more than three lives at risk to achieve that.

Surely Callix never intended for more than three of them to go out...

Is it possible that he'll come out and tell them the test doesn't involve going out into the ocean? Nova's pulse jerks, and she knows it's fear and hope battling again.

She's had two days of hoping against hope that Wren could be right.

Two days of knowing that just like humans believed their destruction could be reversed, sometimes hope isn't enough. What happens next will be inevitable. Nova will follow in her father's footsteps and harvest pods from the ocean.

Her hand drops to her side as she straightens her shoulders. She can't forget why they're doing this. That this is her Proving.

That this is what Bounds do.

Voices trickle behind her, and she turns toward the tree line, squinting in the sun as she adjusts the shawl shading her face. The others, including Kian, went to get what they'll need for this test. At least the equipment is simple—two round drums to hold the pteropods, several nets to scoop them up.

Nova stayed back to collect the oozing sap from the rafts, figuring she can use it if anyone's injured while they're out on the water. She'd quizzed Wren about the sap as they'd stripped the mangrove pines of branches, but Wren had spent more time deflecting than answering. It had quickly become apparent that any talk of the Outlands was off limits.

Nova had moved away, wondering why she was wasting her breath, only to notice the others had already done the same. More often than not, Wren worked on her own.

The only time she didn't, was when Dex wandered past, dragging branches with his one hand. Sometimes he would stop, warning Wren not to touch him, or the sap could glue them together forever. Other times, he'd keep walking, jovially stating he'd give her a thumbs up if he could, but his hand was full.

Wren never smiled, although once or twice, Nova swore she saw her lips twitch.

In the end, Nova went back to work beside her. Whether this girl came from the Outlands, whether she'll be Unbound, didn't matter. No matter what Wren said or did, no one should be treated like an outsider.

This time, instead of asking questions, though, Nova had told Wren about Askala. She told her about the gardens they've tended for generations, no matter how many storms have wiped them out. She told her about how they share out any food they harvest equally. She told Wren about the pteropods, the lifeblood of Askala in a world where fish are toxic, protein is scarce, and plants grow too fast to have much nutritional content.

Wren had barely looked at Nova, had only asked the odd question, but Nova knew she was listening. It was in that hawk-like gaze darting to study Nova's face, in the way her hands stilled occasionally.

Wren may not want to show it, but she's fascinated with Askala.

"Let's get them on." Kian's voice returns Nova to the present.

Two people, nothing more than arms wrapped around wooden drums and legs striding beneath, appear from the trees. Nova instantly recognizes Kian in the lead—she knows those limbs as if they were her own. Those arms have held her, those hands stroked her face. Those legs chased her when they were children, then as they filled out for manhood, became the foundation of her future.

The other drum is held by Jay. No doubt he'll be happy to appear useful.

Nova walks toward them, like Kian's steel and she's a magnet. Her spine stiffens when she sees Shiloh is right behind him, carrying the nets. She hates the stab of jealousy that pierces her. She goes to twist the bracelet again but stops herself. After the Proving it will be gone, replaced by the chip in her hand.

Then, she and Kian will be together and Shiloh can carry nets and flutter her dark lashes all she wants.

The world will know what their hearts already do—they belong to each other.

Kian lowers the barrel to the sand while Jay places his beside it.

Kian surveys the boat and raft beside the water. "The last thing we need to do is get these strapped down."

Kian already has his lifted again, while Jay stretches his arms like they're in pain. Nova goes to pick it up for him, but Thom is already beside it. They both pause.

Thom steps a little closer. "Best if one of the stronger people get this one, Nova."

Nova hesitates, conscious of the cameras pointing down on them from high up in the trees. It's the first thing she looked for when they came down here this morning. Callix and Lana would had to have installed them in a rush last night.

"I'm sure I can carry it, Thom."

Wren appears beside Nova, her hands on her hips. "I reckon she could, too."

Nova blinks. Why is Wren weighing in on this?

Thom frowns. "I just figured..."

Wren angles her head. "That 'cause you wimped out on going, you should do something to help?"

Thom's frown multiplies, his brows practically reaching his nose as his square shoulders hunch. "I was trying to be helpful."

Wren snorts. "Of course you were." She turns to Nova. "You going to let him call the shots?"

Nova feels tension rise in her like mercury, her body starting to feel warm. Does she insist on picking up the barrel, to prove she's capable? That she's willing to do her part?

Or does she let Thom do it? Acknowledging that he's stronger and better suited to this task?

Despite feeling suddenly hot, her lungs freeze. Or does she let Thom do it, so he can have the opportunity to prove he's kind and helpful, especially considering he's chosen to stay behind which is surely a bad move?

What should she do? What would a Bound do? She resists glancing at the trees, frustrated that every small decision is being watched and weighed.

She smiles at Thom as she steps back. "It's all yours."

Thom relaxes and grins. "Sure thing, Nova."

He lifts the barrel easily and heads to the raft.

Nova watches as Kian instructs them on placing it in the center to keep the raft balanced and checks they're all tied down securely. She has no doubt Callix would be noting that Kian is a natural leader. Everyone's safety has been his priority.

Wren's shaking her head beside Nova. "Why didn't you just pick up the damned barrel, Nova?"

Nova shrugs, ignoring the twinge in her chest. "To give Thom the chance to do it."

"You keep doing that sort of stuff, and you're going to fail. I thought you wanted nothing more than to be with Kian and have his babies?"

Nova flushes, not sure she likes the image Wren is painting. Kian is her world, but she has a life outside of him...doesn't she? She shakes her head—Wren is probably trying to get Nova second-guessing herself. "I disagree, Wren. The Proving isn't about proving your own strength or superiority. It's about demonstrating kindness and consideration for others."

"Like in the first test, with the blocks? You're showing that you'll put others before you?"

Nova nods, relaxing a little. "Yes. That's what Bounds do."

Wren angles her head. "Kind of like Kian is doing? By making himself the self-appointed leader of this little mission?"

Nova's muscles go rigid, once again feeling on the defense. It's not the same for Kian. This mission is dangerous. It's necessary for someone to ensure everything is done right. Their lives depend on it.

Shock has Nova going still, wondering if she's about to snap with all the tension winding through her muscles. Or is Wren suggesting that Kian is sabotaging his chances of success in this test by taking a leadership role?

Wren waves her hand like she's flicking away a fly. "Forget I said anything. What do I know?" She huffs and Nova expects another of her snarky comments. "There's a weather change coming."

Surprised, Nova scans the horizon, seeing nothing but clear sky, although she knows that doesn't mean much nowadays. Weather changes can be rapid and extreme in this post-global warming world. She's about to ask Wren how she can tell when another question strikes her. "Why are you telling me?"

Surely, the others should know this.

Wren raises a brow. "You really think they'll listen to me?"

Nova clamps her mouth shut. Wren's right. Everyone will

assume she's saying this to sabotage the task. The few words Wren has said over the past two days have largely involved grouching that the Bound have got them doing this so they can save their own hides.

Nova's glance slides away. Unless that's exactly what Wren's doing...and she's smart enough to realize that Nova is the most gullible of them all.

Wren shrugs again. "Plus, I think you should pull out. You're too nice to end up in the gut of some leatherskin."

Nova's mouth pops open, only to quickly form into a smile. "You almost sound like you care, Wren."

Wren snorts so hard Nova wonders how her nose stayed intact. "Nice isn't a quality I respect, Nova. Nice gets you killed where I come from."

Nova turns away, hiding the fact her smile may have diminished, but it hasn't gone anywhere. "Forget I said anything," she chides, using Wren's own words. "I'll be fine. I hear leatherskins don't really like white meat."

There's a half-choke, half-chuckle behind her as Nova walks away but she doesn't look back. Who knows what Wren's motivation is, but she needs to tell Kian what Wren said about the storm.

She needs to stop second-guessing every decision she and the others make.

Kian is still busy tying down the barrels, so Nova holds back, willing to wait. The lifeboat is already packed, so now it's just the raft. Felicia rushes forward, practically pushing herself between Kian and the barrel. Kian frowns but simply steps around her, resuming the lashing of the branches.

Nova scans the horizon again, seeing nothing but clear sky. How odd to think the ocean used to be blue. That was before it absorbed tons of atmospheric carbon and progressively heated. The coral was the first to go, bleached and cooked, along with any species that depended on it. Then deep-sea species slowly suffocated. It's their dead bodies that seared the ocean floor rust red.

Nova stares out over the sea. It's the color of watery blood.

The blood of her dead father.

The knowledge that this is how he died has weighed heavily on Nova since the moment she heard this is what the next test would be. No one knows how dangerous this is more intimately than her.

It's why she hoped Wren was right—that Callix would come out and give them a reprieve by saying they would never use those undertaking the Proving to harvest pods.

Dex comes to stand beside Nova, dusting his hand on his pants. "We're almost done."

And there's no sign of Callix.

Nova nods, her heart punching at her ribs. "Good."

Dex goes silent as they watch everyone. Their faces all hold varying shades of frown, all conscious they need to get this right. At least everyone else is tense, which means Nova's short response isn't out of place.

Dex nudges her with his shoulder. "Remember when I dared you to eat a fish out of there?"

Something inside Nova unwinds as she rolls her eyes. "I couldn't kill it once we'd caught it."

He chuckles. "You teared up just taking the hook out of its mouth."

"Give me a break! It was looking at me with its fishy eyes, mouthing 'help me' over and over!"

Dex's chuckle fades. "Exactly. You knew you wouldn't be able to eat it, so you couldn't bear to see it die for no reason."

"It was more because it's full of toxic heavy metals, and I realized it wasn't worth the dare." She'd felt like such a soft-touch, but she couldn't bring herself to do it.

"Not true." Dex shakes his head. "It could've been the most delicious, nutritious fish in the ocean and you wouldn't have eaten it. That's why you're going out on this mission, Nova, even though it scares the heck out of you."

Because this comes first. The mission is more important than her own, selfish fear.

Impulsively, Nova throws her arms around Dex. He knows exactly how much this test is weighing on her, and because Dex is Dex, he's trying to cheer her up.

He's telling her she's acting like a Bound.

For a moment, Dex hugs her back, his arms strong and tight around her. Then he pulls back. "Hey, don't be ruining my chances with Shiloh, okay?"

Nova shakes her head. Dex has commented that he could never be with anyone who has 'hi' and 'lo' in their name because he won't know if he's coming or going. She wonders if he's also noticed Shiloh's lash fluttering with Kian.

They return to standing side by side and Nova notes the preparations are almost complete. Kian is checking the saplings that have been used to lash together the trunks again. He commented under his breath yesterday that they seemed like the weakest part of the rafts. After all, he was the one to watch the raft Wren arrived on fall to pieces and kill all but one on board.

Dex lets out a breath. "If it's any consolation, I don't think my father intended for you to go out."

Nova swallows. She doubts Callix intended for Dex to go out, either. Dex realized this, which is exactly why he was the first to join Wren on her raft. All through their childhood, Dex worked to prove that the loss of his hand didn't make him...less.

Nova wonders if he realizes it's to prove that to his father far more than anyone else.

She crosses her arms, hoping Dex isn't going to make the same suggestion that Wren did. "But we are going out."

Dex swallows as he nods. "And we're going to make Askala proud."

Nova lets out the breath she was holding. "Yes, we will."

Dex grins as he turns to her. "I can't wait to show Dad the double crop of pods we're going to bring in."

Nova almost hugs him again. Dex is probably imagining the light in his father's eyes. She hopes he sees it, but already wants to comfort him considering he probably won't.

A voice tickles her ear. "You know, I can tell when you're about to hug someone."

Nova turns to Kian, her heart skipping as it always does when he's this close. "You cannot," she scoffs.

He nods, his dark eyes twinkling. "You lean forward on the balls of your feet and your shoulders do this thing." He hunches forward an inch.

Instinctively, Nova straightens. Sweet Terra, he's right!

"I've had a Nova special today," Dex boasts. "What about you?"

The smug smile that was just blooming across Kian's face dies. "You know we can't..."

Dex's grin grows. "But I can." He grabs Nova in an enthusiastic hug.

Rolling her eyes over Dex's shoulder, Nova embraces him back. Kian watches them, his lips in a flat line as his eyes twinkle.

Dex pulls back, his grin practically devilish as he saunters toward the raft. "It must suck to have to wait," he calls over his shoulder.

As alone as she's going to get with Kian during their Proving, Nova finds herself a little tongue-tied. How can everything seem so sure and yet so uncertain at the same time?

Kian shifts a little closer to her. "You doing okay?"

Nova has to stop herself from leaning against him. "We always knew it would be tough."

"Yeah, we did."

Kian's words hang in the air, like he's not sure what to say either. Nova's chest tightens. It's never been like this before.

Knowing this isn't the time to talk about it, Nova sighs. "Wren said there's a weather change coming."

"She's probably lying." Kian shoots a glare at Wren, but she's focused on triple-checking the raft. He crosses his arms. "Just in case, we'd better get this over and done with quickly, though."

For a moment, Nova's surprised, but the feeling quickly dissipates. Of course that's what Kian would say. Although he doesn't trust Wren, he's not going to let that risk the lives of everyone here. If there's a chance Wren is right, they need to be prepared for a storm.

Fern is standing beside the raft, her hands on her hips as though she's making sure she gets noticed. "Let's get this show on the ocean, guys."

The others filter down, each moving toward their allocated vessel.

It's time.

Nova turns to Kian, her eyes tracing the strong lines of his face, the smooth angles, the dark hair. Her gaze connects with his, finding his earth-colored eyes full of longing.

Her breath evaporates. It feels like they've waited a lifetime.

And in a few days, the wait will be over.

Everything will be decided.

Kian steps forward, leaving an inch between them. "We've got this."

Nova nods, her hand coming up of its own volition. Her fingers brush the caramel skin of his cheek, tingling as they move from smooth to stubble.

Realizing what she's done, she jerks her hand away. Stepping back, she tries to smile. "We have to, Kian."

If one of them doesn't pass, her heart will fracture into so many pieces, no amount of healing could fix it.

Kian pulls in a steadying breath, doing a better of job of managing a smile. "Good thing we've got this then, huh?"

"Come on, you two!" It's Dex, waving at them. "These things ain't gonna row themselves."

Starting to head down, Nova's pulse feels too big for her body. Kian's hand reaches and grasps hers before releasing it. It's a brief caress, but a loaded one.

He's focusing on the part he's sure of—their love.

The lifeboat and raft are sitting on wet sand, but far back enough that the waves can't reach them. The less time they have in contact with the water, the better.

Everyone stands around, staring at them, contemplating what's ahead of them. Thom and Felicia take a few steps back, probably full of relief they're not about to embark on this.

Everyone except Wren. She stands back, arms crossed, a few feet away from the raft.

Jay shuffles his feet in the sand, never seeming to be able to stand still. "You're not going, Wren?" His voice ends on a squeak.

Fern glances from Wren to the raft. "Of course she's not. She wouldn't risk something as precious as her hide to get pods for Askala."

Nova goes to defend Wren—she was the one who suggested this after all—only to find herself stopping. Wren said she thought a storm was coming. Of course she'd pull out.

Wren narrows her eyes as she scans them all. "Why should I go? What do I owe any of you?"

Nova waits for Kian to jump in and point out they saved her, clothed her, fed her, and included her in the Proving. Nova almost winces. Wren won't see the last point as an act of grace.

But Kian remains beside her, the only sign of his anger is his hands clenching.

Wren huffs as she stalks toward the raft. "Exactly. I'm going, but not for you people. I plan on showing you what close-minded fools you all are. This raft is going to be your link to the Outlands, and I'm not going to let any of you idiots ruin my chance to prove that."

Wren squats down and pushes the raft along the sand, the heavy half-logs only scraping a few inches.

Nova is about to rush forward, not wanting Wren to look like a fool herself, but Dex beats her to it. Putting a hand and forearm against it, he pushes too. Another few inches and the edge of the raft is licked by a wave.

With a sigh, Kian braces his hands against the lifeboat. "Let's get these things out there."

Everyone jolts into action. Seven bodies begin to strain and push.

Kian, Shiloh, Jay, and Nova get the lifeboat bobbing in the water the quickest seeing as it's the lightest and there are four of them. Nova doesn't comment that Shiloh isn't even coming in the lifeboat.

The water is lapping at Nova's ankles, mimicking the nervousness licking at her consciousness, when Kian turns to her. "Hop in, I'll push the rest of the way."

Nova is about to point out she can help get it out further when she stops. This is an opportunity for Kian to shine. No matter what Wren said, his confidence and leadership are a strength.

Nova climbs in, and Kian turns to Jay to do the same, probably thinking Shiloh should join the raft. Jay climbs in, his long limbs making the process an awkward one. Nova grips the side as she waits for the boat to stop its wild rocking.

Shiloh holds up her hand. "I'll just push it a little further out."

Kian nods, but Nova notices the slight frown on his brow. Turning back out to face the ocean, Nova reminds herself she needs to stop second guessing every decision. Would Callix even have noticed that small interaction when they're so close to shore? The tiny choice she and Shiloh just made?

A moment later Kian tells Shiloh to head to the raft and climb in. Nova looks around to see the raft not far behind them. Kian passes Jay an oar and they head out to sea. It takes several minutes for the two of them to develop enough of a rhythm to get past the waves trying to push them back to shore, but they manage it. Behind them, the others encourage each other as they struggle to do the same.

Nova sits at the back of the lifeboat, trying to be as still as possible until it's her turn to row. Behind her, the barrel is strapped down, waiting to be filled with sea water and pods. Her palms begin to sweat, and she knows it has nothing to do with the harsh sun beating down on them.

She's surrounded by ocean, the very monster who took her father. She clenches her jaw. It's the most terrifying and beautiful thing Nova has ever seen.

Miles of rusted water stretches out before them, empty of diversity but so full of danger. Nova glances down, thinking maybe she'll see a school of fish, but all she sees is the burnt sand beneath them.

Straightening in a rush, she decides to focus on something else. Kian is in front of her, rowing on the left, his back to her. She knows his face would be tight with focus, his eyes constantly scanning. She knows he'd be highly conscious of her behind him.

She watches his biceps bunch as he pulls the oar. So much strength. So much beauty.

All she wants is to earn the right to be able to touch, to hold that. To call it hers.

Which means she needs to be Bound. Pushing back her shoulders, Nova scans the horizon they're moving toward. The sun is high and bright, looking too dazzling and oversized to allow room for storm clouds. Hopefully Wren was wrong. Maybe even lying.

Glancing over her shoulder, she confirms the others aren't

far behind. Everyone is quiet and focused. The sooner they find pods, the sooner they can return.

Keeping his gaze straight ahead, Kian calls out. "Start scanning for pteropods. If we're lucky, we'll find them closer to shore."

Nova carefully leans over the side, seeing anyone who's not paddling the raft do the same. There's very little wind, but there's a roar in her ears. What if they don't find a shoal soon? How long before they turn around?

And what happens if they go back empty handed?

Askala has become a hazy blur on the horizon when Nova sees it. "Kian!" she gasps. "Look!"

It's a shoal of pteropods, but not just that. A huge shoal of pteropods.

Kian's paddle freezes midair. "Sweet Terra, they're beautiful!"

He's right. In a blink, they find themselves floating above a pulsing, glowing cloud of life. Nova slides to the other side of the boat to see them there, too. Hundreds, probably thousands, of translucent orange, glimmering bodies are moving through the water.

"Guys, guys!" Jay has shot up to standing, once again wildly rocking the boat. "We've found some!"

Nova looks to Kian and they smile at each other. She wishes she could launch herself across the boat and throw her arms around him.

Not only have they found pods, they've found more than enough to fill the barrels.

They'll be returning to Askala with a feast.

KIAN

*G*rowing up and helping his mother with the pteropods means Kian's seen shoals of their glowing bodies quietly swimming together far more than most people. He's sat beside the edge of the pool countless times just to marvel at their beauty and grace.

But he's never seen this many.

It's like their boat is floating over a luminescent cloud. It throbs with pulses of light, all gliding and drifting like slow moving stars. Kian gently lowers the oar into the boat, not wanting to disturb the small orbs below. His mind reels with what such a harvest could mean for Askala.

Looking back toward Nova, he watches the same awe that's filled his chest move over her face. It seems to lighten her skin, making her blue eyes shine as she watches and smiles.

His heart constricts. He's watching the most beautiful girl in the world shine from within.

Wishing he could tell her, Kian turns back to the water. Right now, they need to get these pods in the barrels and head back to shore.

The raft nudges the boat from behind and Kian tries not to

wince, his mind already imagining the vulnerable dent it just left in the side. No one on the raft is paying attention, though. Everyone is focused on the unbelievable, magnificent display below them.

Dex reaches down, his fingers dipping into the water. "There are so many..." As the surface breaks, the pods below jolt away, looking like tiny comets.

The only one who isn't marveling at what they've discovered is Wren. Her gaze remains fastened on the horizon. "Let's get this over and done with."

As much as he hates to agree with her, Kian nods. "We need to get some seawater in the barrels."

Nova is the first to move, grabbing a bucket and passing another to Jay. With the same efficiency he's seen in the infirmary, she gets to work, dipping it in the water and tipping it in the barrel.

Her smile grows as she does it. "They're so close."

Kian can't help but smile back. Seeing joy on Nova's face has been his life's mission.

Shiloh and Fern leap to do the same on the raft, tussling for a moment as they grab the same bucket. Wren rolls her eyes as she passes them a second one.

Shiloh glances at Kian then flushes as she looks back at Wren. "Thanks," she mumbles.

As the barrels are filled, Kian catches Dex's eye. There's an excitement there that echoes the buzzing feeling in his gut. They nod at each other, both trying to contain a smile.

"So, who's going in the water?" Jay's voice is soft and tremulous. "Are we sticking with what we decided yesterday?"

Kian straightens his shoulders. "Like we said, it's logical that it needs to be the two strongest swimmers."

The key to surviving the acidic ocean is to be in there for as little time as possible. One of those is him, but he already knew that.

Jay's shoulders sag with relief. "I hated the water as a kid." He glances over the edge of the lifeboat, a small shudder rippling down his skinny back. "Never wanted to spend too much time in it. I used to have dreams that I got eaten by a leatherskin."

Shiloh puts her hand up. "I'm still happy to go in. My dad would take me to the lake on really hot days. I can swim well enough."

Kian nods. "Thanks, Shiloh." He walks over to Nova who's finished bucketing the water and grabs a net. "Let's get this done as quickly as possible."

Dex walks to edge of the raft. "Everyone else, we're on lookout."

For leatherskins.

Nova must think the same thing, because her hand grips his arm. Kian finds her looking at him, her eyes wide and tremulous. She knows he has to go…but she wishes he wouldn't.

Kian takes her hand and squeezes it. "There are so many pods, it won't take long. I'll be back before you know it."

She shakes her head. "I doubt it. You don't have to be gone for me to miss you, Kian."

His breath disintegrates. How he wishes he could kiss her. It would be something he could leave with her until he returns. A promise of things to come.

Instead, he tries to lighten the mood. "I'd better be quick, then."

He turns away, resting the net against the barrel so he can pull off his shirt.

Nova's gasp is soft but sharp, and it's enough to have Kian pausing as he realizes he just did the opposite of lightening the mood.

There was a time that he and Nova would swim in the lake, too. He'd be shirtless, she'd wear little more than a slip of hemp. They'd laugh and splash and enjoy the freedom they knew was going to be short lived.

134

But that's before their awareness of each other became something neither of them could ignore.

Slowly Kian looks back at Nova, stomach clenched, nervous at what he's going to see on her face.

Her eyes are the widest he's seen since they went out, her cheeks flushed with a delicious rosy glow. Her lips are parted and her tongue darts out to wet them.

Feeling like he's just been slammed in the gut with the trunk of a mangrove pine, Kian tries to clear his throat. How can he be doing the most dangerous thing he's ever done, and all he can think of is Nova?

"You need to put some sap on that golden skin of his, Nova."

It's Wren's voice that jolts them out of the awareness that just swallowed them. Kian feels like the air has turned to the same sap Wren is so fond of.

Nova startles. "What?"

Wren jams a hand on her hip, grinning at them across the distance. "The sap. It'll protect his precious skin while he's in the water."

Impossibly, Nova's eyes widen even further. She swallows. "I don't know that I—"

Dex looks over his shoulder from his lookout post at the corner of the raft. "Now, Nova, Bounds always work for the greater good. Those are some pretty impressive muscles, and we wouldn't want anyone missing out on that breathtaking sight."

Kian almost wishes he'd kept his shirt on. Although something primal in him is loving the look in Nova's eyes... He turns to his best friend, wishing he was closer so he could throw something at him. "Zip it, Dex."

Dex raises his arms in a conciliatory gesture. "Hey, just looking out for you, cousin. We both know that stuff works."

Wren turns to Shiloh. "Fern can do yours."

Shiloh's head snaps to Wren, making Kian aware of how

closely everyone is watching him and Nova. Shiloh frowns, probably looking forward to having that stuff on her as much as he is.

Kian holds his hand out to Nova. "It'll probably never wash off, but I might as well put it on."

Nova turns to the bag she has beside her, her lashes fluttering down. "I'll do it." Kian is about to object, not sure how much torture he can endure at the hands of the girl he loves, when her blue gaze captures his. "I'd like to."

He nods wordlessly. Nova's wish has always been his command.

Nova bites her lip as she opens the jar and dips her fingers in the dark, sticky liquid. "I don't have a lot, so I should focus on your face and your hands."

Kian nods again, wondering if he'll ever find the power of speech again.

Nova starts on his forehead, brushing the sap across in long streaks. At first Kian notices the thick, tarry feel of it, but then he registers Nova's fingers against his skin.

Within seconds, it's all he can feel.

He closes his eyes, barely allowing himself to breathe.

There's a pause and her fingers stroke across one cheek and then the other. "The face is the most vulnerable to the acid seawater because of your eyes and mouth," Nova half-whispers. She traces his cheekbones, then glides down to his chin. Her fluttering fingers pause, and he knows she's staring at his lips.

Sharply, she pulls away. This time when she speaks, her voice regains some of its strength. "Your hands will have the most contact with it, though."

Kian swallows only to find his throat is dry and parched. He needs to focus on the sticky mess that smells strongly of pine. They're about to harvest pods from the ocean, for Pete's sake.

Except then she's touching him again. She takes his right

hand and holds it gently, palm up. He doesn't notice the sap, only the fingers stroking...the warmth of the skin cradling his.

He goes from breathless to lightheaded. Thank Terra there isn't enough sap to do the rest of him. He's already imagining her hands on his shoulders, hot and soft, gliding down to his chest...

Nova clears her throat and steps back. "All done."

Telling himself he's thankful the moment is over, but deep down wishing it would never end, Kian straightens, unable to make eye contact. He can already sense the effect this has had on Nova. He felt it in the way her hands trembled and lingered. Seeing it would snap his self-control. "Ah, thanks."

"Whoa!" It's Dex's voice from the raft floating a few feet away. "You look like a creature of the deep!"

Kian glances down at his hands like it's the first time he's seeing them. They're several shades darker and kind of shiny.

A strangled chortle comes from Jay's direction.

Kian looks at Nova ruefully. "It looks pretty terrible, doesn't it?"

Nova tries to contain her smile. "It really does." Her gaze steadies. "But I still want you, sticky mess and all."

Kian is about to reply that he knows the feeling—he'd want Nova in his life no matter how she looked or what she was covered in—but she's already speaking again.

"Be careful, okay? And be quick."

Kian grins, feeling the layer of sap push up in the process. "You can bet on it. I've got an amazing future to come back to."

"Those pods are going to die of old age at the rate we're going!" Wren's voice is full of impatience. "Let's get moving."

Fern glances down at the raft beneath her. "Are you worried this thing won't last?"

"No." Wren points toward the lifeboat. "I *know* that thing won't."

Kian holds in his frown. Once again, Wren is right. The boat's demise began the moment it touched the water.

He grabs Nova's hand. "Don't forget. Askala was built on love."

She squeezes it, ignoring the sap, a wealth of emotion shining from her blue eyes. "We were forged with love."

Our future will be filled with love.

Before he can let himself think about everything that could go wrong, Kian grabs the net and dives into the water.

The warm wetness instantly envelops him, almost feeling pleasant. But the moment Kian opens his eyes to scan for the pods, he feels the truth. Hot stinging needles spear through him and he instantly slams them shut again.

The pods are straight ahead, only a few feet down. He'll scoop the net through them, hoping for the best.

Kicking his legs, he shoots down, straining as he arcs the net through the water. Knowing he needs to maintain the momentum so the pteropods remain trapped within it, he kicks for the surface.

As his lungs find air again he opens his eyes. The boat has floated a few feet away and Kian is suddenly conscious that a breeze has picked up.

"Kian, are you okay?" Nova's leaning over the edge of the boat, holding out her arm although he's too far away to reach him.

Drawing the net up, he notes that it's writhing with the masses of pods it holds. He swims over as quickly as he can considering one hand has to hold the net above the water.

Jay rushes over. "Go, Kian!" He grabs the net, quickly tipping the pods into the barrel.

Kian treads water, ignoring the stinging as droplets fall into his eyes. "You need to keep swapping the seawater in the barrel. It'll stop the water from fouling and will also keep the pods warm."

Jay salutes him. "Will do, Kian!"

Nova's face is alight with excitement. "Shiloh is getting just as many."

"That's awesome." Kian keeps his lips tight despite the happiness blooming in his belly. He doesn't want any more seawater in his mouth than necessary. "I'll go get some more."

"Be carefu—"

Nova's words are cut off as Kian dives again. The best thing he can do right now is to be fast. The sooner they fill the barrels, the sooner they can head back to Askala.

The sooner he can get Nova and the others out of this deadly monster called the ocean.

Kian quickly establishes a rhythm. Dive with eyes tightly shut. Scoop. Kick for the surface with a netful of wriggling pods. Watch Nova's eyes light up as he dumps the load in the barrel.

Over and over he dives, his eyes stinging more and more, and his skin starting to feel like it's sunburned. His lungs begin to ache with the repeated lack of oxygen, but he ignores it all. Each time he surfaces, the boat has drifted further than he'd expect, but his sight is getting too blurry to scan the horizon.

Wren's warning of a storm is weighing heavily on his mind.

Let alone the fact that he's sharing space with leatherskins.

It's not long before the back of the lifeboat is sagging in the water. Nova's eyes are full of pride. "We've got so many, Kian! Even the Unbound could have some."

Kian's heart swells. Of course Nova would think of the Unbound—those who have to work for pods.

Jay is tugging on his hair. "We've scored big time, that's for sure. I think that's enough, though. We have to get them all back, yet."

Kian eyes the boat then the raft. Shiloh is already pulling herself out, her skin pink from the water. Dex and Fern are busily bucketing old water out and fresh seawater in.

139

Wren has her arms crossed as she stares out to sea.

Kian hauls himself into the lifeboat, conscious of Nova's hands on him as she helps him in. He flops onto the floor of the boat, panting a little. His whole body burns and he can feel his eyes watering. The sky up above is gray and blurry.

He frowns. It was blue when he went in. Although he's struggling to focus, the shades of ash above him are unmistakable.

"Kian!" It's Dex, standing on the raft which is bobbing a few yards away. "I say we have some celebration pods!"

Fern jumps up and down on the balls of her feet, clapping her hands. "Yes! We have so many."

Jay has already sidled up beside the barrel.

Kian looks to Nova, finding her eyes alight with anticipation. "We probably have extra. The boat might be too heavy, yet."

Pushing himself upright, Kian looks around. The world looks like it's been filtered through thick glass. He turns to Wren. "Five minutes and we head back?"

Even though her outline is smudged, Kian swears he sees surprise on her face. He waits for her response, not caring what she thinks. It's possible this test was all about deciding who was the best person to lead, and Remnant or not, Wren is one of those. No amount of dislike for a person would stop him from acknowledging that.

She hasn't realized there's nothing he won't do for Askala.

Even Kian's blurry gaze can tell Wren doesn't like the idea, but then Dex nudges her with his shoulder. "Aw, come on, Wren. Five minutes won't hurt."

She shakes her head and Kian's pretty sure she rolls her eyes. "Trust me. Five minutes can hurt a lot."

Dex smiles at Wren, blinking his eyelashes dramatically. "Please?"

"You people and your pods." Wren huffs. "Just be quick about it."

"Of course we'll be quick," says Kian. "We haven't got extra time to waste. Plus, it'll give us energy to get this motherload back."

Everyone takes this as a green light. Fern scoops their net into the barrel on the raft while Jay does the same on theirs.

Taking a seat as he realizes how tired his body is, Kian watches Jay pull up a wriggling, glowing clump. Without looking up, Jay grabs a handful and shoves them in his mouth.

Kian frowns. Handing them to the others would've been what his parents would've done first.

What any Bound would've done first.

Juices dribbling from the corner of his mouth, Jay brings the net over. "There's hundreds in there," he mumbles through his over-full mouth.

Kian indicates to Jay to offer them to Nova and Jay flushes.

Nova takes a pod as she comes to sit beside Kian. "Thank you, Jay."

She puts it in her mouth and bites down, the exact moment the orange body erupts in her mouth apparent when she screws up her face.

Kian takes his own, already anticipating the squishy body and bitter bile that will flood his tongue. He closes his eyes as he focuses on the nutrition his body is about to absorb. His cells will soak it up like parched soil.

Looking around, he takes in the grimacing-smiling faces. No one here has ever had this many pods in one sitting. He can feel the energy and strength returning to his body just watching the opaque bodies flapping about in the net.

Over on the raft, Fern and Shiloh are eating them faster than their hands can catch them, giggling as the pods slip through their fingers. Dex is holding one out to Wren, who's shaking her head vehemently. Kian has to admit, when his mother first presented one to him as a child, he hadn't been keen on the thought of putting it in his mouth.

Nova holds out her hand. "Have another, Kian."

"You've had more yourself?"

She nods. "I will when you do."

Shaking his head, Kian takes six more pods out of the net and passes three to Nova. He doubts Nova even notices that she instinctively puts others first. He'll make sure he notes this in the interviews they all have to attend about what happened out on the ocean. "You remember when we'd play that game where we saw how many berries we could stuff into our mouth at once?"

Nova giggles. "Fun, but messy."

Kian holds up a wriggling, opaque body. "Who thought we'd do it with pods?" He shoves it in his mouth quickly followed by the other two. They flap their tiny wings against the roof of his mouth and he has to stop himself from gagging. Pulling up a grin is hard work as he chomps down, but he manages it.

Nova's laugh dances through his body, making it all worth it. Watching her shove the pods in and eat them just heightens his joy. The girl he loves is getting the nutrition she deserves.

"Ew!" Wren's voice has them both spinning toward the raft. "These things are disgusting!"

Dex grins. "We haven't figured out whether they feel or taste worse." He passes her another and she takes it, popping it in her mouth as she screws her eyes shut.

"She ate it!" Nova whispers beside him, her voice full of pleasant surprise.

Kian brings his brows back down before anyone notices. "I suppose Dex could make a leatherskin smile."

If anyone could convince prickly Wren to have a pteropod, it would be him.

A gust of wind rocks the boat and Kian glances around. In

the short space of time they took to enjoy the fruits of their harvest, the sky has turned the color of granite.

Nova stills. "We need to get going, don't we?"

Kian tries to keep the tension out of his voice. "It'll be fine. We didn't have to go out as far as we thought, but yeah, we'd better head back."

The boat and the raft are going to be heavy with the bumper crop they have.

He stands up. "Right, everyone, now that we've taken our multivitamins, we can get these pods back in no time."

Dex pumps his fist in the air. "We return victorious, Askala. Come and see the feast we bring you!"

Even Wren is smiling. "I bet Thom and Felicia are going to regret staying back."

Kian picks up the oar as Jay does the same and they start to turn the boat. To their left, Wren and Fern have already got the raft moving.

Wren glances over her shoulder as they move ahead. "It's so much easier when a raft doesn't have a front or a back, huh, Kian?"

Kian grits his teeth as Jay fumbles with his oar. It would be a whole lot quicker turning around if he didn't keep paddling the wrong way.

Then Kian grins. The boat may need to be pointed in the right direction, but it's far lighter and more streamlined than her trunks lashed together. At least they seem to be holding together, unlike the raft she'd arrived in. "Race you back?"

Wren's eyes light up. "You're on."

As they turn their backs on the gray sky behind them, Kian's grin grows as he digs the oar into the water, glad to see Jay do the same as the boat powers forward.

This test couldn't have gone better.

No storm. No leatherskins.

And now his future with Nova starts in a few days.

A flash of lightning yanks a scream from someone on the raft. Jay jumps so high he almost drops his oar.

Simultaneously, they all turn around and Kian's shoulders drop as his gut clenches into a knot.

It seems Mother Nature has other ideas.

DEX

"*Y*ou were right." Dex turns to Wren, the bitter taste of pteropods still fresh on his tongue. "That storm's coming in fast."

"Less talking, more rowing." Wren's face is pale, all hint of the laughter they'd just shared a distant memory. She'd mentioned she thought a storm was coming in on their way out to get the pods, urging everyone to row faster. Shiloh and Fern had seemed suspicious of her motives, but Dex hadn't doubted her. He just hadn't realized it was going to come in so quickly.

"I'm sorry." His words are swept away by a gust of wind that pushes the raft back toward the lifeboat. Even the gathering storm can't steal away the regret he feels. Why had he talked Wren into letting them stay to eat the pods? Why had he pushed so hard, fluttering his eyelashes at her like some kind of fool?

She'd been right.

Again.

Dex pulls on the oar, determined not to let his one hand disadvantage him. It took him a little while but he figured out a way to hold the oar by gripping it with his right hand and tucking the end under his other arm. A little awkward but it's working.

A deafening clap of thunder has them jolting on the raft and Fern lets out another scream, leaving Dex wondering if she's going to do that every single time.

"It's okay," he calls to her over the howling wind. "Just keep rowing."

Poor Fern had been doing so well at pretending she was taking charge until the storm hit. Now she's given up all pretense that she's in control of anything, least of all herself. She's a shivering mess behind him. At least there are no cameras out here. Hopefully, she can pull herself together before his father gets eyes on her again. Unless someone tells on her in their interviews. That's if they ever make it back to be interviewed.

Shiloh isn't doing much better, although her problems are more physical than emotional. Her skin is an angry pink color, apart from her face and hands, which are still stained brown from the sap. Once again, they should've listened more closely to Wren when she'd suggested they collect enough sap to cover the bodies of everyone going out, not just the two who'd be diving.

"This is impossible," calls Shiloh, feeling his eyes on her. "We'll never make it back in this storm."

Some of her hair looks like it may have fallen out and her eyes are bloodshot. If she offered to collect pods as a way to impress Kian, her plan may have just backfired. Not that it matters what she looks like. Everyone's invisible to Kian when Nova's around.

A towering wave hits the raft, sending water spilling over the top and soaking through their clothes. Dex winces from the sting, but as the next wave is about to hit, he realizes he has a bigger problem. He has to make a choice between holding onto his oar or holding on to the raft. And he has only a split second to make it.

Damn his one hand!

He lets go of the oar and grips onto the edge of the raft, only just managing to keep himself on top of it as the raft tips and spins in the strength of the wave. His fingers are slipping but he knows that letting go is certain death.

Please, let them have tied these planks together with enough strength. If the raft breaks up now it won't matter how long he can hold on. They'll be as good as dead.

With his heart hammering and his breath coming in deep gasps, the raft steadies between waves and he's able to let go for a moment and stretch his fingers. The oar is nowhere to be seen.

It's very possible his one hand just cost them all their lives. Rowing back was already a difficult task with four oars and now they only have three. He adds that to the guilt he's already carrying on his shoulders.

Wren spins around and sees his empty hand.

"Don't worry," she calls, although her eyes betray her. She's disappointed. In the situation? Or him? Probably both. He doesn't blame her. He's disappointed in himself.

He wishes he has something funny to say. His usual go-to in these kinds of stressful situations, but the panic has his mind coming up blank. There's absolutely nothing funny about this.

"How will we get back now?" Dex repositions his weight closer to the barrel, looping his fingers through the small branches that are holding it strapped to the center of the raft. Keeping the pods safe is about the only useful thing he can do right now.

"I told you not to worry." Wren points at the lifeboat, her dark hair stuck to the edges of her stoic face. "We'll use their oars."

At first Dex is confused. They can't take the oars from the lifeboat. Kian, Nova and Jay need them.

Then he gasps as he realizes what Wren means. Pretty soon there won't be a lifeboat left to row. It's not faring well in the rough waves and is getting lower and lower in the water. It has to have cracks letting in seawater. Gaping holes, perhaps.

"We have to help them!" Dex's heart picks up an even faster beat as he pushes away the thought of surviving this task only to have to return without his cousin. Magnus and Amity will never forgive him. They won't forgive his father, either, for setting such a dangerous task.

He watches helplessly as Nova buckets water out of the lifeboat while Kian and Jay fight the waves, trying to get some traction in the water. It's a losing battle. They're in even more trouble than a raft with three oars and a man with one hand.

"Over there!" Wren calls to Fern and Shiloh and together they change direction and head toward the lifeboat.

Just when it seems the conditions can't get any more challenging, heavy rain starts. It's almost a sweet relief as is washes the acid from Dex's skin, but it makes visibility almost impossible.

"Don't take your eyes off the boat," Wren says to Dex. "And you two, keep rowing!"

Another flash of lightning streaks across the sky and Fern lets out a yelp this time instead of a scream. She's shaking, barely able to row, and Dex hates that he can't take over from her. He'd be in the water in no time, even less use to them than he already is.

"We're getting closer," Dex calls, seeing the blurred shape of the lifeboat looming. "Keep going! Just a little m—"

A wave, bigger than any of the ones to come before, slams the raft with force and sends it hurtling toward the boat. This time, it's Shiloh's turn to empty her lungs on a shriek.

Dex tightens his grip on the small branches, bracing himself for impact. They wanted to reach the boat, but not like this. The impact is going to be catastrophic. The lifeboat will be torn to shreds. Possibly the raft, too.

He squeezes his eyes closed, blocking out both the view of the lifeboat and the helplessness he feels. There's nothing he can do to stop this and that hurts more than the imminent collision is bound to.

The raft slams down on top of the lifeboat and Dex's eyes spring open as he lurches forward, only just managing to keep his hold. Pain shoots through his fingertips. But it's the noise of the fiberglass hull cracking open that has him gasping. It's a noise far more frightening than any thunder.

As if on cue, Fern screams as she sails over Dex's head and lands in the churning waves. Shiloh is thrown into the sinking lifeboat and clings to the side, shouting words Dex never expected to come from such a sweet girl's mouth.

Somehow Wren has managed to hold on, although that's not a surprise. She'd already told him she didn't plan to go back into the water in a hurry.

He spots Jay, not too far away, using an oar to keep himself afloat.

"Kian!" Dex squints in the rain as he waits for the next wave to hit. He lets go of the barrel to haul Fern back onto the raft, while Wren drags Shiloh back on board. He can't see his cousin or Nova anywhere. "Kian!"

Fern hears his cries and points to the back of the lifeboat. Dex sees Kian treading water as he works madly to untie the barrel before the boat goes down, a familiar look of determination on his face. Nova is doing the same beside him, although seems to be having enough trouble just keeping herself afloat.

"Leave the bloody pods!" cries Dex.

But they either can't hear him or they aren't interested. Kian's determined to complete his mission and bring those pods back for the good of Askala. But there's no way he's ever going to untie that barrel in time. He's going to die being a hero. Maybe that's the only way he knows how to be. After all, he is the son of Magnus.

Dex glances quickly to the sky, hoping that somehow his mother is watching over him, and dives into the water. Closing his eyes tightly, he swims down underneath the waves, kicking his way over to Kian and Nova, bursting through the surface only a few feet away.

Closing the gap, he takes hold of the barrel and tugs at a knot on the other side that Kian hasn't gotten to yet. With the hull cracked in half, the boat is sinking fast and it's about to take this barrel down with it. Hearing the roar of the next wave before he sees it, he's slammed from behind, almost hitting his head on the barrel. Holding on tight, he's determined not to be swept away.

"Get back on the raft," yells Kian, without taking his eyes off his task. "Take Nova with you."

"Not without you," says Dex, wishing they hadn't tied these barrels down quite so well as he resumes working on the knot.

"I'm okay." Nova gets the words out just before taking in a mouthful of water. Her face screws into a ball as she winces.

"You sure?" asks Kian, pausing his busy hands to look at her.

"I'm sure." She nods, with a look of determination. "We're nearly there."

There's something in her eyes that must convince him, because Kian focuses back on the ropes. Perhaps it's more that they don't have time to argue. What's left of the boat is going down any moment now.

Another wave smashes into them and Dex only just has time to squeeze his eyes and mouth closed, hoping that Kian and Nova are able to do the same. They have to get out of this water soon, with or without the barrel. It's been far too long already.

The wave passes and the three of them work quickly. Dex tries hard to stop his hand slipping from the knot, kicking in the water to keep himself afloat as he uses his stump to help hold his head above water. Even if this ocean wasn't filled with acid, he's not sure how much longer he could do this for.

"I've got it!" Kian has triumph written across his exhausted face.

"Me, too!" Nova cries.

Feeling his knot about to undo, Dex jams his fingers into one of the loops and tugs at it.

"Yes!" The knot pulls loose only moments before what remains of the lifeboat sinks into the water, the ocean swallowing it like a hungry shark.

At the thought of these merciless creatures, Dex scans the ocean, but with rain this heavy, it's impossible to make out the difference between the white caps of the ocean and the fin of a leatherskin.

Dex spits out some water, enjoying their brief moment of victory. The barrel has been rescued and as far as he can see there aren't any giant sea monsters trying to eat them.

"Come on," calls Kian, and the moment of victory is over.

There's a break in the waves just long enough for them to push the barrel through the water. The raft is only a few yards away now and Wren is leaning over the edge, her hands outstretched, ready to grab them as soon as they get close enough.

Dex kicks harder, the thought of getting out of this acid soup spurring him on. Or maybe it's the energy from the feast of pods he just had. It's possible he wouldn't have been able to do any of this without that burst of nutrition. Which makes Kian just as right about taking the extra time to eat the pods as it made Wren for wanting to hurry back to shore. There were no right or wrong answers. They were just as doomed no matter what choice they made.

Nova reaches out and Wren takes hold of her, hauling her onto the raft in one swift movement. That girl is strong!

"You next," says Kian.

Dex shakes his head. "You've been in the water longer. Get up there with Nova."

It's the last part of what he says that has his cousin gripping the edge of the raft and dragging himself out of the water, refusing Wren's offer of help. He swivels around and leans out to hold the barrel while Dex gladly takes Wren's hand and allows her to help him aboard.

He lies down on his back, panting heavily, grateful to have survived. The gray clouds are still swirling overhead but seem to be making way for the sun that's determined to shine through once more. The rain has eased slightly and he hopes it's one of those storms that leaves as quickly as it arrives.

"Love you, Mom," he says, certain she'd helped in some way. How else was it possible that all of them had survived such a catastrophe?

"Where's Jay?" calls Nova over the sound of the dying wind.

Dex sits up in a hurry, doing a quick head count. Six. There are only six of them on the raft.

His heart sinks. Or is it his gut? It feels like every part of him just doubled in weight. How can they have lost Jay?

"I saw him holding onto an oar," he says. "It'll keep him afloat until we can get to him."

They face outwards, looking in all directions for any sign of Jay. But it's hard with the ocean so choppy.

"I see him!" calls Shiloh, pointing. "Over there!"

"Careful," warns Wren as they all shift their weight at once, sending the raft tipping.

Regaining their balance, Dex looks to where Shiloh is pointing, catching sight of Jay. He's still holding onto the oar, waving one hand at them, desperate to get their attention.

They wave back and Dex has to stop himself from leaping to his feet and cheering.

"We're coming," calls Shiloh.

But a quick check of the raft reveals they only have one oar remaining.

Raking his fingers through his tangled hair, Dex lets out a sigh. If Jay can't swim to them, they may never be able to reach him.

"A leatherskin!" cries Nova, tugging Kian's shirt as he works on securing the barrel from the lifeboat to the back of the raft.

Dex rubs at his eyes and looks out. Nova's right! There's a fin making its way directly toward Jay, cutting through the water with speed. Jay has no time to get away. And they can't get to him.

Which means he has no hope.

"Jay!" calls Fern, her voice quavering. "Behind you!"

"Don't tell him," says Dex.

Surely it has to be better to be taken without knowing what happened than to spend your last moments of life in a panic.

Like his own mother had.

"Dex is right," says Wren. "We can't help him. Don't scare him."

"I'd say he's scared enough already," says Nova, her face summing up the anguish they all feel.

"Any ideas?" asks Kian, sitting up now that the barrel's secured and fixing his gaze on Wren. "I've seen you kill a leatherskin before."

Wren glares at him. "This is different. I don't like being outnumbered."

Dex looks back to Jay and sees what Wren's talking about. Bile hits the back of his throat. There are at least half a dozen leatherskins circling Jay now. Which means he's seen them. And instead of waving, he's now holding the oar in the water, ready to strike, as he screams for them to help him.

"I can't look," says Fern, burying her face in the back of Shiloh's shirt.

Dex wishes he couldn't watch, but his eyes are glued to the

scene in front of him as his gut churns, mimicking the anger of the ocean.

Poor Jay.

What was his father thinking setting this as one of their tests? How could he have done such a thing? Perhaps Felicia and Thom were the smartest ones out of the lot of them after all. They should never have come out here.

He winces as Jay lets out an ear-piercing squeal and is dragged under the water. It happens so quickly that he doesn't even have time to swipe his oar and it bobs away from him as the top of his head disappears. They're left with nothing but the memory of his terrified face.

More fins dive under the water, replaced by a dark red liquid bubbling to the surface.

The feeding frenzy begins and there's thrashing of fins and tails and snapping of jaws as the leatherskins fight each other for a share of their prey.

Shiloh leans over the side of the raft and vomits, exposing Fern to the horror before them.

"No!" Fern cries, drawing her knees up to her chest and hugging them tightly. "Jay."

Shiloh wipes her mouth and crawls over to Dex in the middle of the raft. She's shaking now and Dex tries to stop himself from thinking what a waste of pteropods that just was.

"He's dead," sobs Fern. "He's really dead."

"Quiet!" It's Wren now, talking in a loud whisper. She holds up her hand, demanding their attention. "I want everyone to sit perfectly still. Don't move a muscle and don't say a word. The leatherskins' bellies aren't full yet."

There's nothing she could have said that would have had more impact. Everyone immediately freezes as they fall silent. Even Kian, who Dex knows hates following Wren's orders. He might be stubborn, but he isn't a fool.

It's just lucky that Felicia isn't here.

Dex can feel Shiloh's shivering worsen, so he dares to move very slowly to wrap his arm around her shoulders, pinning her to his side.

Wren glares at him and he decides to pretend she's jealous, rather than fearful of the risk his movements may have just put them in.

The leatherskins are settling now, their thrashing slowing. Clearly there's not much of poor Jay left to fight over.

Dex is struck with the memory of Jay telling them that he used to dream of being eaten by a leatherskin. Had he somehow known? Surely not. But…it's still strange. Maybe there's more to this world than what they can see in front of them? Maybe his mother *can* watch over him from the clouds. In all this misery, this is a thought that brings him comfort.

Jay's blood is drifting in the currents now, a trail of it reaching the raft and Dex closes his eyes for a moment, sending his thanks to Jay for everything he did for Askala. He'll never be Bound now. Or Unbound. But if Dex has anything to do with it, instead, he'll be a hero. Always remembered and honored for the sacrifice he made to help secure their future.

The leatherskins have broken apart now. A few have been chased away by the larger, more dominant sharks and Dex holds his breath, hoping they remain unnoticed. The square shape of the raft doesn't look like prey. If they can just sit still for long enough, there's a chance they'll be okay. At least the storm is passing with only a few drops of rain in the cool breeze.

A leatherskin turns toward them and swims to the raft, following the trail of red. Shiloh's shaking intensifies and Dex grips her tightly, praying she can stay still.

The large gray fin approaches and Dex studies the ridges and patterns of the tough skin, desperate to distract himself from the thought of what it's attached to. Wren pulls her knife from her belt, her movements swift but restrained. He knows she'll only use it if she has to.

The shark nudges the raft and they spin, a silent waltz through the bloody water. Dex joins Shiloh in shaking now. He's pretty sure they're all shaking. The next few moments are going to be the most important of their lives.

Another nudge from the giant creature sends them skimming across the water, toward the area where Jay lost his life.

With a flick of its tail, the leatherskin loses interest and swims away, the huge fin getting smaller and smaller in the distance until it disappears altogether.

But they hold still, nobody yet daring to believe they've survived.

"Good job," says Wren, eventually.

They let out a collective sigh and Dex feels the weight on his shoulders shift just a little bit.

"I thought we were all dead," says Shiloh, hiding her face in Dex's chest.

He presses his cheek to the top of her head and hushes her. "We're okay."

Kian releases himself from Nova's side, stroking her face as he makes sure she's okay, then stands beside the barrel, levering off the lid.

"What are you doing?" asks Nova.

"This can't all be for nothing," he says, studying the contents of the barrel. "We have to make sure the pods are healthy."

Dex nods. Amity would be so proud if she could see her son right now. He lives for those pods. In some way, they all do.

"An oar!" cries Fern, uncurling herself to lean over the side of the raft and scoop it up.

"Jay's oar." Shiloh bursts into loud sobs.

"We couldn't have rowed back with one oar," says Wren. "This is a good thing."

Fern beams and Dex knows she's wishing there was a

camera out here to see her. Which makes this whole test even more ridiculous. How can his father possibly rank them based on a test he wasn't here to witness, no matter how many interviews he does? So much has happened.

Too much.

"They're dying." Kian groans as he pokes about in the barrel, concern written all over his sap-stained face. "The temperature dropped too much with the storm. They're never going to survive."

"Throw the barrel overboard then." Wren shrugs. "We'll move faster without the weight. Especially now that we have two extra passengers on board."

"No way." Kian puts the lid back on the barrel and shakes his head. "Collecting these pods was the whole point of this test. Do you know just how much they can do for the diversity of the population we have back on the Oasis?"

"We still have the other barrel," says Nova. "Wren's right, Kian. Let's reduce the weight and get back home safely."

Kian pauses as he stares at Nova. Dex doubts she's ever disagreed with him on anything.

"I agree," moans Fern.

"Let me check the other barrel," says Kian, looking away with a frown as he goes to it and leans out to work on the lid.

Dex lets go of Shiloh to help him.

The lid comes free and Kian peers inside. "They're fine. The water's keeping them warm. Let's tie the other barrel next to it."

"Or just let the other barrel go," Wren mutters, tucking her knife back into her belt. "Towing a weight like that makes it no easier than having it on board."

"Listen here, Wr-Wren," says Kian, practically choking as he spits out her name. "We all listened to you when you told us to build this raft. We listened when you told us to put sap on our faces. When you told us to sit still and hope the leatherskins didn't notice us. And we did that because we accepted that you knew more about this stuff than we do. But when it comes to the pteropods, you need to listen to me. Askala depends on the nutrition the pods provide. Without them, we're as good as dead. That's why Callix set this as our test. Not to be cruel. But because he knows better than anybody what life's like without the pods. If we can't make the sacrifice for Askala and bring back those pods then what kind of Bounds would we make?"

"Nice speech." Wren shrugs and Dex has to suppress a smile. "But you forget I have no interest in becoming Bound."

"He does, though." Kian tilts his head toward Dex as he puts the lid back on the barrel. "Do it for him."

"Hey!" says Dex, nudging his cousin. "I belong to Shiloh now."

Shiloh visibly blanches as she shakes her head.

"That was a joke." He holds up the palm of his hand, glad the flush to his cheeks can't be seen under the irritation from the ocean. After all he's done to comfort Shiloh! She didn't have to be quite so offended. He really had only been trying to lighten the mood.

"Get your barrel in the water then," says Wren. "We need to get moving. That leatherskin could always decide to come back for seconds."

"Poor Jay!" howls Shiloh.

Dex doesn't comfort her this time. He joins Kian at the barrel still strapped to the raft and together they untie it, tip it to its side and roll it off the back of the raft.

It lands with a splash in the water and Kian secures it as the rest of them try to regain their balance in a raft that seems considerably happier without the extra weight of the barrel.

Wren doesn't wait for Kian to finish. She grabs the oar from Fern's hands and shoves it at Dex, before picking up the other one.

"We need our strongest to row," she says to him. "Given that pod boy is busy, we're up."

Dex nods at her, aware that his chest just puffed out a few inches.

Shiloh may have rebuffed him in the harshest way, but Wren just made up for it one hundred times over. She sees him as one of the strongest. And a compliment coming from Wren means so much more than one that comes from anyone else.

Because if there's anything he knows about her, it's that she speaks the truth.

He takes his place at the edge of the raft and dips the oar in the water, determined to prove he's worthy of the compliment she just gave him.

"Ready?" Wren asks, looking at him.

He nods. "Ready."

As they drag their heavy load through the water, he wonders if they'll be returning as winners or losers. They're bringing back the biggest haul of pteropods Askala has ever seen. Which is a massive success.

But they're coming back with six when they'd set out with seven. Which is the worst possible kind of failure.

He hopes his father has fun analyzing that.

WREN

*W*ren looks across the round table at Dex, having chosen not to sit beside him for the interview session. He has a way of making her agree to things she doesn't want to do. Which is dangerous. She hadn't planned on liking anybody in Askala.

She glances at Nova. Someone else who's impossible not to like.

Switching her gaze to Shiloh is a little more comfortable. Now there's someone she finds easy not to like. The way she'd humiliated Dex when he'd joked with her was unacceptable.

But she'll keep. People always do.

Like Kian.

Although, her hatred for that obnoxiously loyal Bound has simmered somewhat recently. It helps that he uses her name now, but it's more than that. Despite herself, she's starting to understand why Dex and Nova think so highly of him.

She looks at him now, observing the way he has his hand on the back of Nova's chair, naively believing he can protect her from the evils of the world.

But there's more to him than that.

He's smart. He's strong. He fights for what he believes in.

Wren blanches, realizing why she's drawn to those traits. It's exactly how she sees herself. Only her loyalty is to the Outlands.

Kian's is to Askala.

Which means it doesn't matter how much progress they've made. They'll never be on the same team.

"How long will we have to wait?" asks Felicia, her curls seeming to have been regenerated while they were gone. She and Thom are looking noticeably healthier than the rest of them with their pink, peeling skin and bloodshot eyes. A wash, a meal, and a good night's sleep had helped them recover from the effects of the ocean, but it will take some time to feel normal again.

Felicia drums her fingertips on the table when nobody answers.

It's the same table they sat around for their first test with the blocks. A test that feels like it was a decade ago instead of only a few days. So much has changed.

Nine have become eight. And all Felicia seems to care about is how long they have to wait to relive the story of Jay's death. Wren would be quite happy if Callix keeps them waiting all day.

She'd been surprised at how difficult it had been to watch the last moments of Jay's life. In the Outlands, comments are often made about killing all those who live in Askala. Wren has punched her own fist in the air many times at such comments and cheered along with her companions.

But seeing it with her own eyes? Watching the terror on Jay's face and hearing his screams as he'd been pulled under the water, then the pool of red liquid bubbling to the surface... well, that was nothing to cheer about. Jay was a guy with his own hopes, dreams and fears just like anyone in the Outlands. He was still human.

The door opens and Callix and Lana walk in. Callix is wearing his usual irritating frown. Lana, her usual irritating smile. What gives these people the right to place such judgment upon them? They bleed and shit just like anyone else.

They take two empty chairs, which places Lana next to Wren. The chair that Jay would have sat in remains empty. Strange that they haven't removed it.

Wren shuffles over slightly. Then, not wanting to get too close to Thom, she shuffles back. These people sure don't seem to value the need for personal space.

"May I say something before we start?" asks Felicia, smiling widely at Callix.

Thom smiles, too, folding his stocky hands on the table. Clearly, whatever it is she wants to say is something they planned together.

Callix's frown deepens. "There's no n—"

"I'd just like to state our reasons for staying behind." Felicia pats down her curls, betraying the shaking in her hands. "Just so things are clear. You see—"

"No. You see." Callix holds up his hand. "We're well aware of your reasons. There's no need to go over that now. We'd like to keep this interview as short as possible. You all need your rest."

"So, did we make the right choice?" asks Felicia, glancing at Thom.

Wren suppresses an eye roll. Callix isn't going to tell her that. Is she really that stupid?

"You made the choice you felt was best, given the information you had in your possession." Callix stares blankly at her. "Now, let's—"

"But it was the best decision, wasn't it?" Felicia smiles in a way she seems to think is charming.

Thom winces, smart enough to see she's not doing their cause any favors.

"Now, let's talk about the pteropods," says Callix, flatly ignoring her. "You collected more pods yesterday than any team has ever collected before. Amity… informed me this morning that our population has never been healthier."

Wren notices the pause that came at the mention of Kian's mother's name. And the wince that crossed Callix's brow. Interesting. But something she'll have to ponder later. Callix seems to be forgetting something quite important. Or rather, *someone*.

"Jay's not too healthy," she quips. "Although, the chair you put out for him seems to indicate you believe otherwise."

"Would you rather we put the chair away and pretend he never existed?" Lana asks with a gentle smile. "It's important to have that chair there as a reminder of the part Jay played in this. A sign of respect for his sacrifice."

"What sacrifice?" Wren crosses her arms and meets Lana's smile with a glare. "He gave up his life for a bunch of squishy pods."

"Pods that will save dozens, if not hundreds, of lives," says Kian. "Those pods give us strength and immunity from disease. Askala saw firsthand what happened when our pod population was wiped out seventeen years ago and it wasn't pretty."

Wren shrugs, accepting that he has a point but not willing to admit it.

Felicia clears her throat. "Can I also remind you that if you hadn't suggested the raft idea then Jay may not have gone out at all? He might still be alive today."

Wren grips the arms of her chair, resisting the urge to grab Felicia by the throat. She seems to have forgotten the lesson she taught her last time.

"Hold on." Nova sits forward. "That's not fair. If Wren hadn't suggested the raft, we'd have three empty chairs today, instead of one."

That's exactly the kind of thing that makes Nova impossible not to like. Wren loosens her hold on the chair. Having Jay's death on her shoulders isn't a burden she wants to carry.

"Thanks," she says, shooting Nova a smile.

"Can you tell me a little more about your decision to eat the pods?" Callix directs his question at Kian, who shifts in his chair.

"We made that decision together," says Nova.

"That's true," says Kian. "Everyone agreed. Except her."

Wren doesn't need to look at him to know he's pointing at her, fixing her gaze instead on Callix.

"How do you know we ate the pods?" she asks him.

They'd all been too tired and emotionally wrung out to discuss anything when they got back. There's no way Callix could know about the pods.

"We had a camera on each of the barrels." He holds her stare without an ounce of apology. "A small one in the knots of the timber."

"You mean a hidden camera," she says, calling it what it is. "That's not very honest of you. Not very *Bound*."

"We knew coming in here that everything would be filmed," says Kian. "I don't have a problem with my actions being judged."

Wren does.

Not because she's worried about being judged for making heartless or foolish decisions. But because she knows that her behavior during that test would be hard to fault. Which makes it another test she's likely to have scored well on.

As Kian explains to Callix the reasons behind their decision to eat the pods, Wren considers why the thought of having done well on the test isn't quite as abhorrent as it was at the beginning of the week.

Is it because if she's Unbound, she'll have to spend the rest of her life on the upper decks of the Oasis with the likes of Felicia? Or is it because the thought of being Bound alongside Dex and Nova isn't an idea that offends her as much as it used to? Assuming they both become Bound, of course. Although, it's hard to imagine a scenario where they aren't.

"And what about Jay?" asks Lana, her smile dropping as she replaces it with an expression filled with compassion. "Can anyone tell us how it was that none of you noticed how far away he'd drifted?"

They all look at each other and it becomes obvious that they've all already asked themselves this exact question over and over since it happened. If they had their time again, Jay would never get so far away.

"It was crazy out there," says Fern in a whisper. "It was hard enough to save ourselves."

"Yet somehow Wren managed to haul both you and Shiloh to safety, while Kian, Nova and Dex prioritized the pods." Lana taps a long finger on the table, her Bound ring flashing in the overhead light.

"We didn't prioritize them over Jay." Dex sits forward in his chair and crosses his arms to hide his missing hand. Wren wishes he wouldn't do that.

"Sorry, but I hope you understand that's what it seemed like when you decided to help your cousin rather than Jay." Lana says this in such a gentle tone that it almost sounds like she's not hitting Dex with such a wild accusation. This woman has a nerve!

"No!" Dex shouts, standing up and releasing his arms. "I didn't realize Jay was in trouble. I would never have made that choice if I knew."

"There really was a lot going on out there," says Fern, running a hand through her fluffy brown hair that's been standing on end ever since they returned from the ocean. "None of us saw him."

"That's right," says Callix. "None of you saw him, which is what we're asking you about. If you'd gone out in a group of three as instructed it would have been far easier to keep track of everyone."

Felicia nudges Thom and gives him a smug nod.

Dex sits back in his chair and shakes his head. "A bit hard to keep track of people when you're dead."

Wren resists the urge to clap. Good on Dex for standing up to Callix like that.

"Would you like to say that a bit louder, please?" asks Callix.

"I would actually." Dex shoots his father a poisonous look. "I said it's hard to keep track of people when you're dead, which is exactly what would have happened to the three people who went out in that lifeboat if we hadn't had a raft to bring them back. I'm not sure who those three would have been, but I can guarantee you that one of them would have been your nephew. Is that what you wanted?"

"Of course not." Callix seems unmoved by his son's heartfelt speech. "Now let's move on to the decision to bring both barrels back at the expense of a speedier journey. Wren, I believe you were against that decision, as was Nova?"

Nova shifts in her seat, her face flushing.

"We were," says Wren. "Nova was worried about getting everyone back safely. But Kian convinced us otherwise. I agree now that it was the right decision."

Kian's eyebrows shoot up and Wren feels the warmth of the smile Nova is beaming her across the table.

"Don't get too excited," Wren says to them. "It's just the truth. The second barrel slowed us down less than I thought it would. And Kian did more than his share of the rowing."

Callix and Lana look at each other and nod. It seems they've covered what they wanted to ask. Thank goodness. She'd expected far more questions than this. But I guess there's no need to ask questions when you've already watched the whole unfortunate scene play out over the cameras.

"When's the final test?" asks Shiloh, yawning. Wren can't blame her. She'd like nothing better than to crawl underneath the bunks into the small space she's created for herself and go to sleep.

"Tomorrow," says Lana, in her cheery voice. "Rest up today because you're going to need your energy."

"Don't worry," says Felicia. "Thom and I have plenty of energy having followed all the rules so far."

This time Thom rolls his eyes.

"It's okay," he whispers to her. "They know why we stayed behind."

"Terrific!" Lana smiles as she pushes back her chair and waits for Callix.

"Thanks for your cooperation today," says Callix as he stands. "It's been illuminating."

Wren shakes her head at the word, certain that the hidden cameras were illuminating enough.

"May the Proving serve you well," Callix and Lana say in unison as they leave the room.

And now it's the eight of them again.

"I don't like the sound of that," says Fern. "I was hoping for something a little less stressful next test."

"Each test has been getting more challenging." Shiloh glances at Kian as she speaks, even though she's talking to Fern. "I'm not sure that less stressful is a realistic expectation."

"Surely, the next one can't be worse than the last," says Nova, shifting her chair a little closer to Kian's. "I can't imagine anything worse."

"There's always worse," says Wren.

"Not likely," Felicia scoffs.

"Yesterday resulted in one death out of seven people," says Wren. "The day I arrived here we had one survivor out of twelve people. Trust me, there's far worse."

The room falls silent and Wren's pleased her words seem to have had some kind of impact.

"The people who tried to cross the ocean with me were no different to you." She moves her gaze around the table, her point not quite made yet. "Mothers, children, brothers, friends. Two of them were even in love."

She looks directly at Nova and Kian, happy to see them flinch.

"That's why we need a link to the Outlands. And it seems we have one now. That new technique with the raft worked beautifully. Because nobody should ever have to die when all they're trying to do is make sure they continue to live."

"That's beautiful," says Felicia, the sarcasm dripping from her lips.

Wren clenches her fists. Violence won't help her here. She's only just starting to manage to get these people on her side. Well, the ones who count anyway.

"It actually is beautiful." Dex stands and walks around the table to stand beside Wren. "Maybe if you become Bound, you'll be able to do something about all of this injustice."

Wren's mouth falls open. Dex is right.

This whole time she's been doing her hardest not to be connected to the people who make all the decisions around here. If she wants to make change—if she wants to make Cy proud—she needs to come at this another way.

"Just something to keep in mind." Dex winks at her. "Now that you've aced your third test."

Tugging at the pendant hanging from her neck, an unfamiliar sensation sweeps over her. A sensation that the other seven people in the room are very familiar with.

It's not the desire to beat this last test since she's already decided to try her hardest.

This feeling is a little different.

It's a freshly born desire to become Bound.

NOVA

ova runs her hand over the smooth metal of the table. She's not surprised that on the eve of her last test she was drawn to the one room that's a replica of the infirmary. It's the closest place she has to somewhere familiar. Somewhere she can gain a shred of comfort.

She hesitates in the center of the room. It's late and she should be in bed, but although she's exhausted, she can't sleep. Her head feels too full. Her body too tight.

Three tests have been completed. There's only one to go. Two more days and she'll be Bound or Unbound.

With Kian.

Or her whole world ripped apart.

Taking a few more steps into the gloomy space, Nova can see everything is much the same as after the second test. The shelves, the cots, the chairs. They've drawn back the curtain, revealing the two seats on the other side of the table.

Sam and a Bound sat on those chairs, their arms bleeding. Both waiting to be chosen and healed.

Deep down, Nova knows she made the wrong decision

when she suggested they sew them both up, but only in half-measures. Kian and Dex know it.

They would've chosen the Bound.

Except Nova has chosen Sam before. In a place so similar to the one she's in now. Her knees weaken as the memory of the choice she made refuses to be shunted away. She slips into a seat in the corner of the room, her head falling into her hands.

Sam. Drunk with blood seeping from a deep gash high in his hairline after falling over.

An Unbound. Doing nothing productive for the colony. And yet she sewed him up anyway.

She couldn't let him leave knowing the cut would be held together with nothing but hemp.

She hasn't told anyone about it. Not her mother.

Not Kian.

The sound of the door sliding open has Nova stilling. It doesn't surprise her others can't sleep but she was hoping for some solitude. She was hoping to distract her mind from its persistent desire to relive every choice she's made over the three tests.

Weak light filters in from the hallway as the door opens wider. Nova freezes when she considers it might be Callix. She's supposed to be in the dorm, at least in her bed if she can't sleep.

Has she been caught out failing to follow the rules again?

There's a pause and the door begins to close again. Relief is a hot flush through Nova's body. Whoever it was hasn't seen her tucked in the corner. She slowly lets out the breath she was holding. Once this person's gone, she's heading straight to bed.

She can go back to staring at the ceiling.

Except the door halts, causing Nova to freeze again. She didn't move, didn't make a sound.

It slides open again, the pale square of light growing, and this time it keeps going. It reveals the outline of the body standing in the doorway.

One Nova instantly recognizes.

She holds very still even though she's no longer alarmed. The body enters the doorway, scanning the room.

Nova doesn't move even though she's in the shadows. She waits for those earthy eyes to fall on her.

Kian will find her. He always does.

The moment he does his whole body unwinds. "I had a feeling you'd be here."

Nova smiles weakly. "Couldn't sleep."

Kian's corresponding smile is a crooked one. "Yeah, me neither."

Nova notes that he stays in the doorway. A week ago they would've gravitated toward each other, never questioning the magnetism that pulled them together. Just being within touching distance could always provide such comfort, such reassurance that they had each other.

After the past few days though, things have changed.

Their future no longer feels certain...

A band tightens around Nova's chest. How could something so simple and true have become so complicated?

She stands. "I should probably head back. We have a big day tomorrow."

In one swift motion Kian enters the room and scans his bracelet so the door behind him closes. Quiet hangs in the new darkness, their breath the only thing disturbing it.

"Kian?" Nova doesn't think she's ever felt uncertain when she's spoken his name before, but her voice wavers. She doesn't even know what she's asking him.

Is he okay?

Is he as scared as she is?

She swallows. Is he disappointed in her?

"Do you know you're one of my first memories, Nova?"

She goes so still she thinks she might shatter. "I am?"

Kian nods in the dark. "We would've been four or five, I'm

guessing. I was at the pod tank with Mom when your mother brought you. I'm sure we'd played together countless times before, but this is the first time I remember it."

Nova allows the words to wrap around her, weaving a sweet image as if she recollects it herself.

"Mom had just scooped out a netful of pods to show us. Even back then I was fascinated by them. We both peered over as they flapped about. You stared for the longest time and I figured you were counting them, just like I was."

Nova almost smiles. That's exactly what Kian would've been doing, even at that age.

"But then you reached down, Nova. I was about to tell you we're not allowed to touch them when your hand came back out and you held it up. On the tip of your finger was a small black insect."

Nova tries to imagine the unexpected twist in the story, but she's not sure what Kian's getting at. Insects are numerous in their world thanks to the warmer temperatures, she doubts it would've been anything significant.

"As that bug crawled down to your hand, you looked at me with such a big smile. It was a beautiful smile. A proud smile that you saved that insect's life. A bug I never would've noticed."

Nova tries to talk but finds she can't. Her throat is tight as she works to contain the tempest of emotion that just erupted in her.

She and Kian have known each other so long, the rhythm of their days twined together as tightly as the roots of the mangrove pine. They'd wake and seek each other out. They'd eat together, play together when they were young, dream together as they grew older. They know each other, heart and soul.

But she didn't know this.

Just like he doesn't know what she did for Sam.

Nova gives into her heart's longing and takes a step forward. "Everything is just so…" Her shoulders sag. "Complicated."

Kian moves another foot toward her. "It'll only make us stronger."

Another step and Nova's before him. She pulls in a breath, filling her lungs with his scent. She wants to believe that so badly. "Out on the raft…I'd make the same suggestion again."

To throw the barrel off and lose the pods. To do what she can to save those on board. "And I know you'd do the same."

She's always loved and respected Kian for his dedication to Askala. For his willingness to sacrifice. In the end, it's that thinking that meant they saved the pods without risking everyone.

"It doesn't mean you've failed, Nova. You made that suggestion based on compassion and kindness."

Nova's breath releases on a shudder. The tests have made her realize something. "Maybe I'm not cut out to be Bound, Kian."

Kian's mouth opens to object, but Nova places her fingers over his lips, knowing that's exactly what he'd do.

"I don't like being the one who decides who gets stitches, who gets pods." Nova shrugs, letting the truth tumble out. "I hate choosing, Kian."

His breath puffs against her skin and Nova pulls her finger away before the awareness between them can spark.

"When we're Bound, the decision is made for us. It won't be the same."

Won't it? Nova wonders. If she were to be Bound, would she be okay with not stitching up Sam? With not letting a sick Unbound have pods unless they earn them? With having children when someone she knows and cares about, can't?

Kian takes a step back, his arms arcing out. "Don't you see, Nova? This weighs so heavily because you care so deeply. That's exactly what a Bound does."

His hands spear into his hair but the room's too dark to be able to see his eyes clearly. Nova stands mute, having said the words that have weighed down her heart so completely. She wishes she felt lighter, but she doesn't.

Kian's hands fall to his side and he straightens. Will he leave now? Has he acknowledged they just need to wait until the ceremony?

He looks around the room then heads to one of the cots. He sits on the edge, patting the space beside him. "Come here."

Nova hesitates. If things don't go the way they hope, will it hurt more or less if she were to join him right now?

"I don't know what's going to happen, Nova." Kian sighs. "I don't feel like I know much of anything right now. But I do know how I feel about you." His dark eyes reach to her across the room. "And that I really need to be close to you right now."

Nova's feeble defenses crumble. Who's she kidding? No matter what happens, her heart will always go to him.

The few steps to the cot feel like they take too long, but she's sitting beside him a moment later. Their hands come together, the only expression of their feelings they've allowed themselves.

Their fingers twine, palms connect. They grip tight. Their shoulders press against each other.

"I've imagined it so many times, Nova. What it will look like. What it will feel like."

Nova's heart swells. This time she knows what he's talking about. She's done exactly the same thing. "I'll be in the infirmary, helping those who are hurt." She'll tell her mother about the mangrove pine sap and they'll heal so many more.

"And I'll be with the pods." Nova can hear the smile in his voice. "Breeding them, feeding the colony."

Nova sighs. "Your parents will be so proud." Kian will probably become a High Bound.

Kian grins. "Together, we'll make sure Askala continues to grow in strength."

174

Together... Nova's heart stutters at such a beautiful word.

"We'll have our own cabin. You'll be mine and I'll be yours."

As Kian's softly spoken words hang in the air, Nova realizes they've steadily been leaning closer together. So close, that their faces are only inches apart.

She knows she should pull back, but the magic of what they feel for each other is weaving around her. This is why they've had to be so careful.

It's always been so potent.

Nova waits for Kian to do the right thing. To retreat. They're not meant to do this before the Announcement.

Except Kian doesn't move. His lashes flutter in the gloom, his eyes drawn to Nova's lips. "I can't..." His gaze captures hers, hot and hungry. "I don't want to stop, Nova."

Their self-control has always been stretched tight. But now, with the tests, with losing Jay, with so much uncertainty, Nova has to admit it.

Neither does she. "Kian..."

The distance between them shrinks, their breaths mingling.

"Just a small taste? I promise."

Nova almost smiles at the question in Kian's words. He's checking with her.

It was never going to be a no. Ever.

Plus, she's already proven she's willing to break the rules in the name of following her heart.

They lean in, bodies a hairbreadth apart. Simultaneously, they stop, an unspoken agreement that they should treasure what's hanging between them. This moment has been years in the making, thousands of heartbeats have counted down to it.

The anticipation builds. The need heightens.

Nova's body stretches tight, not sure how much longer she can wait. Kian's groan tells her when he concedes defeat and her heart soars.

The last remaining millimeters dissolve as they fall into each other.

Their lips touch, caress, taste with the gentlest of weight. Nova's heart stutters. Sweet, hot pleasure sparks from their touch and charges through her body. How could such a gentle touch ricochet through her with such power? Every cell screams to discover what more pressure, more Kian, could mean.

Except what they've already done is a stolen moment. Something that shouldn't have happened.

Pulling back, Nova realizes she's panting. They hover, wanting more, but knowing they can't. Kian's breath seems to have come to a halt.

Carefully, they rest their foreheads against each other.

Their first kiss. How long have they waited for this moment?

And of all the moments, it happened now.

Nova pulls back, startled by the thought. Her hand flies to her mouth, touching the lips that will never be the same again. "We shouldn't have done that, Kian."

Against the odds, Kian grins. "We really shouldn't have."

Her shoulders flop. "How in the world are we going to hold back now?" Her words are a half-whisper, half-wail.

Kian chuckles, the sound like warm syrup down her spine. "We just had a taste of heaven."

Nova's heart doesn't know if it should dance at hearing that Kian feels the same way, or ache because what they've discovered is still so far out of reach.

Silence descends between them as they try to process what this is going to mean. Nova's hands tighten in her lap. In part, because she wants to hold him so bad.

In part, because she's already tense at the thought this moment has to end.

That tomorrow is their final test.

Nova opens her mouth to tell him they should head back but

she can't find the words. In this moment, after the sweet kiss they just shared, she doesn't want to talk of responsibility. She doesn't want to pretend she doesn't want to be here.

Kian sighs. "All these decisions…it's so tiring."

Those are the words Nova needs to hear to spur her into action. Kian needs sleep. They really should go. And now that he's said the words, Nova realizes she's exhausted herself.

Except Kian grips her hand. "Stay with me, Nova?"

"Here? On the cot?"

"We'll head back first thing, before anyone is up." His grin softens. "Here. On the super uncomfortable cot." His face becomes serious, almost vulnerable. "Together."

This time, Nova doesn't hesitate. "Always, Kian."

Kian's grin returns and this time it's blinding. He shuffles around her and lies down, opening his arms.

She looks at him, his sharp lines soft in the gloom, his eyes so full of hopes and promises. Her whole body suffuses with emotion as she pictures a future with this moment in it, over and over and over.

As Nova settles in, her head on his shoulder, she's conscious of so many things. She's keenly aware of the hard, muscled body pressed against hers. All she can hear is the sound of Kian's steady heartbeat. The gentle pulse of desire wanting more is refusing to be ignored.

But then she remembers how over the past few days, they've seen failure. They've seen death.

And the knowledge that there's a chance this could be all they have is never far from Nova's mind.

There's no way she's moving from this cot.

The gentle brush of Kian's lips on her head has Nova's eyes drifting closed in pleasure. His strong arm around her shoulder gives her a sense of comfort she's never experienced.

As sleep steals over her, the three words that hold the most truth of all, three words she's never said, settle on her tongue. Wanting desperately to be spoken.

I love you, Kian.

Please let this last test be the final gauntlet before she can say them out loud.

KIAN

The sense of déjà vu as they stand in the walled yard beside the lab isn't a pleasant one. Kian resists the urge to cross his arms. The others will think it's a defensive gesture as they all stare at whatever is under the sheet before them.

But they'll be wrong.

Sure, he's worried about what's coming next. He'd be stupid not to be. But last night is what he's trying to hold as close to his body as he can. What he's having problems letting go of.

The feeling of Nova lying against him, their bodies twined, their hearts so close.

They'd kissed.

Such a small kiss, little more than a taste of what lies between them.

But it'd been amazing. So much more than he imagined.

And now all he wants is more. More touch. More passion.

More Nova.

He'd woken before dawn and lain there, listening to her soft, steady breathing. Having every morning like that would be his heaven.

Surely, that's not too much to ask for?

She'd stirred and his body had responded, firing hot and fast from each place they brushed. They'd stared at each other for long moments, not needing to speak. Both knowing there's too much to say. Nova's hand had stroked his cheek, her gaze the softest he'd seen.

He'd done nothing but tighten his arms, just like they are now. If he'd allowed himself to caress her the way he wanted, he'd never be able to stop.

He'd tried to keep their parting light, to focus on the future that's waiting for them just around the corner. But Nova's eyes had been tinged with goodbye, heavy with worry.

And there's nothing he could do to make that go away.

All he'd allowed himself was a lingering press of his lips on her forehead as they'd parted at the doorway. Nova would go back to the bunkroom, and he'd follow a few minutes later.

It'd be like last night never happened.

Kian glances at her on the other side of the yard, but Nova is staring at the large square with strange lumps on the top that stands between them. Whatever is beneath is as unknown as their future.

He drops his arms to his sides. He knows exactly what his future is going to be.

He'll follow in his ancestors' footsteps. He'll be Bound. He'll do what it takes to make Askala everything it's destined to be.

And so will Nova.

Dex nudges him with his elbow. "Nice day for it, huh?"

Kian throws him an exasperated eyeroll. "The weather wasn't exactly on my mind."

Dex shrugs. "Seems better to focus on sweet sunshine than that." He indicates the mysterious entity not far away.

Felicia steps around the centerpiece, sighing. "They sure do like making us wait."

Wren snorts. "Builds the suspense."

"I'm pretty sure we don't want to rush into this, anyway," says Thom, rubbing his palms down his pants. "I'm kinda happy to wait."

Kian almost shakes his head. He hopes Callix didn't hear that. Bounds have to be willing to do what it takes.

The door to the building whooshes open and Callix steps through. Kian straightens as he goes on high alert. Beside him, he senses Dex does the same. It must be so much harder for him knowing his father is watching his every move.

His every choice.

Lana isn't far behind Callix, already smiling serenely. Instead of following him though, she turns and heads to one of the gates that are part of the yard. A few of the others glance at each other, noticing her movements, too. Kian figures they should probably be relieved she chose that gate, and not the one on the opposite side that heads to the beach.

Callix stops beside the shape beneath the sheet. "Welcome. For your final task, two teams will be chosen."

Kian resists looking at Nova. He doesn't plan on getting separated from her. Doing this final task together is one way he can make sure they get the outcome they want.

They can't afford for Nova to make another decision ruled by her kind heart.

His uncle lifts the sheet with a short, sharp movement. Beneath is a square block about waist high, eight wooden handles protruding from it. They're all about a foot long, all identical.

"Each person will select a weapon. The choice will dictate which team you'll be on."

Alarm rings through Kian's body. Weapons? And random selection of teams?

Callix steps back. "Please select a handle each and remove it from the block."

Everyone pauses, conscious that the test just started. Do you stride right up there and show courage and determination? Or do you wait, and let others go first?

Wren rolls her eyes. "What happens when you people need to decide who eats first in the dining hall?"

She steps forward, a slight hesitation as she reaches out the only sign she might be nervous. She grips one of the handles and yanks only to find it slip out smoothly. Stepping back, she surveys what she holds. "Now that's cool."

"A slingshot?" asks Fern, her pale brown eyes wide with disbelief.

That's exactly what's protruding from the wooden handle. Two short arms, a thick band of rubber with a slip of leather in the middle dangling between them. Everyone looks to Callix, wondering what's in store for them, but his face remains impassive as he speaks.

"Wren, please stand by the gate." He extends his left arm in the direction of the empty gate.

The one Lana isn't standing beside.

Wren glances back at them, particularly at Dex and Nova. With a shrug, she walks over, stretching the slingshot as she stares down at the taut rubber.

Dex straightens his shoulders, stepping away from Kian. "I'll take the next one." He watches his father as he approaches the block, but Callix's face never changes.

Dex takes a moment to scan the seven handles pointed at him, then grabs the one that was beside Wren's. There's almost an imperceptible slide of metal on wood as Dex pulls out a knife.

He pauses as he holds it before him and a ripple moves through the others. It's a large knife, almost the size of a machete. "Probably a good thing I didn't get the slingshot, huh?"

Callix's gaze slides to Dex's stump before jerking away. He moves his right arm. "Dex, could you please join Lana."

Although Lana's smile brightens like Dex just won a prize, Callix's voice remains emotionless.

Kian glances over at Nova to find her stricken eyes on him. Not only does this test involve large knives and slingshots, there's a possibility they're going to be separated. Kian isn't sure which prospect scares him more.

Felicia and Thom move forward at the same time, then glance at each other nervously. They step back simultaneously. "You go first," Thom offers.

Flicking her hair, Felicia smiles at Thom graciously. "Why thank you, Thom."

She flounces over, smiling at Callix although he doesn't acknowledge it. Moving to the other end of the block, she grabs a handle and pulls.

She pauses as she holds the slingshot awkwardly in her hand.

"You've got to be kidding me," Wren groans.

Felicia turns her back on Callix and glares at her as she walks over. "Wren, we're going to make such a good team," she chirps.

Kian almost rolls his eyes. Doesn't Felicia realize that Lana can see her expression?

Thom steps up and almost haphazardly grabs at a handle. He pulls out a knife, for some reason looking relieved. He joins Dex beside the opposite gate.

Kian's surprised when Nova steps up next, wondering at her strategy. Maybe she's thinking that the middle road is the best option for this test. Don't draw attention to yourself by choosing to go first or last.

With shoulders straight, Nova walks to the block. She scans the remaining four handles. So far there's been no rhyme or reason as to where the knives or slingshots are. There's no way of telling who will get what.

Taking a lone handle sitting in the top corner, Nova draws it out.

She turns to show him the knife in her hand, her face taut within the shade of her shawl. Everything about her is hoping he pulls one out, too.

"Nova," Callix speaks in his same measured tone. "Please move toward Lana."

Shiloh steps up, throwing Kian a reassuring smile as she passes him. He pulls up a tight one in return, trying to be encouraging. All he can think about is needing to pull out a knife.

There's no doubt in his mind this test is going to be dangerous.

Shiloh pulls out a slingshot, glancing over her shoulder at Kian again. He nods, unsure why she's focusing her attention on him. Is it because she assumes he'll lead this again somehow? Or is she reassuring him that there's still a good chance he'll be on the same team as Nova?

Two handles remain. One has to be a slingshot, the other a knife.

Fern looks to Kian. "Maybe we should do it together?"

"Actually, that's a great idea."

A show of solidarity, and it means this unbearable tension will be over sooner.

Fern beams, then glances at Callix. "Thanks, Kian. I think it's important we work as a team whenever we can."

Kian's gut roils at Fern's words. Everyone is so conscious their every move is being weighed and measured, but Bounds are expected to be humble and modest. These tests mean it's hard to be either of those.

Kian is conscious of Nova's eyes on him as he walks up with Fern. Although he wants to stride up and grab a handle, he hangs back half a step, letting Fern take a subtle lead.

It's what a Bound would do.

Fern is focused intensely on the remaining two handles, one before her on the right, the other on the left. That's the one Kian heads toward, hoping against hope it's a knife.

At the last moment, Fern steps to the side. She smiles up at Kian. "I think we should swap sides."

Unsure why it matters, Kian hesitates. He'd already set his sights on the handle closest to him. But then he nods. A Bound wouldn't make an issue. A Bound would graciously incline his head like he's seen his father do so many times and move to the right.

Which is exactly what Kian does, resisting the urge to look at Callix. He refuses to be someone who acts for the cameras.

Stepping up to the block, Kian tells himself maybe this is a good thing. Maybe fate is looking after him and the other handle is the knife.

He hears Fern suck in a breath as she lifts her hand. He does the same, and they grip the handles together.

There's very little resistance, a gentle *whoosh*, as they simultaneously pull them out.

Kian looks from the weapon he's holding to Fern's, struggling to register what's happened.

Fern has a knife.

He has a slingshot.

"Kian, please join the others by the second gate. Fern, please join Lana."

He almost objects. Almost. But before the words can fly out, he clamps his mouth shut. This is the way it's meant to be.

One glance at Nova shows her face is full of anguish. Walking away from her physically hurts. It's like something is tearing, like a part of him is determined to stay with her.

He repeats the words to himself. This is the way it's meant to be.

The teams chosen, Callix nods to Lana then joins Kian,

Wren, Shiloh, and Felicia. He opens the gate and walks through. "Please follow me."

Straightening his spine, Kian does as he's told, the others filing behind him. He tries to cover the wince as he hears the gate shut behind him.

On the other side of the wall, the forest quickly envelops them. Callix doesn't turn around as he strides away.

They all glance at each other, Wren the only one to look at the closed gate behind them. Kian hunches his shoulders as he follows, indicating the others should do the same.

"Of course we just head into the forest without asking any questions," Wren mutters. "Do they even realize the polar grizzlies exist?"

Kian grits his teeth. Those massive, mottled bears were the first things that came to mind as they left the safety of the yard. As Askala had warmed, grizzlies had steadily migrated north along with the forests. They'd hybridized with polar bears, creating a new species...one the size of a polar bear, but with the ferocious temperament of a grizzly.

As he realizes this, Nova is probably leaving the yard as well.

Callix strikes west, weaving through the trees in silence. Saying without words that's what everyone else should be doing.

Shiloh comes up beside Kian, her shoulder brushing his. He tenses as he resists the urge to create some space between them. She's probably scared. She leans in a little closer, whispering. "Do you know where we're going?"

Kian shakes his head, keeping his gaze straight ahead. It's obvious they're not meant to ask questions.

Felicia huffs behind him, muttering under her breath. "Even a hint would be nice."

Kian's brows hike in surprise when Wren marches past them and straight up to Callix. She glares back at them, obviously frustrated with their silence, before falling beside Callix.

"Where exactly are we going?"

Callix doesn't break stride as he barely glances at Wren. "To the final test."

"Which is pretty obvious, Wren," Felicia calls out. "We're happy to find out where we're going when we arrive."

Wren ignores her. "Enough with the sidestepping, Callix. If you're taking us to the ocean again—"

"We're heading inland, Wren." Callix keeps his gaze straight ahead, seemingly focused on their destination. "There's no ocean in this test."

"Also pretty obvious, Wren." Felicia pipes in. "I would've thought you had a better sense of direction."

Wren's glare is so full of threat that Felicia falls back a step. "It's easy to lose your bearings in the forest, Felicia." She practically spits out her name. "We could circle back to the ocean without even realizing it."

Kian catches her gaze. "Callix wouldn't lie."

The moment he says the words, he realizes they were the wrong ones. He was trying to calm Wren, not placate Callix. He wanted to reassure her that Callix would be telling them the truth. Hoping Wren would get the hint it's in her best interest to back off.

Except the words only infuriate her. She spins around and catches up with Callix. "Do you even care that Jay died? In one of *your* tests?"

The only sign that Callix heard the question is a tightening of his shoulder blades. And the fact that he picks up his pace.

Striding like a polar grizzly is on his tail he calls out without looking back. "We're almost there."

Wren's hands clench into fists. She's practically vibrating with fury. She's already made it clear she doesn't care if she fails these tests and becomes Unbound, but she's not doing any of them any favors by angering Callix.

Except there's no way she's going to listen if Kian points that out.

So far, Dex has been the only one to get Wren to see reason. Maybe even Nova could've. But neither of them are here right now.

"Wren," Kian calls out, holding up his slingshot. Maybe he can distract her. "Did you want me to hold yours until we get to wherever we're going?"

Wren opens her mouth and Kian braces himself for the onslaught, only to find there is none. Wren snaps her mouth shut, narrowing her eyes at him. "I was using one of those when you were paddling about in the pool, pod boy."

Kian shrugs, a smile playing on his lips. "Just making sure you weren't going to take out something you might regret."

Wren glances at Callix, who's now several feet ahead. She stops long enough that the other three catch up then starts walking again. She glares at Kian. "I've found regret to be a fleeting emotion."

Kian lets out a breath of relief. An angry Wren is a formidable thing. And an angry Wren with a weapon is down-right dangerous.

Shiloh's shoulder brushes his again. "Good thinking," she whispers.

Kian looks away, wondering why every time Shiloh's close he thinks of Nova.

Suddenly, in the middle of the forest, Callix stops. He turns to the group of four. "This is where I leave you."

Wren opens her mouth but Callix lifts a hand.

"For your final test, you will need to find a raven's nest and collect four eggs. As most of you know, the shells of their eggs are used to purify acidic rainwater." He looks around and everyone nods apart from Wren. "These eggs are important for our freshwater supply."

Which is true. Bird shells are an excellent way to neutralize the damage done to something so essential to human survival.

Callix looks at each of them in turn. "You cannot let the opposing team know of your plans. They have been tasked with sabotaging you and stealing the eggs."

Wren sucks in a breath. "You're pitting us against each other?"

Callix doesn't even glance at Wren. "You have your task. May the Proving serve you well."

Without another word, Callix strides past, quickly disappearing amongst the army of trees.

Wren crosses her arms. "I've seen cowards run away from polar grizzlies slower than that."

Felicia fills her chest. "Callix is a deeply respected High Bound, Wren. I'll not have you—"

"Oh, shut up, Felicia," Wren growls. "I doubt he can hear you, although that doesn't really matter, because if you don't zip it, I'm going to use your gob to sight this baby in." Wren lifts the slingshot and easily draws it back.

It's obvious she's familiar with the weapon.

Kian slowly turns on the spot, getting his bearings. Finish the test. Get back to Nova. "The ravens nest in the cliffs, which are due west." Callix has already brought them part of the distance. "My guess is they're not that far away."

Shiloh shuffles her feet. "Their eggs aren't easy to get."

"Of course they aren't," responds Wren.

Kian shrugs. "But they're the most prolific of all the bird species. Taking some of their eggs won't hurt their population numbers."

Felicia lifts up her slingshot. "Then what in the world are these for? They're not going to help us climb a cliff face."

Wren rolls her eyes. "For protection. How have you not been bear fodder yet with questions like that?"

Felicia flushes bright red as she slices a glare at Wren.

"I suggest we get to the cliffs and come up with a plan there," Kian offers.

"Great idea, Kian." Shiloh slips closer and he grits his teeth. He's going to have to remind himself she's doing this because she's scared.

And the truth of the matter is, she should be.

Too many people of Askala have lost their lives to polar grizzlies.

Wren places her hands on her hips as she turns around. "They've probably planted cameras around here, anyway."

Felicia freezes. "Oh no, they're watching us again?"

Glancing up at the breaks in the canopy and the angle of the light streaking through, Kian gets his bearings. "Let's go get these eggs."

They start hiking in the opposite direction, creating more distance between them and Callix. And the lab.

Kian glances at the slingshot in his hand and frowns. He turns to Wren. "Anything I should know about using one of these things?"

Most people of Askala are familiar with a slingshot, particularly those who work out in the gardens. But Kian's spent his life focusing on the pteropods. He hasn't handled one for a very long time.

Wren's brows shoot up. "It's pretty straightforward. You pull back, aim, and release."

Kian does exactly that, lifting it, pulling back the leather pouch then releasing it. The rubber smacks against his arm then twists around the prongs of the slingshot.

Wren snorts. "Not like that. Are you trying to hurt yourself?"

She pulls back her own slingshot, holding the leather close to her cheek as she stares down the taut rubber. "Keep it all straight. Line it up, pull it back all the way, then exhale."

"Exhale?"

Wren releases the pouch and it flicks through the arms. "Yep.

Releasing the breath completely eliminates any chance that a slight body movement could mess up your shot."

There's a snap of a branch behind them. "I'm pretty sure the knife team has an advantage when it comes to the weapons department," Felicia mutters.

"They certainly have an advantage if everyone in their team isn't stomping through the forest pretending they're an elephant," Wren mutters.

Shiloh's eyes widen as she suppresses a giggle. Everyone knows elephants went extinct a long time ago.

Kian holds his slingshot up again and pulls it back. "I'd suggest it's in your best interest to practice with it, Felicia. We might need them to get the ravens away from their nests."

Felicia huffs as she tucks the slingshot under her arm, striding forward with a frown on her face.

Shiloh holds hers out. "Will you show me, Kian?"

Kian's about to point out that Wren is much better placed to do that when a scream pierces the air. And not just any scream.

One that's high and shrill, wrenched from terrified lungs.

One that's far closer than Kian would've expected.

He freezes, his veins turning ice cold. "That was Nova."

Wren's slingshot is already up and loaded. "Are you sure?"

Kian's heart jackknifes in his chest. "Without a doubt."

"It's a trap." Felicia is looking around in alarm. "Callix said they're going to try and sabotage us. They want us to come running."

Shiloh rests her hands on Kian's arm. "Felicia's probably right. We were given our instructions."

For the second time that day, Kian feels something tear inside him. His heart is begging him to go to Nova.

His mind is already replaying what Callix told them.

For your final test, you will need to find a raven's nest and collect four eggs...

They have been tasked with sabotaging you...

191

Wren slowly lowers her slingshot, her eyes wide. "You're seriously thinking of not going."

The second scream, a sound bleeding with terror, has Kian making a decision.

Locking his muscles, he prepares himself for what he has to do next.

DEX

*D*ex's heart is thumping so hard, he's finding it difficult to hear. Or think. Or see. Everything is swirling.

But he knows that's not good enough. Nova needs him.

Shaking his head to regain his senses, he takes a step toward the polar grizzly, even though everything inside him is telling him to run.

The giant beast has backed Nova against a rockface and is only a few feet away from her.

Nova is pale and shaking, holding her knife in front of her chest. Her eyes are fixed on the bear as they study each other, waiting to see who's going to make the first move.

The grizzly is so much calmer than Nova. A large male with mottled fur, it's on all fours with its nose twitching as it draws in Nova's scent. There isn't much food around here for a bear this size. Nova must be very tempting. No wonder it's so interested in her—it's probably deciding how much risk is involved in killing her...

But Dex knows the bear's calm demeanor can change in a

deadly split second. The next few minutes are crucial. It's a miracle the bear didn't attack when Nova screamed.

Twice.

Two miracles. Could they hope for a third?

Dex grips the knife clutched in his fingers, extra glad he wasn't given a slingshot.

"It's no use," whispers Thom beside him, the smell of fear oozing from his pores. "We need guns, not knives. We'll never be able to get close enough to use these things."

"He's right," says Fern, gripping her knife so tightly her knuckles have turned white. "We should get away while that thing's distracted."

"We can't do that." Dex holds still. "It's distracted with Nova!"

"But we could all be killed," hisses Thom, taking a step back. "That thing could eat every one of us and still have room for seconds. Look at the size of it!"

Fern nods wildly, her face pale and her eyes darting from the bear to a huge boulder behind them that she seems to think might offer some protection.

"It won't look good for you to leave," says Dex. If their concern for Nova isn't enough to make them stay, maybe concern for themselves will do it.

But Thom and Fern take another step back, shaking their heads, unable to swallow down their fear.

"If that's what it takes to be Bound, you can count me out," says Thom, even though they all know there's very little chance of him growing old with all ten fingers intact, no matter what decisions he makes in the rest of this test.

"They're right," says Nova, tearing her gaze from the grizzly to look at Dex. Her eyes are dark with fear, her knife rattling in her fingertips. "You should go."

The grizzly leans forward, sniffing at Nova. She knows if she runs the game is over. And she won't be the winner. For now, she has no choice but to stay exactly where she is—staring down the snout of a giant death machine as it decides if it's going to eat her.

Nova takes a step to her left, only for the grizzly to snarl, jamming its nose into her stomach and forcing her back to where she was.

She whimpers, squeezing her eyes closed as she presses herself against the rockface and waits to see what the beast is going to do with her. A beast that doesn't seem to be in a hurry.

"Go, Dex," she pleads.

"I'm not going anywhere," says Dex, his mind racing to find a way out of this mess. Hopefully, with Nova safely by his side. But he keeps coming up blank. "I'm not going to leave you."

But Thom and Fern are making no such promise. They back away clutching their knives with shaking hands to stand behind the boulder. Dex wants to tell them a large rock isn't going to keep them alive, but he's not as interested in their safety right now as he is in Nova's. She's the one in peril. She's the one he can't leave.

Even if it means he'll likely become the dessert to Nova's main course.

They'd been foolish, walking through the dense forest speculating about how they're going to collect four raven eggs so the yolk can be used to feed the pteropods. With all the noise they'd made, they'd practically invited that grizzly to come and eat them.

At first, they'd thought the noise of breaking branches and heavy footsteps had been the other team coming to sabotage them. But very quickly they'd realized the danger they were in when the giant bear had appeared. They'd done a pretty good job of ducking and weaving, until that rockface had loomed in front of them and somehow Nova had been the only one not to be able to navigate her way around it.

"Don't move," Dex says to Nova, trying to remember what

195

Magnus had taught them to do if they were ever unlucky enough to encounter a polar grizzly.

Damn it! Kian would know what to do. He's always been far better at listening to instructions than Dex. Why did Kian have to select a slingshot, leaving Dex and Nova stuck with Thom and Fern?

"Run, Dex. Get yourself to safety." Nova's pleading now and Dex's heart hurts so badly it feels like it's going to split open inside his chest. He looks down at his knife, certain if he were to slam it into the bear's back it would only result in disaster. A wounded bear is an angry bear.

The bear turns its head and looks at Dex. Is that a warning?

"Come and get me!" calls Dex, waving his knife.

The beast roars so loudly it shakes the leaves on the trees around them. It's telling Dex to back off, unaware that it's a wasted effort. He's not going anywhere.

Dex holds his ground as the bear turns its eyes back to Nova, sniffing at her once more, like it's deciding which part of her to eat first.

Maybe Thom's right. They need guns, not knives. Why would his dad send them out here with such useless weapons? What was he thinking, setting a task like this? They aren't going to end up Bound or Unbound. They're going to end up dead.

Dex draws in a deep breath in an attempt to slow down his heart before it runs out of beats, but it's no use. Maybe it doesn't matter. If that grizzly gets him, his heart won't be beating for too much longer, anyway.

There's a rustle nearby and Dex turns, relieved that Thom and Fern have changed their minds about deserting him. If the worst happens to Nova, he can't bear to have to witness it alone.

But his eyes widen to see it's Kian and Wren beside him, with the huddle of frightened onlookers behind the useless rock having grown to include Shiloh and Felicia.

Wren's cheeks are pink and Kian has sweat beading on his

furrowed brow. They must've run to get here after hearing Nova scream.

"Holy crap," says Wren, stooping down to pick up something from the ground and putting it in her pocket. "He's a big one."

Kian is frozen, staring at the girl he loves. "Nova." Her name is a breath on his lips as his wide eyes take in what he's seeing.

Nova's looking at Kian now, twitching as if she wants to run to him, but smart enough to know she can't. The bear has stepped even closer to her now, its face only inches from Nova's, with long lines of drool hanging from its mouth.

"Don't move!" Kian snaps into action. "I'm going to distract it and lure it away from you."

"I'm not sure that's a good idea," says Wren, bending to pick up something else from the ground.

"We have no choice," Kian says to her. "We can't stand by and wait for that bear to decide what happens next."

"Suit yourself." Wren shrugs.

Dex has never seen Kian use a slingshot but there's no arguing that he seems to know what he's doing. He tucks a rock into the leather pouch, pulls it back, lines up his shot, does some strange breathing out thing and lets the pouch go.

But the shot lacks technique and the rock skids along the ground behind the bear. Perhaps Kian doesn't know how to use that thing, after all.

Kian curses and tucks the slingshot into his pocket, just as the bear turns and lets out another almighty roar, this one even louder than the last.

Dex swallows, but the fear remains lodged in his throat.

"Just say the word," says Wren, taking a rock from her bulging pocket and holding her weapon in front of her.

So, that's what she's been picking up! She's been one step ahead, knowing she'd need more ammunition than what had been supplied to her.

"Don't shoot yet," says Kian. "You were right. It wasn't a great idea. Rocks will be useless with a bear that size."

Wren nods, but keeps her position, ready to fire if needed.

"Nova, hold your hands up in the air," says Kian, keeping his voice level. "Do it slowly. It'll make you look bigger. More of a threat. Don't show him you're scared. We're right here with you."

Nova does as she's told. The grizzly doesn't back away, but at least it doesn't close the small gap Nova just created. It shoves its snout in Nova's armpit and sniffs, its mottled fur standing on end as it makes its assessment of her. Is it possible this beast is just curious and not hungry?

"Talk to me," says Kian. "Show him that you're human, not his lunch."

Dex mentally kicks himself, remembering Magnus telling them this. He should've kept Nova talking this whole time. He may not have the strength to attack a bear but talking has always been one of his special talents and he'd missed his opportunity to use it.

"I can't talk." Nova's voice is shaking, doing a great job at demonstrating what she just said.

"Yes, you can," says Kian. "And don't look directly at the bear. But don't look away. Look just past his head."

"I can't." The knife in Nova's hand is wobbling now. It's amazing she's managing to keep her hands raised.

"You can." Kian's voice is far calmer than Dex knows his cousin is feeling. "Look at me. I'm going to stand right where I want you to keep looking. Don't take your eyes off me, okay?"

Nova's hands start to drop. "It's not going away, Kian."

"It's not attacking either," says Wren, fiddling with her slingshot. "Kian's right. Hold still. And keep talking to us."

Dex shoots Wren a look. Since when did she ever agree with anything Kian said?

"Talk to us, Nova," says Kian.

"I can't think of anything to say." Nova's eyes are glued to Kian. Dex can only hope it's helping to reassure her.

"Hey N-nova," says Dex, trying to project his words over his fear. There's plenty Nova can talk about. He just has to think of something to get her started. "Remember when we were kids and we stole those rotten berries from the compost and threw them at each other until we were both covered head to toe in juice."

Nova doesn't smile like she usually does at this memory, but she nods. "When I turned up at the infirmary later, Mom screamed because she thought it was blood."

The bear pulls back its head and makes a strange noise. More like a groan than a growl.

"That's perfect, Nova," says Kian. "Now, wave your arms slowly and keep talking, but while you're doing that, start to take small sideways steps, away from the bear. Move very slowly."

Nova attempts the smallest of steps and the bear tilts its head, still not prepared to take its eyes off her. One of the long lines of saliva hanging from its mouth falls and hits the forest floor. At least its jaws are closed. Nova might faint if she sees those giant teeth. Come to think of it, Dex might faint, too.

Dex clears his throat. "Do you remember what happened next, Nova? After your mom realized it was juice, not blood."

Nova takes another step, her shaking hands waving above her head. This time the bear lets her.

"What happened, Nova?" asks Dex. "What did you and your mom see?"

"We saw your dad dragging you past the infirmary by the back of your shirt. He was taking you to the lake to make you wash it all off. Mom asked him to take me with you, but your dad said that would be a reward, not a punishment. He knew we'd have fun if we went together."

"That's right," says Dex, hoping it's possible her next step will go as well as her first two. She's only widened the gap by a small amount, but still, it's progress.

Nova steps again and the bear holds steady.

"Good job, Nova," says Kian. "We're in his territory. But you're showing him we're leaving."

From the corner of his eye, Dex can see that Nova isn't the only one trying to leave. Thom has left his position behind the boulder and is turning to walk away. Perhaps he realizes that if Nova can get back to the group, they're all even prey once more.

"Get back here, Thom!" screeches Felicia, grabbing at the back of his shirt.

Dex holds up his hands, waving at them to keep quiet.

"Let go of me." Thom wrenches his solid frame away from Felicia, sending her curls bouncing. "You can all be good Bounds. Dead Bounds. I honestly don't care anymore. I'm done!"

He bolts into the forest, leaving Felicia gaping.

Dex spins back to find the bear standing on its hind legs with its teeth bared. Its deadly claws swipe the air in front of Nova. The beast is colossal now that it's reached its full height, at least twice as tall as Nova, who's dropped her knife and is crouched over, cowering behind her hands.

"Do it, Wren!" shouts Kian.

She lets go of the pouch on the slingshot and Dex holds his breath as he watches a rock streak through the air toward the bear. This is either going to scare it off or... really piss it off.

Her aim is perfect and the rock hits the bear on the back of the head.

The noise the beast makes is so thunderous, Dex feels it vibrate in his chest. Beating its massive paws in the air, the bear roars as it advances on Nova.

But Wren is too quick for it. She lets fly a volley of rocks, one after the other, pelting the bear on its snout, its chin, its ears. Her movements are lightning fast, her hand dipping into her pocket to retrieve her store of rocks and sending them flinging at her target. Dex's eyes can hardly keep up.

The bear turns its face, looking for the source of the attack and Wren lands two quick shots, a rock catapulting squarely into each of its eyes.

The bear drops down to three paws, using its fourth to swipe at its face as it howls in pain. But Wren doesn't pause her assault, sending rock after rock sailing through the air.

Kian sees his moment. He dashes toward Nova, scooping her up from the ground and whisking her away.

"Let's go," he calls over his shoulder.

Dex doesn't need to be told twice. He'd asked the universe for a third miracle and it was just granted. He doubts they'll be awarded a fourth.

As the grizzly lopes off blindly in one direction, they all follow Kian in the other.

Nova is still cradled in Kian's arms as he runs. Dex wouldn't be surprised if he never lets her go again. Actually, Dex would feel a whole lot more comfortable if Kian never lets her go. His heart is still pounding from the thought of how close he came to losing his friend.

Kian drops his run to a jog, then a brisk walk, bending their direction west. It seems Kian's team is heading to the same place as Dex's.

The cliffs.

Nobody has said a word just yet, everyone too wrapped up in their own thoughts and fears to want to talk.

Even Dex is happy to remain silent as he mulls over the fact that technically this final test hasn't even really started yet. They haven't made it anywhere near a raven's nest to steal the required eggs. And Lana had made it very clear that if they're to score well, they aren't supposed to let the other team know about their task. Plus, the other team is going to try to sabotage them.

Dex can't imagine Kian trying to sabotage anyone, especially a team with Nova on it. Just something to be aware of, he supposes. The others in his team might try to pull some kind of stunt.

"Should we look for Thom?" asks Felicia, her words sounding like a foreign noise in the silence of the forest.

"Oh." Dex had forgotten about him.

Kian stops and sets Nova down. She brushes herself off and stretches out her back, looking more like the old Nova.

"He could be anywhere," says Kian. "Looking for him would be the same as quitting our task. Do we want to do that?"

Felicia bites down on her bottom lip, seeming to be considering that as an option.

"He ran off," says Wren, fidgeting with the pendant she wears around her neck. "He'll be headed back to the lab for sure. All he has to do is go downhill. He can't get lost. Kian's right. We should stick to the task."

"Again!" Dex shakes his head. "You did it again!"

"What?" asks Wren, raising a brow at him.

"You agreed with Kian. What's going on here?" He looks to Kian who gives him the hint of a smile. "Is this part of your task or something? You two never agree on anything."

"That's not true," says Kian. "We agree on things. Sometimes. And no, it's not part of our task."

"Well, I vote we look for Thom." Felicia crosses her arms as she steers the conversation back to her original question. "All those in favor, raise your hand."

All hands remain firmly by their sides, except for Felicia whose hand is waving as she looks at each of them.

"Great," she huffs, shoving back her curls as they flop over her face. "Some Bounds you're all going to make, leaving someone for dead."

"He's fine," says Fern. "Wren's right. He can't get lost heading back. Callix has probably already picked him up by now. Let's just get these eggs and get out of here."

"You need eggs as well?" asks Shiloh.

Fern slaps a hand over her mouth, realizing she said too much. So much for keeping their task secret.

"As well?" asks Dex. "You said *as well*. Are you collecting raven's eggs, too?"

"I'm not supposed to tell you." Shiloh turns a shade of pink. "I already said too much, and that was an accident."

A noise in the bushes behind them has Nova jumping. She clutches Kian's arm.

"It's just a rabbit," says Fern, leaning to one side and squinting.

"How about we work as one larger team for now?" Kian wraps an arm around Nova. "At least until we find a raven's nest."

"You don't need to convince me." Dex takes a step forward and waves his stump in the air. "I mean, I know there's less of me for a bear to eat but I reckon I'd still be pretty delicious."

Kian shakes his head and smiles. "Yeah, real delicious."

Dex pokes out his tongue at his cousin, stopping short of making a crack about how Nova is clearly the preferred bear snack. It's way too soon for that.

"Let's get moving," says Fern. "The sooner we get those eggs, the sooner we can get back to the lab."

"So, we're not going to look for Thom then?" Felicia pouts, stopping short of stamping her foot.

"No, Felicia." Wren doesn't hide her eye roll. "We're not going to look for Thom."

Kian takes the lead, this time with Nova walking closely behind him. Wren takes up the rear, her slingshot at the ready.

Dex drops back in line to walk in front of her, feeling safer to know she's nearby.

So much has already happened on this task.

Danger. Decisions. Defiance.

Perhaps his father knew exactly what he was doing when he set such a dangerous task. It's impossible to hide your true personality under times of intense stress.

Surely, things can't get any worse from this point on?

Although, something in his gut tells him that they absolutely can.

WREN

*W*ren looks at the six people walking ahead of her, wondering how it's possible she's come to care for them. Well, perhaps not all of them. Felicia's not someone she thinks she'll ever care for. It's a shame she didn't run off with Thom instead of trying to stop him and almost killing Nova in the process.

Dex is keeping close, as usual. The only one in his group who hadn't left Nova for dead. But that doesn't surprise Wren. He didn't leave her for dead either when she'd arrived in Askala.

It's a shame his mother didn't live long enough to see her son grow up. Wren's certain she would have been proud of him. Prouder than his father seems to be.

But Wren already knew she liked Dex. And Nova. Kian's the one who's taken her by surprise in the last few days. Annoyingly, this is something Dex seems to have noticed. She'll have to make more of an effort to disagree with Kian when Dex is around. Can't have anyone thinking her heart has gone soft.

What's most frustrating about all of this is that she now officially cares about three people in Askala. Which is one more than the total number of people she cares about in the Outlands.

Cy and Phoenix.

The thought of them tugs at her heart. They feel so far away.

What are they doing? Are they thinking of her? Do they miss her?

Her fingertips flutter to her pendant as she wonders if Phoenix is still wearing his matching one? Their promise to each other that they'll always remain connected. Except she's not feeling particularly connected to him right now. She still loves him, though. That will never change.

Before she came to Askala, she didn't think any of the people who lived here were capable of feeling love. How could they, when they so cruelly refused to share what they have with the rest of the world?

But it's become clear that's not true. She's never witnessed a love as powerful as the one shared by Kian and Nova. He'd have swapped places with her in front of that bear if he could have.

Would anyone do that for Wren? She's not even sure Phoenix or Cy would put their hand up for that.

Dex turns to check she's still following behind and throws her a smile.

"Nearly there," he says.

She nods, realizing the sad truth that the new friends she's found here would be far more likely to sacrifice themselves for her than anyone back home.

Friends. Such a strange word. And not one she ever expected would apply to herself.

But she can't deny that's what these people have become to her. Which is throwing everything she ever believed into question. How can Askala be evil when it's managed to produce people capable of such generosity and kindness?

They break through some trees and Wren sees they're standing on top of a rocky cliff.

She gasps as she looks down on the thick green canopy of the forest below, keeping a safe distance from the edge. It's like some kind of blanket covering their ravaged Earth. And it stretches all the way to the horizon. There's nothing like this in the Outlands. Trees back home are used for fuel and to build shelter. And they're in short supply. Phoenix's eyes would fall out of his head if he could see what she's looking at right now.

"You okay?" asks Dex, coming up next to her. "You look like you're crying."

She blinks, wondering if she actually is.

"It's beautiful," she breathes.

Dex opens his mouth to say something but seems to change his mind.

"It's like we're sitting on a cloud," she says. "Look at all those trees."

"We're doing what we can to heal the Earth." Dex points to a flock of birds, flying in a vee formation. "Slowly, it's working. We're finding new species all the time that we'd thought had gone extinct."

"Nobody in the Outlands respects the planet like this," she says. "Nobody."

Dex nods. "Are you starting to see why we have to protect what we have here? Why we can't just let everyone in?"

Wren's spine stiffens and she shakes herself back to reality. "The trees are beautiful, but you choose them over people. I'll never understand that."

"We choose life over death," says Nova, stepping forward. "Sacrifices have to be made for the greater good. In time, hopefully we can share that with more people."

Wren's brows shoot up. "Well, that we can agree on."

"Thanks for what you did out there." Nova smiles shyly at her, then without warning she wraps her arms around Wren. "You saved my life."

Wren pats Nova awkwardly on the back, wondering how long she's going to have to endure this hug. People don't hug in the Outlands. It's weird.

"She won't let go until you hug her back," Dex laughs.

Nova giggles. "He's right."

"Fine." Wren squeezes Nova back, not enjoying the experience, but not entirely hating it either.

"I'm glad you came here," says Nova, letting go at last. "I liked you the moment I first saw you. Even if you were a little bit…"

"A little bit what?" Wren steps back to regain her personal space.

"Rough," says Nova, seeming to settle on a word at last.

"She means rude," says Felicia. "Now, are we getting on with this test or what?"

"We do have a test to do," says Kian, lying down on his belly and peering over the edge of the cliff.

Wren swallows, hoping he doesn't fall.

"We should split back into our teams," says Fern in a loud voice, clearly hoping that if Callix has hidden another camera on them she'll be heard.

"We already know both teams have been tasked with collecting eggs from a raven's nest," says Nova. "Perhaps we can work together for the moment and figure out what to do with the eggs once we actually have them?"

Felicia shakes her head. "Sorry, Nova. But I don't trust you."

Wren lets out a laugh before she can stop herself. "You don't trust *Nova?* Have you actually met Nova? She's the most trustworthy person on this planet."

"She's not on my team," says Felicia, flicking her curls. "I'm not supposed to trust her."

"Oh, I get it," says Dex. "You've been told we're trying to sabotage you, haven't you?"

Felicia hesitates, then shakes her head. "It's none of your business what we've been told."

Dex looks to Wren and she gives him a quick nod to confirm his suspicions. Callix didn't really expect them to believe they'd sabotage each other, did he?

"I can see one nest within reach," says Kian, still leaning over the edge of the cliff. "It's not going to be easy to get to, but if we make a chain, we might be able to just do it."

"That's our team's nest," says Felicia positioning herself behind Kian and holding out her hands. "Kian saw it first. You guys will have to find your own."

"What do you want us to make the chain from, Kian?" asks Shiloh, smiling at Felicia.

"People," says Kian, sitting up. "If the seven of us hold hands, we should be able to get far enough down the cliff to reach the nest."

"Seven?" asks Shiloh. "But we only have four in our team. You mean…"

"Yes, that's what I mean." Kian stands up and dusts himself off. "We either work together and get what eggs we can to divide up, or we don't get any. Your choice."

"But no raven has eight eggs at once," whines Felicia. "How about we take four and they can have whatever's left."

"So Bound of you," says Dex. "Thank you for asking us to do equal work and then giving us your leftovers."

"Isn't that exactly what you do with the pteropods?" asks Wren, with a smirk.

She watches as six mouths fall open. Clearly, she hit a nerve.

"Well, it's true!" She holds up the palms of her hands. "Sorry!"

"Can we just focus on the task?" asks Fern. "It's afternoon now. I really don't want to have to spend the night out here."

"She's right," says Kian. "Come over this way. I'll show you where the nest is."

He leads them over to a section of the cliff a bit further away. "If you lie on your belly and lean out, you should be able to see it."

Wren stays back, happy to let the others take a look.

"See, over there," says Kian, pointing.

"I don't see it." Fern is leaning right out and Wren's belly twists at the sight. One false move and she could slip.

"Under that ledge." Nova is pointing now. "You can see the corner of it just poking out a bit."

"Oh. I see it now," says Fern.

"You going to have a look, Wren?" Dex sits up and turns to face her.

"I'm good." She wipes the sweat beading on her brow, avoiding his gaze. "I'll take your word for it."

"I don't believe it." Dex grins at her as he shakes his head in disbelief.

"What?" She crosses her arms, trying to ignore the rapid beat of her heart.

"You're scared of heights." He's laughing now, thoroughly enjoying himself at her expense. "Our great fearless warrior girl is actually afraid of something."

"I am not!" She takes a small step forward and attempts a smile. "I don't need to look. If you say the nest is there, I believe you."

"Come here and prove it then." Dex holds out his hand. "I won't let you fall."

"I told you. I'm good over here, thanks." She knows he's teasing her, but she really wishes he'd let this go before the others notice.

"Leave her alone, Dex," says Nova. "She doesn't have to prove anything. Don't you think she's done enough already?"

Wren smiles. "Thank you, Nova."

"I love it," says Dex, clearly not ready to let this go. "I've watched you kill a leatherskin and blind a polar grizzly with little more than your bare hands and you're scared of a cliff."

"I'm not scared of it." Wren marches toward the edge and grinds to a halt as bile races up the back of her throat and her head spins.

Nova jumps to her feet and leads Wren away from the edge, shooting Dex a stern look.

Wren draws in a deep breath, trying to regain her composure. Damn it! She knew as soon as she heard the word *cliff* that this was going to happen. Cy must have told her a million times that it never pays to let your enemies know your weakness. It's the number one rule in any battle.

But is this still a battle given these people stopped being her enemies a little while ago now?

"How are we going to reach that nest exactly?" asks Fern.

"We'll position ourselves at intervals down the rockface," says Kian. "As long as we can reach the person behind us then we'll be able to pass the eggs up the chain. The person at the end should just be able to reach the nest. When we're in position, if we can all join hands then we know we have it right. And we'll be able to make sure we help each other get back up."

"Umm." Dex waves his missing hand in the air. "Are you forgetting something?"

"You still have an arm we can hold onto." Kian shakes his head at his cousin. "I have full confidence you can do this or I wouldn't have suggested it."

Dex seems to grow a foot taller at the compliment and nods his head.

"It's a great plan, Kian," says Shiloh, blinking up at him and Wren feels like she might vomit now rather than faint. That girl has it so bad and Kian has no idea whatsoever. It would be amusing if it weren't so pathetic. Shiloh doesn't stand a chance.

"Wren's one of our strongest," says Dex. "She should stay at the top."

"You're just saying that because she's scared of heights," says Fern.

"No, I'm not." He shoots Wren an apologetic smile. "I'm saying it because I feel guilty for teasing her about being scared of heights."

This makes Wren smile. "If it's okay with everyone, I think I'd like to stay at the top?"

"Oh," says Fern, slapping her forehead. "I get it now. You're not really scared of heights, are you? This is you trying to sabotage us. If you're at the top, then as soon as you get the eggs, you're going to run off with them, aren't you?"

Wren lets out a sigh. "No, Fern. I'm really not such a fan of heights. You can tie me to a rock if it would make you feel any better. I'm not going to run off with anything."

Fern narrows her eyes. "Nope, sorry. I don't believe you. You're not scared of anything. You can't possibly be scared of this."

Going to the edge of the cliff, Fern leans out, her fine hair catching the breeze.

Wren winces, feeling all the blood leave her face as Fern raises a foot and waves it over the edge. "Stop it, Fern."

"Oh, look, I'm going to fall." Fern laughs, waggling her leg over the edge of oblivion, watching Wren's reaction closely.

"It's not funny." Wren holds out a shaking hand. "Come back."

"You can't fool me," says Fern, with a cockiness Wren hasn't heard before. She seems proud that finally she can do something Wren can't. "I know this is a trick so you can get the eggs. It's just a—"

Her words are cut short as the largest raven Wren's ever seen darts out of a nearby tree and heads straight for Fern, letting out a shrill caw as it swoops.

Wren reaches for her slingshot but it catches in her pocket and she can't get it set up in time.

Fern pulls back her leg too quickly and overbalances, causing her other leg to slip on the loose rocks. As she tries to regain traction, the raven dives down, sending Fern toppling.

"Fern!" Wren pushes down her fear and lunges forward. She

takes several quick steps until she's at the edge of the cliff, Kian and Nova beside her.

They're too late to save her, but not too late to witness Fern plummeting, a deathly scream piercing the silence as she grapples with the empty space above her like one of the air currents might save her.

A scream of her own leaves Wren's lungs and she steps back, crashing directly into Dex. He wraps his arms around her and draws her back from the edge.

"That was my fault." Wren buries her face in Dex's firm chest as he holds her close in an embrace that feels altogether different to the one she shared earlier with Nova.

"It's not your fault," he murmurs into her ear. "It was nobody's fault, except her own. You weren't trying to sabotage her. She got paranoid."

There are sobs echoing around them as the shock of what just happened sets in. Wren lifts her head, but the display of grief she witnesses is too much and she returns to the safety of Dex's chest.

But the sound of crying gets too much after a few minutes, and she breaks away.

"That's why I don't like heights," she says, finding her voice and drying her tears. "If an animal attacks then at least you have a chance. Fern had no chance with a drop like that."

Nova leaves the safety of Kian's arms to stand beside her. "It all happened so quickly."

"Maybe completing this test isn't such a great idea," Wren suggests, realizing she's looking to Kian as she speaks. Their unofficial leader. Their strength. The only one of them who doesn't have tears pouring down his face right now.

If he falls apart, she doesn't know what they'll do.

"We have to complete the test." His face is lined with pain, but his strength is shining through his eyes. "This can't all be for nothing."

"We'll all be at the same disadvantage if we pull out now," says Felicia, looking so distressed that even her curls seem to have fallen. "Wren's right. This isn't a good idea."

Kian sighs, and Wren hopes he's not about to lose his cool.

"Don't you get it?" he asks Felicia. "It's not about advantage or disadvantage. This isn't a competition. It never has been. Callix can make us all Unbound if he likes. It's rare, but it's happened before in Provings. We've come this far. We have to complete the test and get back to the lab before nightfall. Besides, we need those eggs. Askala is counting on us."

There are several nods and sighs as they accept what he has to say. The test must go on. They really don't have a choice.

"Will our chain be long enough now?" asks Shiloh. "Without F-Fern."

"It will be if Wren's prepared to stand on the first footing down from the ledge instead of on top of it." He looks at her and she tries her best to hold his gaze. "Is that okay, Wren?"

She nods, even though nothing about that sounds remotely okay.

"Let's go," he says. "This won't be any easier in an hour than it is now."

"Who's going to go down the bottom?" asks Nova.

"We need our lightest person," he says. "Shiloh?"

Shiloh swallows as she nods. "I can do it, Kian."

"Right. Shiloh first, then—"

"I'd feel safer if you were right behind me." Shiloh blinks up at him.

Kian gives her a quick nod. "Okay. Shiloh, then me, then Nova. Then… Dex, then Felicia then Wren. Everyone good with that?"

Wren tries to push down the apprehension she feels. She really would rather face a polar grizzly than attempt what Callix has set for them to do here. But she can't let the team down. Especially after what happened to Fern.

They assemble themselves into position and Kian takes hold of Shiloh's hand as she climbs down from the edge to the rocky outcrop just below. Having just witnessed what happens if things go wrong, Wren is certain that everyone's holding their breath, just like she is.

Shiloh disappears from sight and Kian takes his first step down, holding onto Nova with his free hand. She soon follows, taking hold of Dex's stump as he holds out his hand to Felicia.

Wren swallows. She can't possibly pull out now. It's going to be a stretch with six people as it is. There's no way they can do it with five.

Placing her palm on her pendant she shoots a quick glance east, thinking of Phoenix and Cy. She can do this. For them. She can do it for Fern. She can do it for her new friends, too.

She holds on to Felicia as she leans over the edge of the cliff and gets her first glance of the others. A human chain inching its way toward its target.

But she's not the only one who can see them. It soon becomes clear that the raven is just as aware of what's happening here. It's circling overhead, readying itself to dive.

"Watch out! Raven swooping!" Wren warns, knowing that the surprise of a bird attack can often be worse than the attack itself.

Everyone steadies their footing and breaks hands to shelter their heads.

Wren tucks her pendant into her shirt, not wanting any reflections off the metallic surface to draw undue attention to herself. It's going to be hard enough to hold her nerve here without a bird trying to scare her away. And there's no way she's going to be able to use her slingshot when she's busy using her two hands to hold on for her life. Besides, even if she were alone, this can't be one of Cy's ravens. They don't nest in Askala.

The bird swoops, flies away and swoops again, coming down on Shiloh's shielded head, given she's the one closest to the nest.

"I'm okay!" she calls up the cliff, although Wren can see blood on her hands. That bird means business.

"Keep moving," shouts Kian. "We're almost there. Everyone's doing so well."

Wren feels the pressure on her hand as Felicia tries to move further down the cliff.

"You can do it, Wren," says Felicia, smiling up at her. "You can do anything."

Wren looks down at Felicia, trying to figure out where the sarcasm lies in her words, but fails to find any.

"I mean it," says Felicia. "You're braver than all of us put together. You can do this."

Wren nods at her, wondering how Felicia managed to hide this pleasant side to her personality until now.

Lying on her stomach, she draws in a deep breath as she lifts her foot over the edge, searching for where she's supposed to put it.

"Just a little further down," Felicia's voice floats up to her.

She edges herself down a little more and her foot touches a solid surface.

"That's it!" Felicia sounds excited now. "Just a little more and you'll hit a rock. It'll hold you."

Closing her eyes, Wren does as she's told. If she can't see where she is, maybe she can fool her brain into thinking she's on solid ground. Her foot finds the rock and she tests it for strength, deciding it might just do as Felicia says and hold her weight.

"Good job!" calls Kian. "I think we're right. You can release hands now if you feel it's safe."

"Are you right for me to let go?" Wren asks Felicia, not daring to look down.

Felicia breaks their hold and Wren lifts her face to the sky, concentrating on her breathing. Fainting now wouldn't exactly go down very well. She'd topple off the cliff, taking any number of her companions down with her.

She sees a shadow about to swoop again.

"Raven!" she calls.

There's a shriek from Shiloh.

Then a pause.

"I'm okay!" Shiloh shouts up to them. "I'm about to take the first egg. I can feel it. There's a few of them."

"You need to hurry," says Dex. "That raven isn't happy."

Wren's urge to see what's happening fights her desire to pretend she's standing on solid ground. Ultimately, her curiosity wins out and her eyes spring open.

Focusing on the people, rather than the steep drop below, she sees Shiloh pass an egg to Kian, who quickly sends it up the chain to Nova, then Dex. It's only small. Pale blue in color, its speckles are glinting in the afternoon sun.

Felicia takes the egg and holds it up for Wren.

Which means she has to release one of her hand holds.

Wincing as she lets go and takes the egg, Wren reminds herself not to squeeze too hard. If she breaks it, this will all be for nothing. Although, at least she'll still have the shell, which is what this is all about.

Reaching up, she places the egg on top of the cliff, making sure it doesn't roll right back off.

This process is repeated four more times, with several more swoops from the raven, and shrieks by Shiloh until she announces that the nest is empty.

Five eggs. Great. An odd number. This reminds Wren of their first test with the blocks. It was like Callix knew they weren't going to be able to retrieve a number of eggs that would divide evenly by their teams. Because there's no way they're taking Felicia's suggestion and keeping four eggs, leaving Dex and Nova with only one.

"Time to move on up," calls Kian.

Wren reaches down for Felicia's hand and works her way back up to the top of the cliff, being careful to avoid the eggs nestled safely on top.

The relief that surges through her body when she makes it to solid ground is instant and intense. She lies there for a few beats of her heart, grateful to have made it.

"Hold up for a moment," she calls down, letting go of Felicia's hand. "I need to move the eggs."

Quickly scooping them up, she carries them carefully to a tuft of grass a few feet away and settles them down.

"You're not running off with them, are you?" calls Felicia.

"Not a chance," she calls back. "These eggs belong to all of us. We're one team now."

She takes a deep breath and returns to the edge of the cliff, catching the hint of a scowl on Felicia's face.

Putting out her hand, she hauls her up.

Felicia scrambles off behind her, clearly just as keen as Wren was to set foot on solid ground once more.

Wren reaches back down for Dex and helps him up. Together, she and Dex lift Nova back up, followed by Kian.

"Shiloh's bleeding badly," Kian whispers when he gets to the top. "We need to be careful."

Wren looks down at Shiloh's outstretched hands. They're dripping with blood. That raven's beak had been sharp. Too sharp. They're going to need to find some mangrove pine sap to heal her so she doesn't get an infection.

Nine have already become six. There's no way they're going to end up as five.

Kian gently lifts Shiloh up, reaching down to grab her by her wrists instead of her hands.

"You did an amazing job," says Wren, wondering if she'd misjudged Shiloh out on the water when she'd snapped at Dex. People say all kinds of stupid things every day. She really shouldn't hold one comment against her.

Shiloh beams at Wren before she sits down, allowing Nova to fuss over her hands by tearing strips off the bottom of her shirt to soak up the blood.

"Where are the eggs?" asks Kian, looking around.

"Just over here." Wren leads him to the tuft of grass, her brow furrowing as she realizes it must be the wrong one. "That's strange…"

"Where's Felicia?" asks Dex, bounding up to them. "She's not here."

Wren and Kian look around, but Dex is right. She's nowhere to be seen.

Kian gasps as his hand flies to his brow. "She's gone."

"It gets worse," says Wren, feeling her whole world drop out of her stomach. "She's taken the eggs with her."

NOVA

$\mathcal{N}$ova straightens as she looks around the scrubby bush. "Surely Felicia wouldn't do such a thing."

She glances at Shiloh, who's cradling her bloody hands. They need to be focusing on helping her, not on getting the eggs back. They've already lost Fern, for Terra's sake!

"I knew I should've finished the job when I had my hands around her throat," says Wren as she flexes her shoulders.

Kian finishes the full turn he just completed. "It's true. Felicia's taken the eggs."

"You know what?" Wren grabs the slingshot out of her back pocket. "I reckon I can track her."

Dex leaps in front of her. "No, Wren. You can't."

Wren arches a brow. "You don't think I can track her?"

"Of course you can track her. Is there anything you can't do? I meant you can't go after her. It would be a mistake."

Wren pauses, sizing Dex up. She looks like she's deciding whether she should go around him or go over the top of him. "She can't do something like that and get away with it."

Dex shakes his head. "She thinks she's won by taking the eggs. But believe me, there'll be consequences."

Felicia will be Unbound.

Wren's hand flexes around her slingshot. She's obviously weighing up what her next move will be.

Nova steps up next to Dex. "Plus, I could use your help right now, Wren. I need you to show me how to get the sap."

Nova glances at Shiloh, knowing Wren will notice the way the girl's shoulders are hunched protectively around her hands. Hopefully, she'll notice how pale her skin is and how shallow her breathing is. Shiloh's in pain. She needs help, fast.

Shiloh looks up. "Please, Wren?" She holds up her hands, showing how she's already bled through the flimsy strips of fabric Nova wrapped around them. The jagged gashes gouged into her skin track across the back of her hands, but several extend up her forearms.

Wren tucks the slingshot back in her pocket. "We'll be back in ten."

Nova relaxes and she glimpses a slight smile on Dex's face. Wren is probably totally unaware of how instinctive it is for her to protect and care for others.

Kian's lips settle into a firm line. "I'll come with you. The sooner we head back, the better."

Nova's about to smile her thanks when Shiloh speaks.

"Kian, will you stay with me? You can use your slingshot if the raven comes back."

Nova grits her teeth. Shiloh's voice has developed a tremor and her eyes seemed to have doubled in her face.

Kian glances at Nova, looking torn. For the briefest of moments, Nova considers telling Shiloh they won't be long. But she stops herself. She would never be someone who would ask Kian to choose between his duty and his heart.

Nova forces the smile to climb up her face. "You stay. Shiloh needs to feel safe."

Grabbing Wren's arm, Nova tugs her away before Kian can

respond. She doesn't want to see the battle playing out of Kian's face.

Or worse. She doesn't want to see relief now that he hasn't had to make a choice.

Nova releases Wren's arm, surprised she didn't shake her off, and they strike down the rocky slope.

Wren glances over her shoulder. "I noticed a mangrove pine not far away. This won't take long," she says loudly.

Nova's brows go up. Wren is making sure the others hear her.

Then Wren leans in closer to Nova. "You know, you're not doing yourself any favors by letting Miss Eyelashes take advantage of Kian's protective streak."

Nova opens her mouth to point out Shiloh's genuinely injured, but she snaps it shut again. Wren isn't talking about that.

She's actually glad Wren's noticed Shiloh's tactics. And it's nice to be honest about it for a change.

But it doesn't mean she's going to do anything about it. "I trust him."

"I can see why. You're the center of his universe. It's Shiloh I don't trust." Wren snorts. "People do some pretty extreme stuff in the name of love."

Wren says the last word with such derision that Nova's about to ask where she's learned such a reaction but Wren stops, indicating the thick trunk of a mangrove pine beside them.

She holds out her hand. "Pass me your knife."

Nova does as she's told and watches as Wren grips it tightly. With several short, sharp movements, she hacks away at the bark of the tree.

"First thing is to clear away a section of bark."

She exposes a smooth, pale section of timber. Nova nods, focusing closely so she can learn how to do this.

"It means we get down to the sap wood." This time, Wren

changes the angle of the knife in her hand and hacks out several vee shaped notches.

Nova watches, wide-eyed, as almost instantly the deep red sap leaks from the gashes. She looks around for something to catch it.

Wren's doing the same. "They bleed worse than polar grizzlies," she mutters. She looks back to Nova. "I think you're going to have to use your hands."

Nova doesn't question the suggestion, stepping up and cupping her hands beneath the oozing sap. It trickles down the pale sapwood and into her hands, smelling strongly of resin. "You're amazing, Wren. This is going to make all the difference to Shiloh's wounds."

Wren leans a shoulder against the tree. "So, what's your strategy with her?"

"Strategy? Ah, spread the sap over her wounds and get her back to the labs as quickly as possible. She'll need to be bandaged properly."

Wren rolls her eyes. "Ah, I meant with Kian. You can't just let her try and move in on your man."

Nova flushes, although she's not really sure why. She's considered Kian 'hers' long before their feelings morphed beyond best friends.

Then why doesn't she feel she has a right to stake her claim?

She shakes her head. "I'm not going to do anything."

"And here I thought you were in love with Kian..."

Nova jerks back only to quickly press her hands against the tree again. "I am!"

Wren shrugs, her shoulder scraping against the bark. "Not enough to fight for him."

Anger flashes through Nova. "I have no right to fight for him. Not until I'm Bound!"

Doesn't Wren see? Trust and faith are all Nova has right now.

Wren shakes her head. "Bound isn't the measure of whether you deserve love, Nova. And if pod boy doesn't realize what he has, then...then I'll..." Her hand flexes around the slingshot at her side, and Nova's reminded of the hard lines of muscle she knows are hidden beneath Wren's shirt.

Nova relaxes, her lips twitching up into a smile. "You're a good friend, Wren."

Wren's eyes fly to Nova's in shock. She pushes away from the tree, all of a sudden full of edgy energy. "Yeah, well..." She glances down at the sap that's collected in Nova's cupped hands. "I reckon we've got enough."

Nova hides the fact her smile just grew. "I agree. Let's get back."

The walk back is a brisk one with Nova focused on the precious sticky cargo she's carrying. The sap is thick enough that it won't drip out of her hands immediately, but she can already feel it oozing between her fingers, no matter how hard she pushes them together.

They reach the plateau at the top of the cliff within a few minutes. Nova almost trips when she sees Kian and Shiloh sitting together on the rocky soil.

The one who holds her heart is sitting beside Shiloh, his arm around her shoulders. Shiloh has rested her head on him as she cups her bloodied hands to her chest.

Wren reaches out to steady Nova. "Yeah, makes me sick, too."

Nova doesn't answer, although the truth is, her gut is churning like an angry sea. When they're both Bound, she'll stake her claim.

As Nova kneels down beside them, Kian shoots her a look full of helplessness. Relief floods her—Kian's obviously uncomfortable with the position he's put in.

Nova sends him a small smile. She should never have let her

insecurities have her doubting their connection. They've loved each other since before they could speak.

Nova leans over Shiloh. "Here, let's get that bleeding under control."

Shiloh extends her hands, her arms trembling. Guilt punches Nova in the solar plexus as she looks at the pale girl, a fine sheen of sweat glistening on her skin. Shiloh would be in too much pain to be trying to come between Kian and her. It's probably the last thing on Shiloh's mind right now.

Realizing her hands are full, Nova looks to Kian. "Do you think you could take the bandages off?"

Kian nods, and something around Nova's heart unwinds as he removes his arm from around Shiloh's shoulders. Gently, he unwraps the blood-soaked strips of hemp that have done little to stem the flow of thick, dark red.

Dex steps forward. "We've been trying to keep her talking, but she's getting quieter and quieter." He shrugs. "I was just telling her the story of when you fell in the pod pool and Kian had to fish you out."

"Can you put one of your hands out for me, Shiloh?" Nova asks. She rolls her eyes for Shiloh's benefit. "Not my proudest moment."

Dex chuckles, having no doubt been working on keeping the mood light the entire time Nova and Wren were gone. "Admittedly, not your best look with all those wriggly overgrown slugs in your hair, but certainly one of Kian's more heroic moments."

Nova pauses for the briefest of seconds. They'd only been twelve and Nova was in near hysterics at the sensation of hundreds of gelatinous bodies sliding over her skin. They'd felt like they were trying to wriggle their way into her mouth, her ears, her nose.

"What did Kian do?" Shiloh asks in a whisper.

Nova starts to spread the thick, tacky sap over the wounds on Shiloh's arms. Dex's strategy to distract Shiloh is working.

Nova smiles as she remembers the moment. "He single-handedly hauled me out of the pool. Then he spent the next twenty minutes peeling pods off me, studying each one, thanking me for letting him get a close look at how healthy the population was."

Dex chuckles. "And then he insisted on taking you to the lake so you could wash off."

Shiloh glances at Kian. "Oh."

Except Kian is staring at nowhere but Nova. "You looked like a wet angel," he whispers.

Dex winks at her and Nova ducks her head, focusing on her task. Of all the stories he could've told, Dex chose the one where she and Kian first discovered the depths of their physical attraction. That was the last time they went alone to the lake. Clothes plastered to wet skin was far too much temptation.

First Wren, now Dex. That's two friends determined to protect her. How did she get so lucky?

The sap slides on easily thanks to the blood covering Shiloh's hands, and it doesn't take long for them to both have a thin coating and each of the cuts to be covered.

"Ah, that's better." Shiloh's whole body relaxes.

Nova stands, finding Wren right beside her. She has her hands on her hips as she watches Shiloh closely. "That's the anesthetic effect the sap has. It should keep the pain under control enough that you can walk back to the lab."

"Thank you, Nova." Her gaze flickers. "And Wren."

Kian moves beside Nova and she relishes his nearness. "Are you okay to walk, Shiloh? We need to get going."

Shiloh goes to stand and Kian steps forward, about to assist her, when Wren quickly slides between them.

She tucks her hands beneath Shiloh's arms and helps her to her feet. "There you go, Shiloh." She steps back once Shiloh has steadied herself. "I know how important it is to you to be independent," she adds sweetly.

"Ah, yeah. Sure." Shiloh looks around, her cheeks slightly pink. "Felicia didn't come back."

"No, she didn't," growls Wren.

"Oh well. At least the water supply will benefit from the shells," Shiloh says to Kian, trying for a smile.

"What did you say?" asks Dex in surprise.

"The eggs. We need their shells to neutralize the acid levels in the water supply."

Nova glances at Dex, finding his eyebrows are just as high as hers. "No wonder they were trying to sabotage us," she breathes.

Wren frowns. "Sabotage you? What are you talking about? Fern was the one who wouldn't believe I'm not keen on heights."

Dex winces. "She was so determined to prove you were lying."

Nova rubs her temples. "We were told we needed the eggs for their yolks. To feed the pteropods."

Shock slams across Kian's face. "We needed different parts of the eggs, and yet he didn't tell us. He had us believing we're adversaries, when all along, we were working toward the same thing. There were enough eggs for both teams to succeed."

Everyone is silent as the knowledge filters down into their consciousness. They were supposed to break the rules and talk to each other? Was this test really about working for Askala, despite their personal desires?

It was the ultimate test of kindness and intelligence.

Kian's expression is full of dread. "And we didn't figure it out." He wipes a hand down his face, but his expression stays. "We were supposed to figure it out."

"We just did," offers Shiloh weakly.

"Without any eggs to show for it," mutters Wren darkly.

Shiloh looks away. Everyone is hoping it isn't too little, too late.

"Bloody Callix," Wren huffs. "If that man wasn't so freaking brilliant, he'd be next on my hit list after Felicia. And that coward, Thom."

Dex is cradling his stump. "This is one of those moments where I wish we weren't blood related."

Nova's stomach is a mass of knots. They're about to walk back, two people less, one person injured.

But unlike the pteropod harvest, they haven't returned with four raven eggs like they were tasked to do. Nova wraps her arms around her middle. They won't be proudly flaunting the knowledge that they realized everyone was working toward the same goal.

The good of Askala.

Sweet Terra, did they all just fail?

KIAN

"*I* hate this room," Felicia mutters, as she stares at nowhere but her clasped hands.

Kian takes in the faded walls, the large, chipped table they're all sitting around. He can't say it's his favorite place in Askala, either.

It's weird to think it was only a week ago they were sitting here, waiting for their first test. They were all so nervous, but still a little excited.

They were so naïve...

Now there are three empty seats. Jay. Dead. Fern. Dead. And Thom who still hasn't returned...assumed dead.

Nova reaches out and places her hand over Felicia's tightly wound ones. "It's almost over."

Shiloh leans across the table, her face soft with compassion. The bandages on her hands look clean and dry. It seems the sap is working its magic. "She's right, Felicia. Plus, we need to remember that being Unbound is just as much a privilege as being Bound."

Wren's head is resting on her crossed arms, muffling her

quiet words. "I can't believe you people still try to tell yourself that."

Kian's about to point out that it's the truth, the Unbound are well cared for, when Dex leans forward with a crooked smile. "Telling yourself that actually helps."

Wren snorts, somehow managing to inject the one sound with a whole lot of scorn, but doesn't say anything else.

Silence descends and Kian tries to catch Nova's gaze, but she's let go of Felicia's hands and is preoccupied tracing something on the tabletop. She must sense something, though, because she looks up.

Her blue eyes soften as their gazes connect, but he can't miss the undercurrents of worry there.

Is she worried for Felicia? For Dex? For Wren?

Or is she worried for herself?

Kian wishes he could stand up, circle the table that separates them and take her in his arms. He'd stroke the worry away, whisper her assurances it's going to be okay. That like she said, it's almost over.

When they're both Bound, nothing will stop him from comforting the girl he loves.

He sends her a small smile, knowing it's not much, but hoping it's something.

Nova's lips kick up at the edges, and Kian's heart lightens. Maybe he's helped her hope. Maybe he's shown her that if anyone they care about becomes Unbound, they'll be there to help them through it.

Except then Nova looks away and her mouth drops along with her gaze. Kian resists frowning. They couldn't have stared at each other forever, but why does it feel like she just pulled away?

Kian's confusion only grows when Nova doesn't look back up. It's as if she's not seeking him out. Not wanting his support.

He clenches his hands as he buries them in his lap. It's the pressure of the Proving, nothing more.

Tomorrow this will all be over.

Doubt will no longer exist.

Silence creeps back into the room, as if it had been waiting in the corner, knowing there's no point in leaving. The *tap, tap, tapping* of Wren's foot beneath the table is the only sound.

The moment the door moves, everyone straightens. Kian feels like steel has just been jammed down his spine. This will be Callix and Lana, wanting to talk through today's test.

The one they just failed.

The door slides open, revealing two people standing there. Kian's body freezes in shock as he registers it's not who he thought it would be.

And yet, it's two people who he never thought he'd be so alarmed to see.

His parents; his father, tall and dark haired, and his mother, slender and willowy, smile at the stunned faces staring at them.

They enter and take the two seats at the head of the table.

Dex glances at Kian, the same question stamped across his face as the one ricocheting through Kian's mind. The leader of Askala is running the interview?

His father smiles at each teen in turn, and Kian feels his heart jolt as their gazes connect. His father's eyes seem laden with something, but he has no idea what. Pride? Disappointment? Warning?

But the moment is short-lived, because Magnus moves on, carefully giving each person the same measured look. His father has always valued fairness. He would never be seen to treat his son unequally, even with something as small as a look.

His father glances at his mother, his whole body tense, probably not even conscious of the unspoken emotion that passes between them. They've always been each other's foundation. Kian can almost feel their love bolstering the other.

As he looks back at those waiting around the table, his father clasps his hands. "It is tradition for the leader of Askala to see you on the eve of the Announcement, allowing me the privilege of congratulating you on completing a difficult week." His gaze flickers with pain. "Before we start, I'd like to acknowledge the loss of the two young lives during this Proving, something we haven't had to deal with before. Jay and Fern were loved members of Askala. The grief at their loss has been felt by all. I'm sorry something so unusual occurred during your Proving."

Kian leans forward. "Have you heard from Thom? It must be dark outside by now."

The moment he asks the question, Kian realizes he probably just spoke out of turn. He's failed to remember that right now, he's talking to the leader of Askala, not his father.

His father's eyebrows twitch, in the way they do when he wants to frown but stops himself. "We haven't been able to find Thom."

A small anguished sound slips from Felicia. Her hands look like they're trying to strangle each other.

Kian's mother nods, her face soft with compassion. "This must've been so difficult for all of you."

Kian half expects Wren to jump in with one of her usual remarks, but nobody responds. The loss of Jay and Fern is something none of them will forget easily.

His father clears his throat. "We did want you to know that the eggshells are already being used in the water purification system. Askala thanks you for that."

"And the yolks have been fed to the pods," his mother adds, her gaze flickering to Kian. "We're expecting to see a boost in their reproduction levels in the next few days. After your collection of two full barrels in the first test we're going to have a very healthy population."

Kian almost nods, but he stops himself. Both outcomes are a good thing. Askala can't survive without either.

Wren's hands grasp the edge of the table. "And that makes it worth it? Two lives for four eggs?"

His father slowly turns his head toward her. "And those in the Outlands? What would they die for?"

Wren frowns as she looks away.

As he watches the interaction, Kian fills with conviction. His father's right. Would Wren's people die for their colony? Kian suspects they kill for far less...like for their own selfish survival.

"Wren," his father continues. "We've been watching you with interest. You've made some unusual decisions throughout the Proving."

Wren looks back, angling her chin. "I bet that made it hard to score."

"You've certainly kept Callix busy," he chuckles. "How have you found the Proving?"

"Brutal," Wren retorts, her eyes narrowed.

His father nods, not in the least offended. "They are difficult tests, but they also need to be. How else will we select those with the heart and wisdom to heal our Earth? It's essential that we set the bar high." He angles his head, his eyes bright with curiosity. "Anything else?"

"It was..." Wren glances around the room, seeming to pause for just a heartbeat as her gaze passes Dex. "Eye opening."

"That, it certainly was. I suspect everyone has learned much over the past week."

There's the odd shuffle, but no one responds. Kian notes that Nova has kept her spine straight and her head upright, but her lips look like they've been sewn together.

She also hasn't glanced his way once.

His mother splays her hands on the timber surface of the table. "We'd like to talk to you about the final test. You came together to fight off the bear," she glances at Nova, smiling warmly.

Kian isn't surprised, Nova spent large amounts of time with

his family as they were growing up, drawn to the noise and laughter missing in her only-child life.

"Which is wonderful." She looks around the table. "Do you think you understand what the test was really about?"

Kian stifles the urge to pull away from the table, but he has no way of stopping the heat that stains his cheeks. "We didn't realize we each needed different parts of the egg."

"There was no time," offers Shiloh weakly.

His father strokes his chin, his expression thoughtful, and for the first time in his life, he has no idea what that means.

"Am I going to fail?" Felicia asks, her voice small.

"No one fails the Proving, Felicia." His father says reassuringly. "Becoming Unbound is not a failure. I'm interested to understand why you took the eggs, though."

Felicia seems to crawl within herself. "I did it for Askala. I wanted to get the eggs back, and..." she hesitates, her gaze flickering around the room. "After letting everyone down so many times, I wanted to make sure our team won. Kian found that nest. It didn't seem fair to have to divide up the eggs."

Kian watches his father closely. It's hard to know whether Felicia's telling the truth. It felt like she was taking the eggs purely so she could be the victor who returned with the bounty.

And so she could get out of the forest as quickly as possible.

His father nods, his eyes gentle. "Thank you for your efforts, Felicia."

She peeks up at him. "There's nothing I wouldn't do for Askala."

Apart from go out on a raft. Or face the bear to save Nova. Or stay back to make sure Shiloh was okay.

His mother leans forward. "This was a dangerous Proving. Far more than past years. I have no doubt you were very frightened when you faced the bear, then the raven and the cliffs."

Kian straightens. Did his mother just read his mind? How would she know that?

234

Wren's chair scrapes across the floor. "I knew you were watching us. Where were the cameras this time?"

Dex's face is fighting a frown. He doesn't like the thought, either.

His father nods. "We weren't watching you this time, but we were listening. There were microphones in the handles of the weapons. They allowed us to record what was said."

"You people sure justify a lot in the name of Askala, Magnus," Wren practically growls.

"We need people who will do what it takes to lead our colony, Wren. Callix has chosen tests that reflect that."

Wren crosses her arms and looks away.

Kian wonders at his father's earlier words that Callix would've struggled to score Wren's tests. She consistently did better than any of them.

And yet, she doesn't believe in Askala. If she were to become Bound, would she be like the others—willing to die for what they've worked so hard for?

"Now"—his father places his hands on the table as he pushes himself upright—"we'll leave you to your dinner. You'll need your sleep, particularly considering the High Bound will also be announced tomorrow."

Kian tries not to act surprised, even though those words punch through his chest. With the intensity of the testing, he'd totally forgotten about the announcement of the High Bound. Those who achieve the top ten scores in the Proving over the last generation. He notices his father glance at him. They'll be expecting Kian to be one of them.

Except, despite his best efforts through every moment of the Proving, he must've failed the last test.

His mother stands, too, and their hands clasp together. They speak simultaneously. "May the Proving serve you well."

They head for the door. Kian cranes his neck to see if either of them will turn back for a last look. Maybe give him some small assurance. He thinks his mother's head angles to glance back, but his father places a hand on the small of her back and she straightens. The door *whooshes* closed and they're gone.

Wren stands. "Well, you guys sure know how to throw a party. It's been fun, but I think Magnus is right about one thing. It's dinner, then bed for me."

Kian isn't surprised when Dex stands, too. "That uncle of mine has always been such a wise fellow."

With Wren shaking her head and Dex shrugging and grinning—probably the only person who could grin at a time like this, they both exit the room.

Felicia drags herself to the door. "I'm outta here. I'm going to eat dinner with a full complement of fingers while I can."

Kian's gut clenches. Although Felicia was trying for humor, the flatness in her eyes is nothing but serious and sad. His hand lifts helplessly as she drags her heavy heart through the door. What can he say to her, when she's probably right?

The prospect of someone he knows becoming Unbound, even Felicia with her frustrating ways, is far more difficult than he ever imagined. How can they tell Felicia this is a privilege when she's about to lose a finger, along with her ability to have children?

Shaking the thought from his head, Kian realizes exactly how much this Proving has rattled him. A week ago, he'd never have thought like that. Flexing his shoulder blades, he tells himself tomorrow can't come soon enough.

Bounds don't have doubts. They've sworn themselves to protect Earth—there are no gray areas when you know this fight is bigger than just yourself.

A chair scrapes back, the sound loud in the almost empty room. "I'll see you guys in the dining room?" Shiloh asks the question as though she's talking to both Kian and Nova, but her gaze rests solely on Kian.

Kian nods, keeping a frown from tightening his features. Shiloh's single-minded focus on him is becoming unsettling.

He turns away before she's slipped out of the room. By tomorrow it won't matter, he and Nova will be together. Surely, Shiloh will accept it then.

Glad to have Nova alone, even if it's only for a few minutes, Kian finds himself smiling as his gaze seeks her out.

Except Nova is standing, already only a few feet away from the door.

It's almost like she's...avoiding him.

He shoots to his feet. "Nova."

She stops, her body practically trembling with tension. Slowly, she turns back. "Kian..."

Something has him leaving his place by the table and striding toward her. Maybe it was her tone, sounding strangely hollow. Maybe it's the fact she hasn't taken a step in his direction.

She puts up her hand. "Please, stop."

Bewildered, Kian halts like he just hit a force field. "I don't understand."

Nova's gaze slowly rises to meet his, and when it does, he gasps at what he sees.

Anguish. Pure, soul wrenching anguish.

He takes another step forward. "Nova..."

But she shakes her head, her hand remaining in the air. "It's too much, Kian. Until we know for sure, this"—she indicates the distance between them—"is easier."

So he wasn't imagining it. The final test has rattled Nova, when her faith in herself was as fractured as the cliff they had to scale.

Kian holds himself where he is, although the space between them feels like a chasm. He never considered the Proving could come between them. He grits his teeth.

It's not going to.

"Tomorrow, Nova. You'll be in my arms, in the same way you've been in my heart for as long as I've known you."

Nova's eyes slam shut, her face twisted in pain as she shakes her head. "The tests. The fact that I couldn't choose who deserved the stitches. That I didn't want to." Her hands open out, full of helplessness. She gazes at him, her eyes deep pools of pain. "The fact that I can't be optimistic right now, that I don't have faith, tells me I can't be Bound." Her shoulders fall so low, Kian's heart aches. "I just can't."

"You will, Nova." He injects those three words with as much certainty as he can. How can he show her what he sees?

"How can you be so sure, Kian?" She half shouts, half wails the question as she hurls it at him.

Kian takes a step forward, relieved when Nova doesn't stop him. "Because you're kind and compassionate and true to your heart."

Another step and Nova simply watches him, looking like she's drowning and he just became her anchor. "Because you care more deeply than anyone I know."

The next step brings him before her. "Because I love you, Nova."

Nova gasps as her eyes become watery blue pools. Heart-breaking happiness floods her face. "Kian…"

Those words have hung between them for so long, aching to be said. He smiles as his heart lightens. It feels good to say them.

Actually, it feels amazing.

It feels like he's just said the most perfect, most binding words he's ever spoken. It's nothing short of what this beautiful girl deserves.

Nova opens her mouth to reply but Kian places his fingers on her lips. Her eyes are already full of the emotion she wants to communicate.

They're full of the word he just gave life to.

Except this is the ultimate show of faith he can give her. "Tell me tomorrow." He steps back, knowing they need to join the others in the dining room.

But not before he tells her one more truth.

"When you're Bound."

DEX

*D*ex pauses at the sensor outside his father's quarters, knowing it's against the rules to open this door. This part of the lab is strictly off limits.

But he doesn't care. It's possible that after the disastrous final test they've all failed anyway. He doesn't feel like he has a lot to lose. Besides, their results will have been presented to the High Bounds by now. That's one of the reasons Magnus and Amity had come to the lab. His fate has already been decided.

It's late. So late that it might be more accurate to call it early. The sun will rise in a few hours. He should be tossing and turning in the bunkroom alongside his restless companions. He's certain Wren's the only one who's actually sleeping. She's told him before how important sleep is to survival. Or perhaps it's that there's not as much at stake for her with the imminent results. She hasn't spent her whole life waiting for this day.

But he has. And now that it's so close, it's like his mind is filled with the twisted roots of a mangrove pine. He can't make sense of anything.

And he can't stand it another moment.

Taking a deep breath, he scans his bracelet on the sensor and the door slides open to reveal his dad perched on the edge of his narrow bed, his head held in his hands. It seems sleep has become as scarce as food in Askala tonight.

This is how his father sits when he's stressed. Or upset. Or feeling guilty. Which is unusually often. Maybe he's feeling all three of these emotions right now.

Dex steps into the small room and lets the door close behind him.

His father's head lifts and Dex sees his eyes are bloodshot, his thinning blond hair hanging limply, crisscrossing shadows across his face from the dim lamp beside his bed.

"What are you doing here?" he asks. "Participants aren't allowed to speak to the leader of the Proving."

Dex takes a seat at the small desk, swiveling the chair around to face the bed. "I'm not here to talk to the leader of the Proving. I'm here to talk to my dad."

His father lets out a long sigh. "Now's not the best time. You should be asleep. We can talk after this is all over."

At least he doesn't seem to be in trouble for coming here. Even if it's obvious he's going to need to be persistent if he's to get any of the answers he came for.

"There's never a good time, Dad. You never have time for any of my questions. There's always something else more important. Now's good."

If he's made Unbound tomorrow, who knows if he'll ever get any answers. He can't move to the upper decks of the Oasis not knowing if he's sharing oxygen with the person who killed his mother. It's time his father told him the truth about what happened that night.

"Look, Dex." His father reaches out a hand, then drops it again. "I know I haven't been the world's greatest father."

Dex isn't going to argue with that. "Lucky I had the world's greatest mother, then."

"You did." Smoothing down his hair, his father sits up

straight, looking more like the self-possessed man Dex recognizes. "I've told you before that I didn't deserve your mother's loyalty. Or her love."

"What happened to her?" Dex asks, more interested in things he hasn't heard before. "You've never told me. Not properly."

Most of what he knows came from Kian, who'd pieced together what he could from listening to his parents talk when they thought he was asleep. His own father's version of events was always far lighter on details.

"You know what happened, Dex. An Unbound snuck into our cabin when I was working late. Your mom woke to find him standing over your crib. She tried to stop him... but he stopped her instead." His voice is calm, impassive, like he's relaying a weather forecast rather than the most catastrophic night of Dex's life.

"But why would anybody do that?" he asks, nowhere near satisfied. "Why me? You must've tried to find out."

"It was revenge, Dex." His father rubs at the stubble sprouting on his chin and Dex notices the dark circles ringing his eyes. "Pure and simple. Revenge."

"I was just an innocent baby!" Dex kicks at the floor. "How could anyone want revenge on me?"

"Not you, Dex. Me." He places his open palms on his chest. "Being a High Bound comes with responsibility. Hard decisions have been made. Not everyone's been happy about them. I include myself in that."

Dex's eyes spring open and he sits forward. He'd always suspected his father hadn't been happy with some of Magnus's decisions but he's never admitted it so openly.

"My brother's made some of the most difficult choices Askala has ever seen," his father says. "I've stood behind him out of duty, not because I agree with him."

Dex swallows. He'd come here for answers, which is exactly

what he's getting. They're just not answers to the questions he thought he had.

"So, if the tough decisions came from Magnus, then why was I targeted? Why not..." He bites down on his bottom lip, losing the courage to finish his question. There's no way to ask it without sounding selfish.

"Why not Kian?" his father asks.

Great. As if it's not enough that he's been listening in to his every word this week, now he's a mind reader, too.

Dex nods, guilt surging through his gut. He doesn't wish it happened to Kian, of course. He wouldn't wish what happened to him on anybody. But maybe it would help if he understood the reasons behind it.

"Kian was more difficult to get to, I expect." His father looks away and leaves it at that, but Dex knows what he means. Magnus would never have left Amity alone with baby Kian at night.

Dex crosses his arms tightly, tucking his stump into the crook of his other arm, aware that his father doesn't like to look at the evidence of his neglect. He never has. "What kind of a sick person would cut off a baby's hand to get revenge on a High Bound?"

"Someone upset about having lost their own finger, perhaps." His father looks down at his own left hand, turning his golden High Bound ring in a circle. "You have to understand that you've grown up with this new system. It's normal for your generation to see people with nine fingers. It wasn't like that when I was young. Not everyone accepted the change in process."

"Do you?" Dex has never thought to question this aspect of life on Askala. His father was right when he said it's normal for him. The way things have always been done. It's hard to imagine a world where everyone gets to keep all their fingers.

His father's eyes are still focused on his ring. On the finger that would be missing if his own Proving hadn't gone so well. "No, I don't accept it."

His words are like a grenade, hitting Dex squarely in his chest.

"It's cruel, Dex." He looks up, lines drawn across his forehead. "There are other less extreme ways of setting Bounds apart from Unbounds. Our colony existed for generations before this. I don't blame the Unbound being so upset when it happened. I'm actually surprised they didn't rebel more."

Dex leans back in the chair, blinking rapidly as if his eyes are trying to keep up with his racing thoughts. "So, you're telling me that my hand was taken as revenge for taking the Unbounds' fingers?"

His father shrugs. "I'm telling you that I think the taking of the fingers is connected to the loss of your hand, yes."

"But why take all five of mine? Why not just one?" Dex rubs at his stump, wondering what it would be like to have a left hand with either five fingers or four. He has no memory of his hand ever existing.

"Most people who choose revenge like to take things up a notch." He lifts his face and Dex sees the sadness spilling from his eyes.

"Killing Mom was a little more than a notch, don't you think?"

His father closes his eyes and nods.

"Did Dean have anything to do with it?" he asks, a persistent memory from his childhood tapping at the back of his mind.

"Dean?" His father's eyes spring open and he rakes a hand through his hair.

"Yeah, that guy with red hair who always stares at me. The one whose brother got banished."

"I know who Dean is. I'm just not sure why you think he had

anything to do with it." He tilts his head as he waits for an answer.

Dex shrugs, not sure he has an answer to give. "He gives me the creeps, that's all. When I was little, he cornered me in the garden and told me he's my uncle. Amity told him if he didn't leave me alone, she'd feed him to her pods."

"And did he leave you alone?"

Dex nods. "Amity can be pretty convincing when she wants to be."

His father shifts on the bed, looking as uncomfortable as he always does whenever his aunt's name comes up. The rumor that he was once in love with her is undoubtedly true. Perhaps he still is. Not that he'd ever admit it.

"Why would Dean say he's my uncle?" Dex asks.

"You know Dean's brother was banished?" his father reminds him. "Ronan."

Dex nods. "The one who killed all the pteropods."

"Ronan loved your mom. He wanted her to promise herself to him. Dean seems to think—how do I put this?—that she already did."

Dex's mouth falls open. He's never once thought about his mother being with anybody except the exhausted man sitting before him. "Is it possible Ronan's my father? I mean—"

"It's not possible. I may not be the world's best dad, but trust me, I *am* your dad."

They lock gazes and Dex chooses to believe what he hears. The alternative isn't something he wishes to contemplate. But no matter who his father is, his question about Dean still hasn't been answered.

"If Dean doesn't like you, wouldn't that be even more reason to believe he's the one who came into our cabin that night?" he asks.

"Not if he thinks he's your uncle. Dex, it doesn't matter who it was that night. If they wanted to cause you further harm, they'd have done it by now. You're safe."

"I'm not worried about me." He unfolds his arms, not caring if the sight of his stump is offensive. It's reality. Sometimes the very nature of reality is offensive.

"Good. You have enough to worry about right now, without that." His father absentmindedly touches some papers beside him on the bed and Dex's blood turns cold.

"Are those my results?"

"They're everyone's results." He picks up the papers and shoves them in a drawer. "I presented them at the High Bound meeting earlier tonight."

"And you think I should be worried? Did I do that badly?" A sick feeling is winding its way through his gut. He'd expected that coming here might give him reassurance, not tip his world on its head. "Is that why you were upset when I found you just now?"

"Dex, everyone needs to be worried. You'd be fools not to be." He closes the drawer, although it does little to dim Dex's desire to read its contents.

"We all failed, didn't we? I knew we screwed up that last test."

"Language, Dex." His father blinks, not giving anything away. "I wasn't talking about anyone's specific results. That's all been finalized, anyway. Your chips have already been programmed."

"Where will mine go?" He rubs at the end of his arm where his hand should be. "Has anyone like me ever been through the Proving before?"

He shakes his head. "The chip can go wherever you want it to. Your left forearm. Your right hand. It's your choice. Lana will put it in. You won't need to use the same machine for your chip as everyone else."

Dex has heard all about the machine where you place your

hand on a glowing plate. There's a humming noise, the chip gets inserted and in most cases a finger comes off. He'll be the only person in Askala to never have to interact with that machine. He feels like he's missing a rite of passage, even if the idea of it terrifies him.

"How will I know if I'm Bound or Unbound without the machine?" he asks.

"You'll have to wait and see if your chip opens your ring box when you're presented to the community. It will be just like the way we used to do it, back in kinder times."

Dex swallows and nods slowly. "But I'll never really know, will I? You could mess with the programming to make sure that box opens. Without my hand, I'll never know for sure what I truly am."

"Your residual limb has nothing to do with this," his father says, looking anywhere but at the body part he's speaking of.

"I prefer to call it a stump, Dad." He waves his arm at his father. "It won't hurt you, you know. You don't need to feel embarrassed to look at it."

"That's where you're wrong. I do look at it. Perhaps it's when you don't know I'm watching you. And it hurts me every single time." He moves his palm to his heart. "It hurts right here."

"Oh." Now, *that* he wasn't expecting. This chat isn't going to help him sleep. He may never sleep again after the things he's just learned.

"I'm sorry I let you down, Dex. I'm sorry I've been such a terrible father." His father crouches in front of him, a gesture that makes Dex feel entirely uncomfortable. Reaching out, his father puts a hand on each of Dex's upper arms and looks him in the eye. "This isn't going to make any sense, but I've been distant because I love you, not because I don't."

"You're right." Dex squirms in the chair. "That makes no sense."

"From the moment you were born, I worried you wouldn't be Bound. That I'd get close to you only to lose you one day." He lets go of him and returns to the bed and Dex can breathe once more. "It hurts to lose people you love."

"Are you talking about Mom or Amity?" he asks, before he can stop himself.

His father lets out a long sigh. "I thought I was talking about you."

"The Announcement's tomorrow," Dex says, noticing his father ignored his question but deciding to let it slide for now. "So, you don't need to worry anymore. I'm the one who needs to worry, according to you. Apparently, we all do."

His father nods, not giving anything away. "How do you think you did on the tests?"

"Better on some than others." Thoughts of the past week surface and he pushes them down, having analyzed them to death enough already. "Did I do enough to pass? If the results are locked in then I don't know why you can't tell me."

"Because I want you to look surprised," he says, plainly. "It's only a few more hours to wait."

Dex rolls his eyes. "Seriously?"

"Seriously." His father's face matches the sentiment.

"So, how did everyone else do, then?" Dex asks, the curiosity almost killing him. "I don't need to look surprised for their results."

"Not everyone can pass," his father says, avoiding his question. "You need to prepare yourself for that."

"Kian and Nova are safe though, aren't they?" Dex studies his father's inscrutable expression. "No way can I see them not passing. Those two are destined to be together."

There's a flicker of something across his father's face. A frown? No, surely not.

"They did both pass, didn't they?" Dex asks, deciding it's

definitely a frown. "Kian's so smart. And there's nobody in Askala kinder than Nova."

"The Bound need to be both kind and smart." The frown falls from his father's face, replaced by a hollow smile.

Dex decides he still can't see any reason either of them would fail.

"Shiloh did well," he says, aware that he's rambling in his desperate hope for some kind of clue as to how any of them went. "She collected both the pods and the eggs. I'd say she's safe. But there's no way Felicia can make it through. Same with Thom if he happens to return before the Announcement."

"I don't think we'll be seeing Thom there." His father scratches his chin again. "You haven't mentioned the Remnant? How do you think she fared?"

"Her name's Wren, Dad." Dex shakes his head, clenching his fist. "Why would you call her that? It's so offensive."

"Because I'm worried you've become too attached. It's important to remember where people come from." He drops his hand and looks to his ring once more. "No matter how brave they are. Or beautiful."

Dex feels a deep flush cross his cheeks.

"I've seen the way you look at her." His father's hollow smile remains plastered to his face.

"And you don't think she'd make a good choice for me if we both end up Bound?" The thought's crossed Dex's mind many times. Could Wren be his choice? Would she even want to be? Perhaps her heart isn't even free to give.

"She's not a safe choice," his father says.

"Was Mom a safe choice for you?" he shoots back.

"She was actually. The safest choice of all. She would never have betrayed me." There's a strange look on his face now. A look he reserves purely for thoughts of Dex's mother.

"It doesn't matter anyway," says Dex. "I doubt we'll both

become Bound. After that last test, it's more likely the whole lot of us will be Unbound."

He searches his father's face for a clue. Something for him to go on. But his face is like stone, his blue eyes vacant of even the tiniest hint.

"You're really not going to tell me, are you?"

"Dex, there's a lot I need to tell you. So much. We're on the cusp of something big—Askala is about to change. It needs to. But now's not the time to discuss it. We need to get tomorrow out of the way first. Then we'll talk."

Dex frowns, wondering if that means what he thinks? If he's Unbound, surely his father wouldn't have anything further to discuss with him. Is that reason enough to hope he's passed? Although, would it be on his own merits or by his father's interference? Then he remembers his father's caution that he should be worried, and he feels just as confused as he did when he stepped into this claustrophobic room.

"Go back to your bunk." His father stands and ruffles his hair, like he sometimes did when he was a kid and he wasn't sure how to interact with him. "Get some sleep. It's going to be a big day."

"You really can't give me a clue if I passed?" Dex stands and looks his father in the eye. "You know, one blink for yes, two for no, that kind of thing?"

"Go to bed." He extends his hand to the door, not blinking at all.

Dex sighs and presses his bracelet to the sensor. The door slides open.

"Hey, Dex." His father's voice is a whisper now. "I *am* proud of you."

Dex swallows, wishing he could return the compliment.

But he can't.

Because no matter how hard he tries, he's not proud of his

father. After the conversation they've just had, he doesn't even know who he is.

He walks back to the bunkroom, head spinning as his father's words echo in his ears.

We're on the cusp of something big.

Askala is about to change.

What does that even mean? He'd come to his father with questions, yet somehow he's left with a thousand more.

WREN

*T*he sun peeks over the top of the wall of the courtyard and Wren dives out of the shadows to stand in its warmth. Her pendant is resting on top of her shirt and she positions herself so it catches the light and reflects it back into the sky.

The cricket she has trapped in her hand flutters, tickling her fingers with its wings. Fingers that she'd very much like to keep attached to her hand.

Swiveling to the side just slightly, she watches the light bounce off her pendant. Surely it can be seen by at least one of Cy's ravens? She only needs one. He has dozens of them. There has to be one circling around here somewhere.

She's been carrying this message in her pocket for a week now, but there are either no ravens or too many people, and neither of those options will do.

Phoenix has to know she's alive. She can't stand the thought of him believing she's dead. Plus, there's vital information she needs him to pass onto Cy for her. And for that she needs a raven.

There's a shadow in the sky and she blinks. But it's gone

before she gets the chance to identify what it was. Hope soars in her chest.

The only consolation in Phoenix thinking she's dead is that in some ways it's the truth. Because even though she's only been in Askala for less than two weeks, she's not the same person she was when she arrived. The old Wren died the moment Dex hauled her out of the water. She just didn't know it at the time.

The old Wren didn't stand a chance. Not against Dex with his crazy sense of humor and his protective streak. Or Nova with the compassion and generosity she's shown her. Not even against Kian with his blind loyalty to the society he's been raised in. A society that he'll likely lead one day.

Which is a problem. Because she came here to bring Askala down. But how can she do that when it's the home of three people she's inconveniently started to care for?

Three people who've changed her so much that she barely recognizes herself.

Tipping her chin up to the sky, she reminds herself that deep down she's still Wren. And she came here to do a job. That hasn't changed. She might just need to go about things in a slightly different way than she'd first intended.

Which is why she needs to get this message to the Outlands.

She squints into the sun, willing a raven to her side. She's running out of time. Soon, everyone will be awake.

When she'd crept out of the bunkroom earlier, it had been to the soft sounds of snoring. After a restless night, her companions had all finally fallen asleep. She'd been the only one to get her sleep when it was actually night-time and the sky was empty of birds. She knew she needed her strength to face this day. She knew she needed to rise early…

Lifting the pendant with her free hand, she tilts it, sending light moving across the sky.

Still nothing.

Hearing a noise behind her, she spins around, expecting to find Dex.

She gasps to see a large raven strutting across the courtyard. It moves lightly and surely, completely unafraid of her. Wren squats down to greet it, her heart beating fast.

It's happening. It's actually happening.

"Hello, beautiful." She extends her hand as she admires the uniform darkness of this creature.

Black glossy feathers, black twig-like legs, a sharp black beak and black beady eyes. This inquisitive creature is a living shadow. A creature of the dark drawn to her by the light reflecting off her pendant.

Her only connection to Phoenix.

"I have something for you," Wren says, and the raven tilts its head to one side as if it understands.

She reaches into her pocket and removes the letter.

"Come here, sweetheart." She opens her palm and holds out the cricket, being careful to keep one of its wings pinched between her fingers so it doesn't jump out of her hand.

The bird hops forward, taking the cricket and swallowing it with a click of its beak.

"You liked that, didn't you?" Wren reaches out slowly, just like Phoenix taught her, and ties her note to the raven's foot using a small piece of string she pilfered from the infirmary.

The bird waits, patiently.

"Go!" she says when the job is done. "Off you go."

The raven lets out an almighty caw, stretches out its impressive wings and takes off into the sky.

She did it! That raven won't stop until it sees Phoenix's matching pendant and delivers her message. Before nightfall he'll know she's alive.

But her joy is short-lived when she stands and looks across the courtyard to see that Dex is watching her.

He doesn't look shocked. He doesn't even look surprised. But he sure looks curious.

"You trained the ravens?" he asks, wide-eyed. "To be your messengers?"

She pauses, then nods. There's no point denying this. Dex is far from stupid. He knows exactly what she was doing. Even someone as thick as Felicia would have known.

"Should I be concerned?" he asks. "I mean... I'm sure what you just did wouldn't be allowed."

"It wasn't anything important." She hates the taste of the lie on her lips.

He nods. She can almost hear the cogs in his brain churning as he tries to decide if he trusts her.

"I just wanted to let my people know I'm okay." This isn't a lie. Certainly, that was part of what her letter was about. There's no need for Dex to know about the full contents. It might put him in danger and that's the last thing she wants. "You believe me, don't you?"

He nods, watching her closely as he walks toward her. "You've never given me any reason not to." The words are half question, half statement.

She lets out a slow breath. "It's nothing to worry about. Just a short message to say I made it here alive."

Dex seems to relax. "I wish I could do that."

"Send a message to the Outlands?" She's confused. Who would he send a message to?

"Not the Outlands." He's standing in front her now, so close she can see the light dusting of freckles across his nose. "Just to the sky. To my family."

"Your mom." This isn't a question. She knows that's the person he misses most. "What would you tell her?"

He shrugs. "Same as you. That I'm okay."

She hopes that's the truth. That he really is okay, because he might be able to fool most people with his sunny exterior but she's seen the dark clouds that lurk behind his smile.

"How are you feeling about today?" she asks, steering the conversation away from messages and ravens before he asks her a question she doesn't want to answer.

"Well, at least I don't need to worry about losing a finger." He waves his stump in the air.

Wren looks down at her left hand. "Reckon I'm going to lose one of mine?"

"Not a chance," he says. "You've been brilliant in every test. Even the one you tried to fail."

She nods, wondering how much bias there is in the scoring. "Dex, it's very possible I'll fail no matter how brilliantly I might have done. Nobody here wants a Remnant to become Bound."

"Don't call yourself that," he snaps. "Someone whose opinion I value told me how offensive that word is."

"What? Remnant? Or Bound? Both are pretty offensive when you think about it." She crosses her arms. "In any case, we need to get used to the idea that by the end of the day I'll likely be one finger closer to matching you."

"When you came here, you said you wanted to be Unbound." Dex touches her gently on the elbow. "Is that still the case? I get the sense you've changed your mind."

Wren bites down on her lip, not willing to answer that. Her reasons for wanting to be Bound aren't entirely noble. She knows she can be more effective if she's working from within. Cy never expected such a bonus. Imagine his glee at discovering she made it to their inner circle...

"Because if you're Unbound, you'll be sterilized. Are you okay with that?" Dex looks to the ground and kicks at a stone, but she can tell he's listening intently for her answer. Listening like her response means something to him personally.

"Dex, I don't want to have children." She leans slightly so she can catch his eye. It's important that he understands this so that he can let go of whatever fantasy it is that he has about her. "I can't bring a child into this world. Being sterilized is the least of my concerns. I'd actually welcome it."

He nods and she hates that she noticed the flinch that crossed his face. People don't do this in the Outlands—have conversations hidden underneath other conversations. In the Outlands people say what they mean. They don't have time to dance around important issues like this.

"I understand that." His voice is a whisper. "I've wondered the same thing myself."

"Hey, maybe we'll both be Unbound and we can hang out by the pool and watch pod boy slave away so he can feed us." She smiles, trying to lift his mood, but it's not working.

"Kian would like that." Dex sighs. "All he's ever wanted is to work with those pods. Come to think of it, I don't mind the sound of it, either. Being Unbound and hanging out with you every day."

"No, you wouldn't!" Wren is shocked. "You've wanted to be Bound your whole life."

"That was before I met you." He's searching her face now, except she's not entirely sure what he's looking for. Who he wants her to be. "You've changed the way I see things, Wren."

"Welcome to my world." She shakes her head. "It seems we've changed each other more than we ever intended to."

"Apparently I get to choose where my chip goes. I was thinking right here..." He presses a finger to the middle of his forehead. "What do you think?"

She lets out a laugh, relief flooding through her. This is the Dex she knows. The guy who makes jokes to cover his pain. The guy who works so hard to put everyone at ease when he's never once been at ease himself.

"Or maybe here," he says, turning to point at his rear end.

"I'd like to see you open a door like that." She shakes her head and he grins at her.

"Seriously though, where should I put it?" The smile falls from his face. "Right hand or stump?"

She doesn't hesitate. "Stump. Everyone else has it in their left hand. Don't go putting it in your right." She doesn't add that she's aware he hates being different to everyone else.

"Even if it draws attention to it?" He rubs at the end of his arm, as if picturing where the chip might go.

"Newsflash, Dex. I think everyone's seen it already. And as a bonus newsflash, nobody cares. It bothers you a whole lot more than it bothers anyone else. I mean, it's just an arm with a hand missing."

He nods. "Thanks, Wren. Nobody's ever said that before."

"Only because they haven't thought to say it. Nova doesn't care if you have a hand missing. Nor does Kian."

"Shiloh clearly does." There's that smile again. "Did you see the way she recoiled from me on the raft when I made a joke about us being together?"

"Yeah." She shrugs. "Made me mad at first until I realized that comment had a whole lot more to do with Kian than it had to do with you."

"She's got it pretty bad, hasn't she?" Dex laughs. "Poor Nova."

"Poor Kian, more like it. He's the one who has to fend her off."

"Oh, Kian," says Dex in a falsetto as he bats his eyelashes. "Please stay with me. I only feel safe when you're around."

"Stop it." Wren laughs as she tilts her head toward the entrance. "She could open that door at any moment."

"Nah. She'll be making puppy dog eyes at Kian over breakfast. Speaking of which, are you ready to go back in?" he asks. "Or do you have more messages to send?"

Wren's brows shoot up as she tries to work out if he's joking.

"About that," she says. "Do you think you could not mention it to anyone?"

"As long as you can look me in the eye and swear you're telling me the truth." He gives her a long stare.

"I'm telling you the truth, Dex." She returns the stare, ramping up the intensity to cover her lie.

"Okay then." He nods.

The tension leaves Wren's gut and she leans over to touch him on the elbow. "Thanks."

Dex tenses at the contact. His arms reach out for her and for a moment she thinks he's going to embrace her. But he must lose the courage as his arms fall to his side. Which is probably a good thing. He already seems to have false hope that they might become more than friends. She doesn't want to encourage him. Even if the idea of a hug is sort of nice.

"I'm glad you trust me," he says, crossing and uncrossing his arms. "I won't tell anyone."

"Thanks, I owe you a favor. Again." Her heart breaks at how uncertain he looks right now. No wonder he yearns to send his mother a message. The poor guy hasn't exactly grown up surrounded by love.

"Any chance I can have that favor straight away?" He looks to the ground again and shuffles his feet. "I mean, your secret's safe with me and all of that. It's not dependent on your answer. It's just that I'd really like to ask if it would be okay if—"

"Dex! You're rambling." She shoves him gently on the arm. "What is it?"

"Any chance I could have a hug? I reckon it's about the only thing that would make me feel better right now."

"Oh." Even though she was certain that was what he'd been wanting from her, it comes as a surprise he asked.

"It's all right," he says, unable to meet her eye. "You don't have to. I'm just nervous and I thought..."

"A hug would be great, Dex. But that's all this is, okay? A hug." It's important he understands this is as far as things go between them.

He nods as he steps toward her and wraps her in his arms. He's taller than she is and she turns her cheek to rest her face on his chest, disappointed at the reminder of how well they fit together.

When he'd held her after Fern's death, it had been him comforting her. But this is different. It's more her comforting him. The loneliness that she's certain he feels is seeping out of his pores and he tightens his grip on her. They're not really all that different. She understands what it's like to be alone.

"You'll be fine, Dex," she says, doing her best to use a soothing voice.

He lets out a deep breath and drops a kiss on the top of her head. Just for one moment she thinks she's in Phoenix's arms and tears sting her eyes.

She pulls away more abruptly than she means to and smooths out an invisible wrinkle on her shirt, hoping he hasn't noticed the effect he just had on her.

Cy would be so disappointed.

Because there's no arguing that she now has another weakness to add to her fear of heights.

Dex.

"Let's go inside," she says.

He nods, despite the confusion spilling from his eyes. But she can't say another word.

Because as complicated as he believes his life is right now... once Cy gets her message, it's going to get a whole lot worse.

NOVA

*D*espite being born and raised on a cruise ship, Nova's never been in a room that's felt more claustrophobic than the one she's in now. The white walls feel too close, the air too thick.

She rubs her arms as she looks around. It's a room they haven't been in before, right at the back of the labs. Lana had escorted them all here, then stopped them before the closed door.

She'd held her hand out with a smile. "Your bracelets, please?"

Everyone had hesitated. In a few hours, they won't need the bracelets they've worn since childhood, allowing them free access around the Oasis.

By the end of today, their chips will be inserted in the back of their hands.

Kian had been the first to pass his over, thanking Lana. The others had followed suit, and Nova was struck at how she used to look forward to this moment. As a child, she'd paraded around her parents' room without her bracelet, tall and proud like a weight had been lifted.

As Lana took Nova's bracelet, she'd felt anything but light. Her smile growing, Lana had waved them through as the door slid open.

Now, they're all in here, silent and waiting. Dex's arms are crossed so tight Nova isn't sure he'll ever unwind. Shiloh keeps rubbing the back of her left hand. Felicia is pacing, Wren is glaring at Felicia pacing.

Kian hasn't left her side.

Nova suppresses a shudder. The room is bigger than the cabins in the Oasis, but it still feels oppressive, even without all of them here. Jay is dead. So is Fern. And Thom is still missing. They've gone from nine to six in the space of a week.

Now they're standing around, waiting to find out whether their choices will mean they'll be Bound.

Or Unbound.

Several chairs line one of the walls, all empty. Nova brushes Kian's arm. "I'm going to sit down."

She doesn't understand how everyone else hasn't done the same. All she wants to do is curl up, tucking her legs up to her chin and wrapping her arms around them. There's an overwhelming urge to protect the heart that feels too heavy, and yet is beating too fast.

Kian gazes at her for several breaths. He's trying to communicate the same words he whispered to her as she woke, her heart trying to climb up her throat as she realized what day it is. The same words he whispered during the breakfast no one could eat, and again just after they startled when Callix's voice crackled through the loudspeaker, asking them to assemble in the hallway. "Askala was built on love."

We were forged with love.

Our future will be filled with love.

Nova nods, attempting a smile, but it feels like she's trying to raise the dead.

Kian frowns. "I'll join you."

Nova slides into one of the seats and Kian settles beside her. She should tell him to stand if he wants, maybe even pace like Felicia is, but she keeps silent. She knows it's selfish, but she needs him beside her right now.

She can't shake the thought that these could be their last moments together.

Hating that she's being so dramatic, Nova focuses on the sensation of Kian's shoulder pressed against hers, of the muscles that are strong and warm, of the memory of his body holding hers.

Kian's right. They have to have faith. Serving Askala with kindness and strength is all she's ever wanted.

With Kian beside her.

Nova looks around, doing another check of those in the room. Wren is leaning against the far wall, one leg propped up against it. She's trying to look bored, except her foot is tapping rapid fire against the wall. Dex is hovering nearby, casting frequent glances her way. Nova doubts he's aware that he's holding his stump, the action almost protective.

Her gut clenches. Because Dex doesn't have a hand to put a chip in. Or a left ring finger to cut off.

How will that even work?

Wren catches Dex's gaze, then with a slight twitch of her chin, invites him to join her. Nova looks away, not wanting to intrude on whatever is happening between the two, but not before she notices the way Dex's shoulders seem to unwind as he moves toward her.

Shiloh moves into Nova's line of sight, a small smile on her face as she drops into the chair on Nova's other side. The bandages are gone from her hands, the cuts still red and angry, but no longer at risk of bleeding again. "Let's hope they don't want us to play the waiting game for this one, huh?"

Nova swallows, trying to moisten her dry throat. "They probably have quite a bit to organize."

The scoring would have to be completed after the final test. The numbers tallied. The chips programmed. Whatever machine is used prepped and readied.

For those who will go from ten fingers to nine.

Shiloh shuffles back in the seat as she straightens her shoulders. "What role do you think you'll take on once you're Bound?"

Nova glances at her in surprise. "Once we're Bound?"

"Sure. Thinking positive is much better for my stress levels right now, so why not? Kian," she glances past Nova. "What do you think you'll do?"

Kian leans forward, resting his elbows on his knees, brows low as he considers the question. "That's always been a tough one for me."

Nova nods, they've spoken about this before. Kian's parents are both High Bound, and he loves them both. How does he choose whose path he follows?

"My father is our leader, and he's always wanted me to do the same. Yet Mom is in charge of the pods and I've spent my life learning about them."

Shiloh smiles. "You'd be so good at both, Kian."

Nova resists the urge to shift closer to Kian, recognizing the possessive gesture for what it is. Shiloh may have feelings for Kian, but she's here, trying to make them both feel better.

And she was the one who's trying to be optimistic.

Shiloh turns back to Nova. "My guess is we'll be working in the infirmary together."

Nova blinks. Of course Shiloh would want to work in the infirmary. She's been helping in there for the past several months. "I suppose we will."

"With you in charge, of course. Your mother's taught you everything she knows. You'll be amazing."

For some reason, Nova almost feels shy. Running the infirmary is a dream she's only discussed with Kian. She'd be happy just to work there. "I'm hoping we can take what we've learned about the sap and use it to help others."

"I thought that, too!" Shiloh glances at Kian. "The Bounds would really benefit from the sap."

Nova tries not to frown. "So will the Unbounds. We should be able to harvest more than enough."

"Of course." Shiloh's smile tenses. "If we have enough."

Nova feels Kian stiffen and her cheeks flush. Of course that's what a Bound would say. Ensuring the survival of those who will heal the Earth always comes first. "Of course," she mumbles, acutely conscious of the tightening in her gut that tells her she's lying. "Only if we have enough."

"Urgh!" Felicia's groan is so loud it has Nova startling. Kian places his hand on her knee, an unconscious touch seeing as he's watching Felicia with a frown.

She's still pacing, but has picked up momentum. She reaches the opposite wall and with another anguished moan pushes away from it. Spinning around, she strikes for the other side of the room.

"I can't. I just can't."

Nova stands, her brow furrowed in concern. "Felicia, is there anything I can do to help?"

Everyone's emotions would feel like shattered glass right now.

Felicia's hands spear into her curls. "I can't do this, Nova. I... I..." She turns to face the door they entered through. "I need to get out of here."

"Felicia, wait—"

But Felicia is already running toward it. She slams into it, holding up her wrist before she realizes they handed their bracelets in. Desperately, she traces the outline of the door, looking for a way out. "No, no, no. They've locked us in!"

Nova's eyes sting. Felicia wouldn't be the first person to realize she probably didn't score well in the tests and decide to run. That door would've been locked the moment the last one of them stepped through it.

Felicia spins around, eyes wild with panic. "I can't be Unbound. I can't have nine fingers!"

She slowly sinks to the ground as Nova rushes over, crouching down beside her. "Felicia," she murmurs. "I know this is hard."

Felicia's teary eyes look up at her. "I'm so scared, Nova."

Nova's legs crumple beside the shivering girl. "We all are." Her gaze softens. "But you're just as brave as any of us."

"No, I'm not. I stole Dex's blocks in the first test. I was useless in the second test. I stayed back rather than going out on the raft." Her head sinks into her hands. "I took the eggs."

"But you've tried your best, Felicia. It's all we could've done. Those who'll be Bound will dedicate their life to Askala. And those of us who'll be Unbound will be cared for."

Felicia blinks, her lip trembling. Nova hopes she's realizing she won't be alone through this. She discovered working in the infirmary that anyone, whether they're Bound or Unbound, can face far more than they believe if they know someone will be there with them.

Dex leans over Nova's shoulder. "And hey, I only have five fingers." He holds up his stump, somehow, managing against the odds to pull up a grin. "As long as you don't get given a sling-shot, it's not as bad as you think."

Felicia looks around the room. "This really sucks, you know."

Nova nods. "It really does."

Suddenly Kian is standing over them. He holds out a hand. "Here, Felicia. Come and sit with us."

Shoulders dropping in defeat, Felicia reaches up and Kian hauls her to her feet. With a comforting smile, he escorts her to the chairs. If there was some water anywhere, they could've offered Felicia a cup, but the room is bare.

Nova takes a seat next to Felicia, who's staring at the ground, her whole body sagging with dejection. "And what really sucks, is that I'm going to fail, and a Remnant is probably going to pass," Felicia wails.

Nova's eyes fly to Wren in alarm. Felicia's already learned what Wren is capable of when someone calls her that.

Except Wren isn't trembling with fury as Nova expected. She narrows her eyes at Felicia. "Might be a good time for you to reconsider that label then, huh? When nothing but humanity's leftovers pass your precious Proving." She looks away. "I doubt anyone expected things to go the way they did."

Wren's right.

This Proving has been so different from the others. The deaths. Wren surprising them all.

And if Wren's changed her mind and wants to be Bound, then Nova is glad for her. The Proving is about finding the smartest and kindest, and Wren is certainly smart.

Wren leans back against the wall, her arms crossed. Their eyes connect and Wren nods, her gaze steady. Nova isn't sure what Wren is trying to communicate, but her heart warms. As much as Wren tries to hide it under her tough shell, she cares. Kindness is just as much a part of her as it is the people of Askala. There were countless times she could've turned her back on any of them, but she didn't. More than once, she's saved several of their lives.

The door on the opposite side of the room slides open almost silently, but the gentle sound has everyone freezing. Nova's heart is thumping so hard it feels like she's bruising her ribs from the inside out.

Lana steps through, a clipboard in her hands. She smiles the same smile she's had throughout this entire ordeal. "Kian, we're ready for you."

She steps back in the room behind her, her smile growing as if she's inviting him into the dining hall.

Kian stands, his movement slow and measured. His gaze locks with Nova's, and she sees what she never thought she'd see in his eyes.

Fear.

Wishing she could comfort him, Nova holds herself still. Of course Kian will be Bound. How could he even doubt that?

Shoulders back, he walks to the door. Nova feels the moment their gazes disconnect as he passes her and she grits her teeth at the pain. It's like something just severed inside her.

Who knows what their world will look like when they reconnect again.

The moment Kian steps through, the door slides closed behind him.

Everyone is silent. It's like no one is even breathing.

Maybe, they too, have two words ricocheting through their brain.

It's time.

KIAN

*T*he next room is much like the one Kian just left. Square, white walls, cameras hanging from the ceiling in each corner.

Except for one glaring difference.

In the center stands a white machine on a metal table.

Lana ticks something off on her clipboard. "This is for you." She passes him a small, black square. His chip. "When you're finished, simply leave through here." Her stock standard smile never slipping, Lana exits through the door on the opposite side.

Leaving Kian alone. With the machine.

He blinks in the bright white space. Is there a reason he was called first?

He knows he needs to move, but his limbs have grown roots. The machine before him holds his future.

An eventuality he's looked forward to for so long, but now that he's here, feels far less certain. What if he or Nova didn't pass? It only takes one point below the cutoff and you're not Bound.

All the plans. All the dreams. Gone. Destroyed.

Made void by a number.

His heart is a battering ram in his chest. What would his parents say? They'd be crushed under that much disappointment.

He jumps when a green light starts flashing on top of the machine. It stays silent, the steady pulsing beckoning him.

Swallowing past the boulder in his throat, Kian approaches it. Smooth and domed, it has a hole in the front like the mouth of a cave. At the base is a clear plastic plate, the outline of a left hand on it.

The chip is digging into his palm and he realizes he's gripping it. The flashing light is above a square slot, one exactly the same size as the chip.

A bead of sweat zigzags frantically down his spine. There's no way he can put off the inevitable.

Kian places the chip in the slot and it slides in smoothly, the machine beginning to hum. The plate pulses with a gentle light.

Sweet Terra, that's where he has to place his future.

Suppressing the tremors, Kian lays his hand within the outline. His fingers sinks into it and the plate glows red as it *whooshes* forward, pulling his hand into the machine.

He stares at his arm, his hand now out of sight. All he can hear is his harsh breathing and his out of control pulse. It almost drowns out the ticking and clicking coming from the machine.

A puff of air almost has him jerking his hand back out, but Kian keeps it there. Sweat is now trickling down his temple.

There's a sting and he winces. It was the chip.

Or the amputation.

A moment later, his hand slides back out.

At first, his brain is too far in overdrive to process what's happened. He lifts his hand to his face. One, two, three, four, five.

Five fingers.

He's Bound.

It takes long seconds for the words, their implications, to register. He's Bound! He feels like dancing. He wants to whoop so loud his ears will ring.

But Callix will be watching, maybe Kian's father, too.

So Kian contains his joy. He savors the happiness singing through his veins. There will be ample time to celebrate soon enough.

Feeling lighter than he ever has before, Kian exits the room. He expects to see another yard on the other side, somewhere for everyone to come together as they each pass through the gauntlet.

But the door opens into a tunnel, walled on either side by timber. Above, the sky is brilliant blue and Kian draws in a lungful of pine. He's never seen this tunnel before. They must've built it just for the Proving, so they can be led to wherever he's meant to go next.

Kian wants to run down it, leap to wherever it's taking him. After all this time, after the heartache and loss and doubt, he's...Bound!

Instead, he walks with pride. Maybe his family will be at the other end. He certainly knows his future will be.

As he makes his way down the tunnel, Kian senses he's getting close to the Oasis. He reaches another door and he stands before it, waiting for it to open. When it remains shut, he takes a step back, glancing around. Is there something he's missed?

Then it strikes him. With a grin he's unable to contain, Kian lifts his hand and swipes it over the panel beside the door.

With a glorious *whoosh*, it slides open.

Feeling more grown up than he ever has before, Kian steps through. He finds himself stepping onto the stage in the center of the old ballroom.

The cracked chandelier high above has a handful of lights

glittering in it, the room is full of people who come to attention as if they were waiting for him. From where he's standing, the cracked paint can't be seen, the worn, faded carpet is lost in shadows.

The decay is lost in the beauty that is this moment.

Kian looks around, wanting to imprint this in his memory. The wooden stage is empty apart from him.

And Callix.

Kian's uncle steps forward, a small wooden box in his hands. He extends it and Kian sees it's been made from the timber of the varnish tree, carvings of the tree etched into it, the roots twisting around each other in intricate patterns. He stares at it, already knowing what's inside.

Callix lifts the box a little higher. "You know what you need to do, son."

His eyes stinging, Kian passes the back of his hand over the box. There's a soft click and the lid springs open. Slowly, he lifts it the remainder of the way.

Inside, nestled on white hemp, is a ring. The ring of the Bound.

Kian picks it up, liking the weight as he admires the soft glow of the silver. Fashioned from the finest roots of the mangrove pine then dipped in silver, three threads interlace each other. Almost feeling like he's watching himself, standing there in the center of the stage, light falling down on him, the people of the colony he loves watching him, he slips it onto his fourth finger.

It fits like a second skin. Like it belongs there.

Like he was destined to be Bound.

Kian turns to the crowd, finding his parents standing at the front. His mother has tears streaming down her face, their steady trickle reaching the smile below. His father's chest is puffed with pride as he nods, just once.

Staring out over the people, Kian feels heavy and light at the same time, excited yet calm.

The moment has come.

In a sure, smooth movement he raises his left arm, holding his hand high in the air.

The crowd surges forward with a roar, his parents leading the explosion of joy. Their elation hits Kian like a wave, lifting him higher.

Their hands match his as they reach for the sky, the multitude of rings catching the light. Each and every one a testament of their commitment to save Earth.

This is the moment he's been waiting for.

Now, all he needs is for Nova to join him.

DEX

*D*ex walks into the small room and eyes off the machine he's been told there's no need for him to touch. It's a white box-like contraption with a base plate of the outline of a hand.

A left hand. Something he doesn't possess.

"I'll be back in a moment," says Lana, holding her clipboard to her chest. "Please wait here."

She slips out a side door and he goes up to the machine and touches it, imagining what it would be like to insert his chip and watch it deal out his future. But it's difficult to picture. Because that would be like imagining he's the same as everyone else. And as that outline of the hand is clearly pointing out to him, he's not.

Running his fingertips along the cool surface of the flat top, he decides in some ways it would be easier to blend in if he's Unbound.

They have no left ring finger. He has no left hand.

Whereas if he's Bound then he'll need to wear his ring on his right hand. Nobody else does that. There will be one more thing that's different about him, instead of one more thing that's the same.

But as Wren pointed out to him as they'd stood in the morning light in the courtyard, nobody else cares. It's only Dex who notices these things. He's making a bigger deal out of it than it is. Better to concentrate on what he thinks and not get caught up worrying about what's running through everyone else's minds.

The wait to be called into this room was excruciating. He'd hoped Wren would be put out of her misery before him. And Nova. Or even Shiloh. But only Kian and Felicia have gone through so far. He won't know their results until he gets to the ballroom. Their faces will tell him immediately if they passed.

The door slides open again and Lana returns holding a tray like the ones used in the infirmary. He doesn't want to look too closely at the items on it, realizing he forgot to ask his father if this is going to hurt.

"Are you okay?" Lana asks, smiling widely.

"Why are you always so happy?" He returns her smile to show he means no malice by his question. "Even when there's little to be happy about."

The smile doesn't leave her mouth, but he sees it drop from her eyes for a moment, until she pulls it back up. "There's plenty to be happy about, Dex. We're very blessed to live here."

He nods at the tray in her hands, his eyes landing on the small, black chip that holds his future. "I guess that depends on what's been programmed into that chip. Did I pass?"

"How many times do we need to tell you there's no pass or fail? Everybody has their place in Askala. The Proving is about figuring out which place that is for you." She sets the tray down on the edge of the table. "Now, where would you like your chip inserted? Callix said he's happy for you to choose."

Holding out his left arm, he points to the end of it. "Right here."

275

Amazingly, a frown crosses her brow. Was holding out his stump all he had to do to wipe the smile from her face?

"You have scar tissue there, Dex. It's a sensitive area. I'm not sure that's the best choice. How about your right hand?"

With Wren's advice still fresh in his mind, he shakes his head. "Then put it a little higher up, but I want it in this arm. I deserve to be like everyone else. At least in this way."

"That will work." Lana nods and she picks up a strange device that looks like a cross between a syringe and a thermometer and inserts the tiny chip into it. He'd been right not to want to look. The sight of it is making him nauseous. "I'm afraid there's no chair for you to sit on, so you're going to need to be steady on your feet, okay?"

"Nothing wrong with my feet." He does a little jig, stopping short when Lana's face tells him it's no time for jokes. "Sorry, Lana. Humor is my coping mechanism."

"I noticed." Her lips purse together as she swabs his arm with a clean cloth.

"Is this going to hurt?" He steadies his feet and draws in a breath.

"Just a sting." She sets down the cloth and picks up the device. "You ready?"

"Count me down from three?" he asks. "No, five?"

"Five." She puts the device on his arm and moves it around a little, and Dex thinks about all the children he may or may not have.

"Four." She settles on a location, and Dex weighs up the possibility that his father might have altered his results to ensure he passes.

"Three." She draws in a breath as she waits, and Dex wonders if he's a fool to crave a future with a girl who craves nothing but her own freedom. The girl his father advised wasn't a safe choice, which somehow only makes her more appealing.

"Two." Lana clicks the button and a sharp pain shoots up the length of his arm.

He winces. "Hey! What happened to counting down to one?" Closing his eyes, he waits for the pain to subside.

"Sorry." She smiles as she pulls the device away from his arm. "I thought it would hurt less if you weren't ready for it."

"You said it wasn't going to hurt at all." He rubs at his aching arm as the pain begins to dull.

"I said it was going to sting." She hands him the cloth she used to clean his arm. "Hold this firmly on the wound site. This process isn't as clean as the one we use with the machine. You must be careful of infection."

He takes the cloth from her and presses it to his arm.

"Good luck, Dex. I hope the Proving served you well." She sweeps from the room, leaving him alone once more.

Lifting the cloth, he looks underneath and sees a small mark on his arm but thankfully no blood. Running his fingertips along his skin he feels for the chip, but it's so small it's impossible to tell it's there.

But it is there. And his future is decided, just like it already has been for Kian and Felicia.

Going back to the machine, he places his right hand on the plate and the surface gives as if it's trying to suck it in. Dex imagines how frightened they must've been to put their hand inside this contraption knowing what was at stake. And how frightened the three yet to pass through here are going to be. Poor Wren. She didn't ask for this when she came to Askala looking for a better life.

The plate lights up and he quickly withdraws his hand, but not before he catches sight of something on the surface.

Bending down, he squints, then gasps, to see it's a drop of blood.

Which can only mean one thing. This machine has recently taken a finger.

It has to be Felicia. Surely, it couldn't have been Kian?

Poor Felicia. She'd been so afraid this would happen.

Not wanting to be in this miserable room another moment, he leaves through the exit door, surprised to find himself in some kind of roofless tunnel.

Kian and Felicia had walked this same path knowing if they were Bound or Unbound, but he's not going to get his answer until he reaches the end.

Which means he doesn't walk. He runs.

Pounding the ground as he puts one foot in front of each other, he propels himself forward, hungry to discover his fate.

Reaching a door at the end, he comes to a halt and draws in a breath, conscious of the rapid beating of his heart. If that chip did contain the sterilizing agent, then he's doing a great job of making sure it travels around his system nice and quickly.

He presses his arm against the sensor and the door slides open, revealing the stage of the ballroom before him. The room is full of people and they hush when he steps forward.

Kian beams at him from one side of the stage, the glimmer of his new Bound ring catching the light.

He made it.

Relief slides through Dex and he returns his cousin's smile. Now all Kian needs is Nova to pass and he'll really be smiling. They're halfway there to their together-forever future.

Felicia is standing on the other side of the stage, her face pale and her left hand clutched to her chest.

Dex lets his smile slip and gives Felicia the most sympathetic look he can muster. If there weren't so many people watching him, he'd go over and give her a hug. Perhaps after his result is revealed, he'll be able to do exactly that. It all depends on who he'll end up standing next to.

He shifts his gaze to his father who's standing in the center of the stage, holding a small wooden box.

Dex goes to him, surprised to see his father smiling with an expression that looks very much like pride. Were his parting words to him last night true? Could his father really be proud of him?

"Are you ready?" His father holds the box out to him.

Dex glances at the crowd, who are craning their necks, keen to see what happens. He imagines his mother standing there watching him from the front of the crowd next to Amity, exactly where she should be.

Amity gives him an encouraging nod, assuming he's looking to her for reassurance, and he nods back before turning to the box and staring at the intricate patterns carved into it.

"I'm glad you didn't put the chip in your forehead," his father whispers. "Or any other inappropriate places."

Dex hesitates, realizing his father had been listening to his conversation with Wren in the courtyard. Which means he knows about the message she sent with the raven. Feeling like his whole world just imploded, he swallows, clenching his right fist as he concentrates on trying to keep himself together.

Wren can't possibly be made Bound now. She'll be seen as a traitor. It doesn't matter how well she did on the tests, there's no way his father is going to let her go through.

Which means that as he holds his arm to the box and it clicks open, he hopes to find it empty. If Wren's Unbound, then that's what he must also be. He can't bear to think of his life without her. Somehow, throughout the hell of the past week, she's become…his someone. The one who understands him. The friend who chased away the loneliness that's plagued him his whole life.

"Come on, open it," his father says, jiggling the box.

Dex uses his right hand to raise the lid, revealing a shiny silver ring waiting for him.

The crowd see the flash of silver and let out an enthusiastic cheer. But the noise is just a hum in the back of his ears almost like he's no longer inside his own body.

Bound. He's Bound. What he's dreamed for his whole life has just come true. Yet he feels like he's stepping into a nightmare.

"Your mother would be so proud," his father says. "Congratulations, son."

Dex picks up the ring and with a little difficulty, he manages to get it onto his ring finger, struggling to push it down without another hand to guide it.

"Let me help." His father takes his hand and slides the ring down to the base of his finger.

And for the first time Dex feels like he understands the origins of the word Bound. He's now tied to Askala, bound to his duty by invisible ropes that he can't remove no matter how much he might want to. Is it selfish of him to hope that somehow he's wrong and Wren will become bound by the same ties?

Holding his right hand up to the people gathered in the ballroom, they return the gesture, pride shining from their eyes as their own rings catch the light and they welcome him as Bound.

Wren was right. Nobody cares that his ring is on his right hand. Nobody really thinks much about his differences other than himself. He's just like everyone else.

But at what price?

He joins Kian on the left of the stage and his cousin pats him enthusiastically on the back. "We're both Bound. I knew it. Now we just need Nova."

"And Wren," he says, forcing a smile to his lips.

"Of course." Kian nods. "And Wren."

Catching Felicia's tear-stained gaze from the other side of the stage, Dex decides to break all kinds of protocol and go to her.

"Just congratulating the Unbound," he says with false joy as he crosses the stage.

Nobody can pick him up on this. The Unbound are supposed to be just as celebrated as the Bound.

"Congratulations, Felicia," he says loud enough for the crowd to hear, reaching out and drawing her shaking body into his arms. She may have been challenging company for the week, but he doesn't believe she's a bad person.

"I knew this was going to happen," she says. "I knew it."

"I'm going to look after you," he whispers. "We all will. I promise you won't be alone."

The events of the Proving had been unusual. And devastating. Which means the six of them who remain are bonded in ways they never could have imagined. And that includes Felicia.

"Thank you, Dex," she sniffs. "That means a lot."

He pulls away and as he does, he sees something in Felicia's eyes that wasn't present when he'd stepped onto the stage.

Hope.

His father clears his throat. "Dex, please take your place. Our next participant is about to arrive."

Dex returns to Kian's side. This time Kian doesn't acknowledge him. Not because of what he just did, but because his eyes are glued to the door, hoping to see Nova walk through next.

But there's just as much chance it will be Wren or Shiloh.

"You'll know soon," he says to Kian.

Kian nods to show he heard but doesn't lose his focus.

Three down.

Three to go.

May the Proving serve them well.

WREN

*W*ren watches Lana leave the room, clipboard in hand, having just called Wren's name. Shiloh moved through the system so much faster than Dex and it's caught her off guard.

"Shiloh didn't muck about," says Nova.

Wren doesn't say what she's sure they're both thinking. Shiloh would have been keen to make it through so she could ogle Kian once more. Poor Kian must be going crazy waiting for Nova. Shiloh is unlikely to be a welcome consolation prize.

"I thought you'd get called next," says Wren, having been certain they were going to leave her until the end.

"Looks like I'm lucky last," says Nova, even though there's nothing lucky about having to wait even longer to find out if she's allowed to spend her life with the guy she loves.

"Real lucky." Wren suppresses an eye roll knowing it won't help her new friend feel any better.

Nova jumps from her chair and gives her a hug. "I'll see you on the other side."

"I hope you get the future you want," she says, squeezing her back. "With Kian."

"Thank you." Nova is smiling but Wren can see the fear that lies beneath. "And I hope the same for you and Dex."

"We're just friends," says Wren, stepping out of the hug.

"Of course. I wish you a lovely life of friendship." Nova smiles and Wren decides to let it go. She means no harm. Nova never means any harm. "Now, go on. Your future awaits."

Wren heads to the door Lana just disappeared through.

She steps inside and looks around the small room, deciding it looks quite innocent for a torture chamber. Apart from that ominous looking machine on the table behind Lana and her clipboard.

The door closes behind her and she knows she's trapped. The only way out of this room is to stick her hand in that machine and hope it comes out the same way it went in.

"This is for you," says Lana, passing her a small, black chip. "When you're finished, you may leave through here."

"Can't wait." Wren pokes out her tongue at the back of Lana's head as she leaves the room through a different door.

Knowing that the longer she takes, the longer Nova has to spend sitting in that room by herself, Wren launches forward to the machine and slides her chip into a tiny slot that has a flashing light above it.

"Is that what I'm supposed to do, Callix?" she asks, glancing up at one of the cameras pointing at her.

A hum fills the room, drawing her attention back to the machine as it lights up.

Giving the camera a thumbs up, she focuses back on what she's here to do.

When she climbed on the raft that would take her to Askala, never did she imagine she'd willingly put her hand inside a machine that has a very high probability of removing one of her fingers. But that's just one of the things she never imagined here. Best to get it over with.

Bringing her hand to her face, she kisses her ring finger,

then drops it to raise only her middle digit. Smiling at the camera she does a dramatic curtsy and gives Callix a one-fingered salute.

"May the Proving serve me well," she says, her voice dripping with sarcasm as she places her hand on the base plate of the machine.

But when the machine pulls her hand inward, she falls silent and her heart rate picks up. Never has this process felt so real. So raw.

Testing the machine to see how tight a grip it has on her, she discovers her hand is trapped inside, her fingers locked into position. Probably smart. There's no way Felicia would have willingly stood here with her fingers inside the jaw of this brutal machine without trying to pull her hand back out.

A clicking noise comes from the machine and Wren decides in some ways fighting off the leatherskin was preferable to this. At least she survived that encounter with all her body parts intact.

She taps a foot, trying to release some of the unbearable tension that's gripping her. If only this machine would hurry up. She's not sure how long she can stand this.

"Hope this doesn't take all day," she says to the camera. "I've got stuff to do."

There's more clicking and she wonders if it's happened yet. Surely, she'd know if she'd lost a finger? Unless they have some kind of anesthetic.

She feels a puff of air, then a sharp sting but it's hard to tell if it's the back of her hand or her finger that's hurting. Everything's getting muddled up now.

The machine spits out her hand and she's almost too afraid to look. But she doesn't want the cameras to see her fear. Callix won't have the satisfaction of knowing he can cause her such distress.

Drawing in a breath, she looks down.

Five fingers.

She turns her hand over a few times, staring at it, scarcely believing what she's looking at.

But there's no doubt about it. Five fingers. Holy hell, she's Bound!

This can't be right. Looking at the machine again, she checks to see if she's finished the process. Perhaps she's meant to put her hand back in and the finger chop happens next. Although, all lights have now switched off and the machine sits in silence once more.

"Well, Callix," she says, looking at the camera as the reality of what just happened sinks in. "It seems I'm not the only one here full of surprises. Touché."

She exits the room through the back door, shaking her head as she turns over the possible reasons behind Callix's decision. She'd been certain he was going to alter the results to ensure she didn't get through, despite Nova's insistence that he'd never do that. It would go against every rule of Askala.

As she steps into some kind of tunnel and blinks in the sunlight, she thinks about the person she cares about most in this strange place.

Dex. Because if Nova's right and these results aren't judged with bias then it's hard to guess if he made it through.

Taking quick steps down the tunnel, she can't help but hope that Dex has made it. It's too difficult to imagine being separated from him, even though the thought of being with him brings her just as much fear.

When she gets to the door at the end of the tunnel, she finds herself shaking, not from fear, but excitement. No matter how much she's told herself the results of today didn't matter to her, she realizes they did.

She's Bound. Which means she was judged as worthy. Something that she can't remember ever happening in the Outlands. She's been deemed to be both clever and kind, which is strange because she'd been raised to believe that being strong and brave are the only two qualities that really matter.

Then she remembers that she's going to use her Bound status to do this society more harm than good and her shoulders sink. It makes her feel duplicitous and that's never been like her. Wren has always been your classic what-you-see-is-what-you-get kind of girl and she's taken great pride in that.

Scanning the back of her hand on the sensor, she breathes in as the door opens. She tucks her left hand in her pocket as she walks through. They made her wait all day to find out her result, it's their turn now.

The first face she sees is Dex. His eyes drop straight from her face to her hand and he shakes his head to see she's hiding it from him.

He's standing to one side of a stage beside Kian and Shiloh, and it's hard to miss their shiny new rings.

Bound. They're all Bound. Is it normal for so many of them to pass?

And with the way Shiloh is gluing herself to Kian's side, Nova better hurry up and get out here with all her fingers intact.

Then she sees Felicia on the other side of the stage, her eyes red with tears, and she realizes that not all of them are Bound.

"Tough luck, Felicia," she says, wincing as she realizes her words sounded more sarcastic than reassuring. "I mean, I'm sorry. Really, I am."

Felicia throws her a scowl.

"Wren, welcome to the Announcement," says Callix and she turns to see him standing in the center of the stage.

"I thought you were watching from the cameras," she says, feeling foolish for having spent the entire process talking to him. Although, she's certain he'll play the footage back later and hear what she had to say to him. She's sure he'll particularly enjoy her curtsy.

"Lana has everything in hand back at the lab." Callix holds out a small wooden box.

"Interesting choice of words," she says, making no move to take the box from him.

There's murmuring in the crowd as the people gathered at the front of the stage crane their necks, waiting for her to pull her hand out of her pocket.

"You want to know if the Remnant's been made Bound?" she asks, walking to the front of the stage and grinning at them. "You're all so certain that I failed, aren't you? You can't wait to see me with a missing finger."

There's a movement beside her and she sees Dex has approached and placed a reassuring hand on her back.

"These people aren't like that," he says. "They were made Bound because of their kind hearts. They don't wish you harm."

She nods slowly as she takes in what he just said. Looking back at the crowd, she sees them a little differently now. These people were put through a Proving just like she was. And although she's been told some of the Unbound come to this ceremony, it's obvious by the rings on their fingers that most of the people at the front of the room are Bound. Which means Dex is right. These people are the best that Askala has to offer. And from what she saw this week, their best can be pretty good.

Turning to Dex, she removes her hand from her pocket and holds it out for him to see. His eyes light up and he pulls her into a hug, spinning her around.

"You made it! I knew it!"

The crowd erupts into wild applause and Dex sets her down and grasps her left hand, raising it above her head for all to see.

People are clapping and smiling, their faces filled with what looks like genuine surprise and joy as the ancient chandeliers shake from all the commotion.

Wren can't help but smile back at them, until she's startled when a face in the crowd draws her attention. Leaning forward, she tries to get a closer look. It can't be...is that Phoenix?

He's staring at her, too, and she blinks as she realizes it can't possibly be Phoenix. This man is far older than him. But there's no question that he has Phoenix's red hair, the same line of his jaw and distinctive upturn at the end of his nose. How strange.

"Go and get your ring," says Dex, drawing her attention away from the man and leading her to Callix. He steps away to re-join Kian at the side of the stage.

"Thanks," she mouths to him. Once again, he's right there when she needs him. The guardian angel to the ghost she'd just seen in the crowd.

Callix holds out the box once more. "Scan your chip on the lid. Your ring will be inside."

Doing as she's told, Wren watches as the lid pops open and she sees the small piece of silver jewelry that means so much to these people. She'll be the first person from the Outlands to ever be given the honor of wearing this ring.

When Cy hears about this, he's going to be gobsmacked. Pleased, but gobsmacked.

She takes it and slides it onto her finger, turning back to the crowd to see them all standing silently with their left hands raised, their rings catching the light from the chandeliers. The man who looks so much like Phoenix is nowhere to be seen.

Returning to the front of the stage, Wren raises her hand to mirror the crowd. Tears sting her eyes as she fights the emotions bubbling to the surface.

Right at this moment she isn't Wren the Remnant. She's not even Wren. She's a small part of a larger whole. She's one of them. She's Bound. And it feels so good.

Which is a problem.

Because that note she sent to the Outlands is proof that no matter how much she's come to feel like she might have a place here, never in her life will she fight for what these people believe in.

Letting both her hand and her smile drop, she draws in a breath.

There's a war coming.

And she's the one who started it.

NOVA

*B*eing the last remaining person leaves Nova feeling like she's now in a cavern. She doesn't move, barely breathes because she doesn't want to hear the echo of her aloneness bouncing around the room.

She closes her eyes, preferring to think of the moments that have been rather than what's coming.

Kian's face, full of fear, flashes through her mind. He'd be Bound by now. Waiting for her.

Then Dex. Nova hopes going through all this, becoming Bound or Unbound, will finally give him peace.

Felicia, so scared she's going to be Unbound, with none of them able to reassure her otherwise.

Shiloh, holding her brave face so tightly as if the mask was about to shatter any moment.

Then Wren.

She rubs her arms as goosebumps flash over her skin, looking around. Maybe the ghosts of Jay and Fern are with her, too. Thom, whether he's dead or alive, has managed to avoid this ordeal. She wouldn't be surprised if he chose to face the danger of the forest rather than the threat of this.

The door slides open and Lana stands there smiling. Her lips move but Nova doesn't hear anything. It doesn't matter, she knows what she just said.

It's time for your judgment.

Nova follows her into the room, her arms still wrapped around herself tightly. Lana's smile is gentle and full as she ticks something on her clipboard. Her lips move again and she's gone.

Nova turns to the machine sitting in the center of the room. The mouth at the front yawns like a gaping hole.

That's where she needs to put her hand.

Afterward, she'll know whether she's Bound.

Or Unbound.

Please, please, please let her be Bound.

She goes to step forward, at least pretending to be brave, but images of Kian flood her, leaving her paralyzed. Kian, arm outstretched, holding her as far out over the lake as the law of physics allows them. Kian determined yet smiling. Kian laughing.

Kian telling Nova he loves her.

His earth-colored eyes had been so clear, so full of sincerity. How her soul had sung to hear those words.

He was so sure she's going to be Bound that he wouldn't let her reply.

It's that feeling that finally gives her the courage to step forward. To face the machine.

A green light flashes above and she slips her chip in, wondering if it would be any better to know what it's been programmed to do.

The outline of the hand flashes and Nova places her palm on it. The soft surface gives under the weight and her hand sinks into it like quicksand. It feels like it's swallowing her future. Smoothly and silently, it draws her into its belly.

Please, please, please let her be Bound.

The machine begins to hum and Nova's pulse spikes with it. Her heart feels like it's overdosed on adrenaline. Her breathing is the same shallow panting of someone going into shock.

She's about to receive everything she's ever wanted...or her whole world is about to disintegrate.

There's a puff of air and a click and a sting. Nova physically jumps only to find her hand stuck tight. She couldn't escape this even if she tried.

The machine pushes her hand back out and Nova stares at it, trying to process what she's seeing. How long has she waited and worried and tormented herself over this moment?

And now she's here, and she can't understand what she's looking at.

She lifts her hand, holding it in the air as she traces the outline with her eyes.

Her knees collapse as a single tear trickles down her frozen cheek. As she crumples, her heart goes from frightened convulsions to a silent stone in her chest.

The acrid smell of cauterized flesh has her stomach recoiling.

"Sweet Terra," she chokes through a strangled throat.

The hand before her only has four fingers.

There's no mistaking it.

Nova is Unbound.

THE END

Ready for the next installment?

Check out Book 2, BREAKING, now!

http://mybook.to/BreakingThaw

BOOK TWO - BREAKING

Only the chosen shall breed.

Four teens must face the fallout of the Proving. Three have made it through. One has not.

Nova. Kian. Dex. Wren.

Four lives defined by the outcome. Four lives who thought the Proving was the most difficult test they would ever have to face.

They all assumed Askala was safe, but a link to the Outlands has been established and a Remnant invasion is now a threat. In a starving, damaged world, Askala has what others want.

Except the fight for survival is far more complicated than right or wrong, or us and them. It's about humanity versus Earth.

As bonds are fractured and new connections are forged, the question becomes - how do you fight for your world, but also your heart?

Lovers of Divergent, The Hunger Games, and The Maze Runner will be blown away by the breathtaking new series from USA Today best-selling author Tamar Sloan and award-winning author Heidi Catherine.

Grab your copy now!
http://mybook.to/BreakingThaw

WANT TO STAY IN TOUCH?

If you'd like to be the first for to hear all the news from Tamar and Heidi, be sure to sign up to our newsletter. Subscribers receive bonus content, early cover reveals and sneaky snippets of upcoming books. We'd love you to join us!

SIGN UP HERE:

https://sendfox.com/tamarandheidi

ABOUT THE AUTHORS

Tamar Sloan hasn't decided whether she's a psychologist who loves writing, or a writer with a lifelong fascination with psychology. She must have been someone pretty awesome in a previous life (past life regression indicated a Care Bear), because she gets to do both. When not reading, writing or working with teens, Tamar can be found with her husband and two children enjoying country life in their small slice of the Australian bush.

Heidi Catherine loves the way her books give her the opportunity to escape into worlds vastly different to her own life in the burbs. While she quite enjoys killing her characters (especially the awful ones), she promises she's far better behaved in real life. Other than writing and reading, Heidi's current obsessions include watching far too much reality TV with the excuse that it's research for her books.

MORE SERIES TO FALL IN LOVE WITH...

ALSO BY TAMAR SLOAN

Keepers of the Grail

Keepers of the Light

Keepers of the Chalice

Keepers of the Excalibur

Zodiac Guardians

Descendants of the Gods

Prime Prophecy

ALSO BY HEIDI CATHERINE

The Kingdoms of Evernow

The Soulweaver

The Woman Who Didn't (written as HC Michaels)

The Girl Who Never (written as HC Michaels)